SHORTS
2

Shorts
2

The Macallan/
Scotland on Sunday
Short Story Collection

Selected by Candia McWilliam

Polygon

© The Contributors, 1999

Polygon
An imprint of Edinburgh University Press Ltd.
22 George Square, Edinburgh

Typeset in Galliard by Hewer Text Ltd, Edinburgh,
and printed and bound in Great Britain by
Bell & Bain Ltd, Glasgow

A CIP record for this book is
available from the British Library

ISBN 0 7486 6268 5

The right of the contributors to be identified as authors
of this work has been asserted in accordance with the
Copyright, Designs and Patents Act 1988.

The Publisher acknowledges subsidy from

THE SCOTTISH ARTS COUNCIL

towards the publication of this volume.

CONTENTS

Contents

FOREWORD

S hort stories are a disputed phenomenon. Are they harder, or easier, to write than novels, writers are asked, as though short stories were front gardens and novels arboreta. There's a certain sizeism at play, and a bit of slack thinking.

Short stories are shorter than novels, and that's it. No proper writer approaches them as a thing to be dealt with frivolously, as it were, in the spare time left by a novel. Short stories are the repositories of life swiftly apprehended. Because they are short, they are often thought easy. There could be no more malicious misrepresentation, luring as it does amateurs and beginners and enthusiasts, who may well get burned in the predictable false flames of pastiche Maupassant (a twist) or Chekhov (a mood).

Agents and publishers are keen to dismiss short stories: 'Nobody reads them.' Yet readers want them, ask for them, and, as may be seen on any bus or train, read them.

The reasons for this are clear. We live in an inattentive time, whose preferred reading is not essays but captions. However, there is a thirst for something more, without the time – for most of us – to read those demanding baggy monsters, novels. I do not suggest that the short story is a tool for social engineering, but it is surely desired, and intensely appreciated.

Foreword

For some years I have had to do with the Macallan short story prize. It is a marvellous institution, with little of the pomposity that word suggests. The judges are invariably chosen with an eye to originality rather than the conformism of the sausage machine. They choose with an eye, in their turn, to quality; they are strikingly attentive and conscientious. The outcome has been the discovery of some fine writers and their exposure.

A very large number of people enter the competition, and the choice is made with the maximum of consideration and debate. This year is very far from an exception. Perhaps the proof of this, in a curious fashion, is the choice of one writer twice over, for two very different stories.

What characterises the Scottish short story? I think it's the only truth to assert that what these stories have in common is intelligence and freshness. The content is so various – female boxing, domestic claustrophobias, bulimia, miscegenation and deracination from points as various as the Mediterranean and the East – that, mercifully, it can't be adduced as tying its authors together, for they are better than that. Equally, the Scots voice is constant, and cannot be ignored; sceptical, intelligent, operative and open to what is droll even in the heart of tragedy, it is audible not only in those stories that address the perennial problem of how to transcribe Scots speech, whether to suggest it through rhythm or through more literal transcription.

Since each writer deserves some sort of singling out in a foreword of this kind, perhaps I might simply work through the stories with a, regrettably short, word for each; then the reader may seek the story that sounds at first most appealing; I assure that reader that they will linger.

Eating Paris is a restrained story of Welsh children on a trip to Paris; the narrator is in love, of a certain, delicate, sort, with his teacher. *Surface Tension* is an apparently predictable, actually perceptive, story of a small boy who is the issue of a chilly union. *Two Wee Mice* is rooted in folk song, a simple and devastating tale of an accident. *The Neighbours' Return* is a wholly realised account of anti-Semitism and human timidity. *Souvenirs* gives an account of contemporary suffering in a form apparently chaotic but carefully deployed. *Timing* is a sophisticated tale of reunion. *Year of the Vezzas* is a marvellous tale of slippage between cultures. *Mother's Boy* is narrated by a boy who lives in a bender with his reckless father and his beloved mother; it is beautifully told. *King of the Castle* tells of the chafe between gangs of boys and girls. It's beautifully done. *A Piece of the Moon* enters Carver country, a sharing of suffering. *The Flood* tells of the consequences of nosiness and interference – a very Scots story. *The Worm Eater* is one of the most shocking things you will read, ever; yet its sweetness convinces. *The Magic Word* attacks each of our anxieties about shoplifting, and being stood up.

Life's Small Miracles is bigger than its quiet subject. It deals with eternity. *Blue* is an uninflected story of tender love and hopelessness. *The Earth is Slowing Down* is a forceful tale of desertion and self-determination. *Painting the Family Pet* is the best fictional account of bulimia I have read. *Harmonious Fist* is a furiously competent account of female aggression, professionally deployed. *Unfortunate Shortbread* belts along, an energetic nod at Iain Banks. *Yellow Man Walking* has an absolute certainty and a fantastically daring subject – time. *Body, remember* is not only beautifully entitled, but unforgettably poignant, leaving its investigation of HIV and AIDS on the mind like an X-ray. *The End of History* takes us to Berlin. *Norway Maple Leaves* interfolds themes of illness and archaeology. *Private Enterprise* is a dramatic tale of heroin dealing.

Ninety-nine Kiss-o-grams tells of a Scots Pakistani boy who goes to Lahore; its dilemma and mood are finely conveyed.

Clunker is a story whose absence of hope is undercut by its articulacy. *The Greatest Whisky Ever* is the funniest story in the book. *Swans in the Spring?* is a superbly confident story about, among other things, though not really, a dog. *A Musing Tale* is a surprising thing – a successful facetiousness.
So, the choice is yours.

Candia McWilliam

Eating Paris

Sian Preece

The red light went on and David counted hippopotam-
uses. Not enough hippos, and she wouldn't have spent
long enough, maybe wouldn't have washed her hands. Too
many, and she would be doing something that he didn't want
to think about too deeply, getting a big seat-smile on her
buttocks . . . whoa! He reined the thought in, and sent the
hippos into slo-mo, a graceful *Fantasia* dance, aware that he
was cheating. But it was okay. The light went out in a respectable eighty hippos, and Miss Rose came out of the toilet,
shaking her hands. A *washer*! He'd known she would be.

He and Howie tensed in frozen yearning as she brushed
past their seat, sashaying her hips in the slim aisle. They
groaned as she turned sideways and Benson oozed past,
advancing on them in a wobbly prowl, nicotined fingers
clawing the headrests. Booze patrol. The stewardesses had
been warned.

'Boys.'

'Alright, Sir? Want a peanut?'

'A moveable feast, eh! Thanks, Howie.'

He formed his yellow fingers into a beak, dabbled them in
the silvery bag. They came out powdered with dry roasting, a
peanut pincered in the fingertips, and he sucked it into his
mouth.

'Now, I'm telling all you boys, right – no drinking, no wacky-baccy, and leave 'les girls' alone. Don't want you getting stabbed by a French pimp. Not on school time anyway.'

The bit about maturity and trust now, thought David.

'We're trusting you, mind. You're mature enough to know how to behave.'

'Yes, Sir.'

Benson's fags made a shape in his shirt pocket; he kept touching them, couldn't wait to get off the plane and light up.

'Not sitting with your sister, David?'

'Aw, Sir, mun!'

'Right, well; remember what I said.' He moved on and they heard him at the next row: 'Now, I'm telling all the boys . . .'

Howie flipped a peanut at David.

'For why'd you bring your sister, Dai?'

'I didn't bring her, right! She *came*.' He shook his head. 'Look, this is me, earning this trip: *swot swot swot, wash the car, David, mow the lawn, David!* And this is my sister, *earning* this trip: *please, Daddy, please, Daddy, please please please!*' He bounced up and down in his seat.

'Phew!' said Howie, 'Glad I've only got a dog.'

'We've got a dog too,' said David glumly.

Howie glanced over his shoulder. 'Never mind; look.' He opened his jacket. The curved shoulder of a bottle nestled in the pocket.

'Whisky! Where'd you get that?'

'Ssh-ut *up*! My dad. For passing my exams.'

'Yeah, that's another thing! All this stuff they promise you to pass your exams – like you'd go and fail otherwise. Like you wouldn't bother!'

'Easy, Davey boy! Have a peanut.' Bouncing one off him.

'I mean, *my* exams! They're *mine*! I don't need a *reward*. Ah, stop it Howie.'

2

'Boing!'

'Howie, stop it.'

'Baa-ding!'

'Oi! Those are *my* peanuts!'

David grabbed him by the throat and throttled him against the window, popping his head in and out of the deep oval frame, rattling the plastic frame.

'Bloody hell, Dai!' Howie struggled free and rubbed his ears. 'Relaxez-vous! You need a holiday, you do.'

David sat back and tried to stretch, but his feet were too big, his Doc Martens in danger of getting wedged under the seat in front. He often felt constrained by his body; felt that he had grown inside during the night, and that, if only he could stretch enough, he would burst out of himself, fingers folding back like ears of corn to make way for the new fingers inside him. It was a constant itching at his seams, making him fidget, making the teachers tell him off in class.

He tuned in to Miss Rose's humming-bird voice at the front of the plane. She was giving the pep talk to the First Year girls. He would ask her a question later, something intelligent about France, to impress her, to hear her say his name.

'You're more mature than the boys,' she was saying.

'Come over here, Miss!' Howie snickered; '*I'm* mature! Ow! Dai, mun!'

Paris smelt of perfume. He hadn't expected that. Everyone had said that it would smell of drains, of garlic, but no. It was the particular essence of sun meeting city; late summer flowers and smoky urban grass. Even the car fumes were different, exotic. He breathed it in, logging it as a memory, better than a photograph. Miss Rose had a poster of the Eiffel Tower in class, an aerial shot of the splayed 'A'. A cliché. But up close, you could use all your senses to make it your own. He focused in on the nearest girder: *I'm touching the Eiffel Tower*. It was brown, not black. He closed his eyes to hear the backdrop of sounds, voices and traffic in an arcing echo; pressed his face to the metal and felt the texture with his tongue. *This is me licking the Effel Tower.* He was certain that no one else had ever licked the Eiffel Tower.

Howie wanted to pee off the top. No imagination.

His sister tapped his shoulder.

'What you doing?'

'I'm licking the Eiffel Tower. Go away.'

'I want to lick it too!'

'Nuh. Go away, Becca.'

'I want to! I want to lick the Eiffel Tower! Let me-e-e!'

He held her at arms length. 'Hmm – yum yum! It tastes of chocolate!'

'I'm telling Mammy!'

Horror-voiced: 'Your Mammy isn't here now, little girl.'

'I'll tell Miss, then.'

But the teachers were off in the distance, relaxed. Benson was playing football with some foreign kids, coughing and gobbing. Miss Rose was eating sorbet from a tub, licking the plastic spoon with a dreamy, creamy look on her face. He'd been surprised and relieved to hear her speak French; in class, he'd had the unworthy suspicion that she wouldn't be able to hack it in France, that she was only two steps ahead of the pupils. But she was great. Her mouth made sweet shapes as she complained to the proprietor about the hostel toilets, waving her arms, pursing her lips. It was like watching your parents at a party, the moment when they leap to their feet and start jiving expertly.

Howie appeared at the far side of the green, looking furtive. David watched as he dipped into a mad, low gallop, running like Groucho, trying to sneak unnoticed across the open space. His arms were cuddled across a large white carrier bag, hiding it uselessly against his chest. He pulled up abruptly, willing himself invisible, and peeked out behind an air-shaped tree; and then he was off again, running erratically left and right, with the wide, wild curves of a coursed hare, his body upright and his legs pedalling frantically below him. Closer, five feet away, and he stopped.

'Invisible Spy Man!' he yelled, then, 'Hush! It's only me.' There was whisky on his breath.

'What you got there, Howie?'

He held up the carrier bag. 'They sold me wine in the shop! Didn't ask, just sold me it!'

'Yeah?'

'Yeah, party tonight! Par-*tay*! Come on, you can get some too, it's just over there.'

On the previous nights, they had stayed in the hostel's games room, where Miss Rose challenged all-comers to vigorous bouts of table tennis.

'Nah, don't think I'll bother.'

'Alright then, we'll break out after dark and find a bar – pick up a couple of girls. Improve your *French*!' Howie wagged his tongue, lewd.

David thought of it. A girl like Pascale in their French book. Long hair that curled up at the shoulder, and a stripey sweater with things happening perkily underneath it. She would talk in speech bubbles, tell him where to find the *église* and the *hôtel de ville*. He'd take her to a café and name all the crockery on the table. Masculine and feminine.

'Mm. Maybe.'

But that night, after dinner, Howie was sick, and the next morning he was worse.

'Hangover!' pronounced Benson with distaste.

Miss Rose put her hand on Howie's forehead.

'Oh, Howell!'

David glared at him over her shoulder, but Howie was grey, sour and malt-smelling, couldn't take advantage of his position.

'You spoil it for everyone,' said Benson. 'Miss Rose will have to stay and look after you now.'

'Me? Why not you?'

They haggled, tossed for it, then couldn't agree which side of the French money was 'heads'. They did scissors–paper–stone, and Miss Rose lost.

'Alright then. But David will have to go with his sister. If you take my boys, he can keep an eye on the First Year girls.'

'*Miss*!'

'Listen to Miss Rose!' Benson was relieved, backing her up to allay his guilt.

David spelt out a sentence in gestures to Howie:

I – KILL – YOU!

Howie signalled back to him with his eyes:

PLEASE! DO!

'The Louvre!' he said. 'Haven't you ever heard of the Louvre?'

The girls blinked up at him, did it together like Midwich Cuckoos.

'He said *loofah*! Hee hee!'

'My mother's got a loofah,' said one of them. 'In her toilet.'

'She said *toilet*!'

'That's not a loofah, it's just a museum. We can tell.'

'That's just the way in,' he said. 'There's paintings inside, of, you know, ponies and things. Come on, it'll be brilliant.'

But he couldn't move them. They ignored him with superb effectiveness, as if his voice were something that they could simply tune out. He couldn't even threaten them, they'd start to cry. Or they'd jump him; there were enough of them. He felt overwhelmed, ineffectual. Was this what it was like to be a teacher?

'Come on, please! Miss Rose said that I have to take you there!'

'Nuh-huh.'

'Don't wanna go.'

'What do you want to do then?' He tried to think what he normally did with his sister, but he couldn't start fighting with her in the middle of Paris. 'Where d'you want to go?'

They sang in chorus:

'SHOPPING!'

He took them to Galeries Lafayette, and they tried on the same clothes as each other, twittering in and out of the changing rooms in reds and purples and bright pinks. Little girl colours.

'How much? How much?'

He translated the prices from francs to pounds and they swore like sailors. While they changed, he fingered a rack of Lacoste shirts, and eyed the sales girls shyly. The sun streamed through the wide windows, piercing the city grime; it seemed to consume time, moved across the sky with greedy speed. One day in Paris, happening outside without him. Not that he'd wanted a reward, but *this*! It wasn't fair.

'This is my holiday!' he said aloud. '*Mes vacances*!'

'*M'sieur*?' A sales girl approached, waved a bottle. She was offering to spray him with cologne. He nodded, held out his wrist as he had seen his mother do; but the girl shook her head. Moving in close, she hooked the tip of her finger into his shirt collar and drew it gently down. He closed his eyes. A little hushing sound, and a cool wetness that dried quickly on the soft, hot skin of his neck. He opened his eyes again. The girl gave him a confidential smile, touched his collar back into place, and was gone. He felt as if he'd been kissed.

When the girls came back out, he was dazed, stared at them.

'Everything's too expensive!'

7

'It's dear!' An old-fashioned word, picked up from a parent. *Dear*, he thought. *Cher. Chérie.*

His sister took his hand and swung it, showing off: *my big brother.*

'David!' she said, 'we're hungry! Hungre-e-e!'

They nodded in unison, skipped on the spot like anxious chorus girls.

'Yeah, right.' He dug out the tourist map that Miss Rose had given him. 'Did you know they have McDonald's in France?'

'HOORAY!'

They walked back singing, arm in arm, stepping into their own long shadows, made even more coltish by the low sun. Just before it closed, they caught a sweet shop that sold sugar models of Parisian landmarks. The assistant wrapped them separately, elaborately, in dainty boxes with curling ribbons, and the girls ripped them open on the pavement outside, scoffing the contents; crunchy little Eiffel Towers and Arcs de Triomphe. Eating Paris. For himself, he bought a sugared wafer with the Mona Lisa printed crudely on it – the nearest that he would get now – and, on a second thought, bought another one for Miss Rose. He would give it to her when they got back. He was pleased that he'd thought of it himself.

He organised the tickets for the Métro, did a head count in whispered increments of two. They were quiet now, slouched in their seats, heads poised sweetly on each other's shoulders while the movement of the train rocked them. His sister shoogled down into the seat beside him.

'David! I got blisters!'

'Hmm.'

'What do I do now?'

'Soak them in salt water when you get back.'

'Oww!' She pulled a horrified face, but he could see she was looking forward to it, relishing the fuss she could make. 'When you're a doctor, you can fix all my blisters.'

'Yeah.'

She put the shoes back on. 'Will you have to go away to be a doctor?'

'I suppose so. After my A levels. I'll have to go to university, and then I'll have to go to a hospital to practise all the doctor stuff. Y'know. Fixing blisters. Chopping people into little bits!'

'Eeee!'

He let her sink her head onto his shoulder. 'What do you want to be, Becca?'

'I want to be a teacher. Like Miss Rose.'

For a moment, he was dressed in a white coat, dressing some minor wound on Miss Rose's hand. Better still, a cracked rib. '*I'm afraid you'll have to take your top off, Miss Rose.*' *Call me Kathy . . . David!*'

He looked down at his hands. They'd have to change. He couldn't see this pair delving into a red, live abdomen, or drawing out a new baby. Writing a prescription across a desk from Miss Rose, or an old lady, or someone like his father. Perhaps the only way would really be to grow new ones, peeling out of his skin, taking off the old ones like rubber gloves. But, even now, he felt different to who he'd been that morning.

He stretched, a real stretch, and his sister's head slid down his chest. She was asleep. Awkwardly, he reached into his pocket for the sugar Mona Lisas. One was cracked, so he ate that, keeping the whole one for Miss Rose. After a while he ate the whole one too. He licked the sugar from his lips, tasting it like a wasp, and, behind the sweetness, there was the lingering taste of French cologne.

Surface Tension

Yseult Ogilvie

T he promenade swept up the coast, pink and grey paving offering a bleak defence against the vast plain of the North Sea. To the east was a lighthouse, tethered to the land by a causeway at low tide; a white vertical against the wide grey horizon.

They lived in a semi-detached house of red brick and pebble dash, the beach-flung finish of a seaside town. An ornate porch of timber and stained glass suggested a small prosperity on a quiet street that fed the promenade perpendicular to the sea front. The wide sands of the beach shock-blasted his legs in the wind that was never still and when the sun shone the expanse was punctured by the striped canvas of wind-breaks, taut as if to set sail. Families sat huddled behind, grinding gritty sandwiches while small children would venture out to paddle only to be driven back by the rolling clouds of sand which crusted around their mouths and nostrils, and the wet tides on their legs.

That morning he crossed the rough concrete causeway, rock pools revealing easy picking as the gulls turned overhead. He lifted the shell-soft fragility of a tiny crab and tossed it to the wind. A seagull caught it in descent. Once when he was throwing stones at the orange buoy off the pier end, a young bird swooped thinking it food. The stone broke its wing and it lay baffled, flapping the water as it was sucked out by the receding tide. Gordon had run home hysterical, unable to say what had happened. He pushed the thought away as he arrived at the whitewashed walls, looked out to the stirring sea and waited for the tide to come in.

He had packed a cigar box beforehand; a short length of string; a bent nail; two fish hooks; matches; a candle stump; compass; plasters; and a collapsing cup. In his pocket he had a sandwich, the jam already turning the bread to pulp. They would never find him here. He wondered if they had ever been as he rolled down a small dip in the close grass. He lay soaking up the warmth from the intermittent sun, the small tufts of pink thrift moving in the tremor of the wind above.

At breakfast his mother had moved ceaselessly from scullery to kitchen. She did not look at him but collected toast racks, jam pots with small frilled lids that resembled her bath hat in miniature, plates. She wore mauve, her favourite colour, a high-necked mauve sweater, a mauve and grey tweed skirt. On the dresser the old mauve of dried-up heather from a brief trip to the moor when it rained continuously and they had tea in an empty hotel, where the only sound was the click of cutlery. Fluffy, mauve slippers clacked her hard, coarse heels. Her eyes were rimmed red and awash, but she was always on the edge of tears. He noticed a white bandage below the edge of her sleeve. Lulled by her movements he drew one knee up, placed his thumb in his mouth and allowed a bare toe to investigate the raised pattern in the carpet. His whole mind was filled with these two particular sensations while a weighty warmth swelled between his legs.

'Get your thumb out of your mouth!' She caught his shin with a stabbing flick from her drying-up cloth. 'And where are your slippers, may I ask? Go and find them at once!'

He left the room and went to lie face down on his bed, caught the smell of moth balls that represented his childhood.

Usually he was alert to her changes of mood but he had been exhausted by the night before.

'Gordon! Come downstairs at once!'

He clambered off the bed and skirted round the bathroom, banishing the image. He slid down the edge of each step on the flats of his feet putting on his slippers at the foot of the stairs.

'You take this cup of tea to your father.'

She still would not look at him though he searched her face for some explanation, caught the fine down on her upper lip, the pink cheeks.

'Your father said I was a doll and look what you've done to me.'

She drew back her arms showing her bulk; said it about once a week. He made the slow progress upstairs, inevitably slopping the tea. He stopped outside the the door to their room and poured it back into the cup, polishing the saucer on the seat of his shorts. His father was lying on his back with his eyes closed. He made a kuh sound with each exhalation and round the edge of his lips a white tide mark had formed. Gordon leant forward intrigued and then reeled away from the rank acrid smell. The varnish on the headboard had been scratched down one side by his mother's hairpins, as if a wild animal had leapt at her from the bed end. His father's trousers lay crushed to the floor, still related to his shoes as if they had come off together. A pound coin had fallen from the pocket and lay tilted in the pattern of the carpet. He picked it up and pressed it to his palm. Now he would have to go. He returned to his bedroom and retrieved the cigar box from under his bed; shoes, socks, he was ready. He ran downstairs.

'Mam! I'm going to the beach!'

And I'm never coming back.

How do you become a lighthouse keeper? He knew the light was automatic now. Maybe no one lived on the island and he could buy the cottage and live there all by himself. He unwrapped the sandwich and ate the soft mush with his fingers; lying in the hollow, his skin polished by the salt air, aware of the churning motion of hairs moving on the surface of his legs. He pressed himself down, his body following the contours of the earth; hugging the warmth below the wind. He dozed and through his closed lids the red disc of the sun became the pool of light that spilled mauve from the bath-room door.

He awoke hungry, thirsty and the tide was only slapping at the base of the causeway. He sat and eased a rough scab from his knee, gently revealing the fine, featureless skin underneath. Round the side of the cottage an iron water butt stood hard against the whitewash. A lone bulrush had seeded itself. Several slender insects with long legs jointed like fingers pressed the surface of the water, skating; large spiralling larvae and the minute plumes of young mosquitoes moved below. He watched for a long time, absorbed by the two worlds, one above and one beneath the surface. His throat was dry but he couldn't drink the rank, iron smell so like blood. He went home, his shoes scuffing the small slip of water that covered the causeway.

His mother was sewing name tapes on to a stiff pile of new, grey clothes. They had talked about it all summer, going to school, proper school, boarding school. That would stop him sucking his thumb, oh yes.

'You're back' she said. 'He's gone out, your father.'

He watched her needle, the bright silver thimble with ER on the side and the writhing scramble of blue veins under the skin of her legs. He looked away.

They were all going by train, several boys together. They took a taxi to the station, the raised cobbles stretching the tyres to a hum. A vast portico centred the soot-grimed facade and he felt the slight tremor of trains underfoot. His mother hauled up her accent, tipping the driver after he had heaved out the trunk and dumped it on the trolley. They pushed it through the huge space, voices reverberating and approached a small group of boys all dressed like him.

'Your father said to give you this.'

She handed him a brown envelope containing a five-pound note. He boarded the train and she kissed him conspicuously and left. Now he would put the memory away, now on the train he would let it slip into his mind and then push it down below the surface. Wakened by his father in the night, rising up through his dreams, through the collapsing frames of images as he burst into his own room. Propelled along the corridor towards the pool of light that spilled from the bathroom door on to the mauve carpet. He could hear the soft sobbing long before they arrived and tried to pull away, but he was gripped by the back of the neck. He looked up to find some clue to this procession but his father's face was blank. They pushed into the bathroom where his mother sat huge in the bath; white pendulous breasts touched the water.

'No' she moaned.

'Look at your bloody mother, stupid bitch.'

His father turned and left the room, the heavy tread leaving the stairs and sharpening through the hard thud of the front door. She trembled, reached up to tidy her hair and he could see a gash in her wrist, the lips of the wound blanched momentarily by the water. The blood resumed its flow, tracing a vein-like pass to her elbow where it dripped and bloomed, a billowing cloud of pink vapour. His mother watched, rapt by the indignity of a gesture that had gone horribly wrong. She looked up as if seeing him for the first time.

'Out! Get out! Get out, you little bastard!'

He backed out, knocked his elbows and knees on the door frame, careered into the walls of the corridor. From his bed he could hear the her keening moan and the plastic flex as she left

15

the bath. He curled up, caressed the satin edge of the cover and with his thumb tried to find the world without meaning.

But it was all right now. The train was moving, the grey town was pulling away and he was chugging into the future with other boys just like him.

Two Wee Mice

Carolyn Mack

'*Down in yonder meadow where the green grass grows . . .*'

Ah'm the best at ba's. Everybody says so. Ah kin dae wan haunies, scissors an' bridges. An' ah kin talk while ah'm daen them. Ma da says ah kin talk while ah dae anythin.'

Ah canny when ah'm singin' right enough. But if ah'm no singin' ah kin talk and dae the ba's at the same time. Lainy Brady's goat tae stick her tongue oot when she's daen them.

'*Where Lizzie Findlay bleaches all her clothes . . .*'

Ah usually get intae trouble for playin' here on Mrs McCann's gable wa'. No' aff ma ma. Aff Mrs McCann.

'Away ye go an' gie's a bit a' peace an' quiet!' she shouts. Ma ma comes oot the windae an' sticks up for me.

'Leave her alane. She's no' daen any herm!' she says. 'At least ah know she's no' at that canal.'

Ah'll no' get intae trouble fur playin' here the day, cos Mrs McCann's no' in. Aw the grown-ups ur away tae chapel fur Danny Williams. We hud tae go yisterday wi' the school. It wis quite good cos we went during sum time. Ah hate sums.

'*And she sang and she sang and sang so sweet . . .*'

We hud tae go an' pray fur Danny Williams' soul. Yer soul's inside yer shoulder, but ye cannae see it. If ye've been good it's gold and shiny, an' ye'd need sunglesses to look at it or ye'd go blind. But if ye've been bad it's grey an' dull. Black, if ye've been really bad. Danny Williams wis bad that's how we hud tae go an' pray for his soul. Yer soul comes oot yer mooth when ye die an' if it's aw shiny, it goes straight up. But if it's aw black, it starts tae go doon. Ma da says Mrs McCann's soul's definitely gon' doon, but ma ma jist tells him tae wheest.

If ye want tae keep a soul fae gon' doon everybudy hus tae pray fur it. Like blowin' oan a feather tae keep it up in the air. The the soul'll go up up up so far. But if ye stoap prayin', or ye laugh when ye're prayin' like Peter Dolan did yesterday, the soul'll start comin' doon. Doon doon doon til it get's tae Hell an' then it kin never get up again.

Danny Williams' should be aboot haufwey up noo. Aboot as high as oor buildin'.

> *'That she sang Danny Williams across her knee. Lizzie made a dumpling, she made it awfy nice. She cut it up in slices and gave us all a slice. Saying taste it, taste it, don't say no. For tomorrow is our wedding day and I must go.'*

Ah kin sing Danny Williams noo, naebudy'll laugh an' say ah fancy him. Cos he's deid. It's a sin tae laugh at deid people. Yer soul'l go black. John Brady's soul'll be black, as well, cos it wis aw his fault. Even though ma ma said last night it wis his da, Mr Brady's, fault. Ah canny understaun it cos Mr Brady wisnae even there. But ah heard her sayin' it tae ma da,

'See whit Brady's belt an' buckle huv done?'

She said it loud like they wir arguin' even though he hudny said anythin'.

'*One, two, buckle my shoe; three, four, knock on the door . . .*'

This is a hard wan tae play cos ye've goat tae dae the actions as well.

Mr Brady hits his weans wi' a belt, sometimes wi' the buckle if they've been really bad. Wan time Lainy showed me a big mark oan her back, jist up fae her bum, where her da hud whacked her wi' the buckle. It wis the time we got caught up at the canal.

Ma ma didnae hit me fur it. She jist hud that look oan her face. The wan that makes me aw horrible inside, an' she jist said tae me.

'Lizzie, ah thoat ye knew better.'

Jist that. That wis aw. Lainy Brady said ah wis lucky. But, ah didnæ feel very lucky.

'*Five, six, pick up sticks . . .*'

He hits them wi' sticks as well. Anythin' that's lyin' aroon'.

'It's no' right.' Ma ma says tae ma da, 'Ah'm gonny report him wan ae these days.'

But he jist says it's nane oor business.

Mr Brady's a bad man awright, but he didnae hit Danny Williams so ah don't know how ma ma kin blame him fur it. Ah asked ma da but he jist patted ma heid an' said ah'm too wee tae understaun.

'*Seven, eight, shut the gate . . .*'

There's a gate at the canal, but some ae the big boays huv dug the dirt underneath so ye kin get in if ye crawl really low. That's where ah wis when ah got caught, haufwey underneath. Lainy wis already through, then we wur gettin' shouted fur wur tea an' ma ma saw me fae the windae.

Everybody gets shouted fur their tea at five roon here. Windaes go up an' wummin are oot oan the streets shouting, 'Lizzie!' 'Lainy!' 'John!' 'Danny!'

That's aw ye hear at five a' clock. Ma da says when he wins the pools he's gonny buy aw the weans bloody watches. Ma ma jist tells him tae wheesht.

> *'The night was dark and the war was over, the battlefield all covered in blood . . .'*

This wan's awful sad, aboot a soldier gettin' killed. Ah always get a lump in ma throat when ah sing it.

Danny Williams' ma wis gonny kill him the other night. No' really kill him like. It's jist wan ae thae things yer ma says. Everybudy wis gettin' shouted fur their tea. Then everybudy went in. The windaes went doon, the doors shut an' it wis aw quiet, except fur Mrs Williams,

'Danny . . . Danny . . . DANNY!'

Her voice wis gettin' louder when ma ma opened the windae an' shouted.

'Kin ye no' find him, Betty?'

'Naw. Ah'll kill him when ah dae.'

'Haud oan an ah'll send Jimmy doon tae gie ye a haun',' Ma ma said.

Ma da rolled his eyes up, but ah knew he didnae really mind. Ma ma pit the rest ae his dinner in the oven. While ah wis eatin' mine ah' tried tae count every time ah heard ma da shoutin' oan Danny.

But then there wis too many voices shouting. Men and wummin. The shoutin' wis gettin' louder. Then people started chappin' the door askin' if we hud seen Danny an' ma ma wid tell them that ma da wis oot lookin' fur him tae.

> *'There I spied a wounded soldier lying dying saying these words . . .'*

Ah knew Danny wis in big trouble noo. Ma ma an' da huv hud tae come oot an' look fur me a couple a' times, but never the whole street!

It wis nine a' clock when ma da came up fur a heat an' a cup a tea. He kept runnin' his hauns through his herr. He always does that when he's worried aboot somethin'. He told ma ma tae keep his dinner in the oven.

He asked me if ah'd seen Danny in school that day an' if he said he wis gon' anywhere. Ah hud tae think. Aw schooldays seem the same tae me. The bell rings, then ye're in class, say prayers, dae sums, dae spelling . . . Then ah remembered that John Brady hud broke ma good pencil at hame time. Ah didnae tell anybudy because ma ma disnae like me telling oan the Bradys, no' even tae the teacher. Danny Williams hud tried tae fix it fur me but it wis snapped right in two.

Ah told him the last time ah seen Danny and John they were running up tae the canal gate.

'But John says he's no' seen him since school,' ma da said as if he didnae believe me.

'*God Bless my home in bonny bonny Scotland, bless my wife and my only child . . .*'

Then he tells ma ma they're callin' the polis, an' she says, 'Oh, dear God!'

But ah don't think she wis prayin'.

She goat gloves an' a scarf fur ma da cos it wis gettin' really cauld noo an' he went away back oot.

The shoutin' stoapped when the polis came. Three motors an' a big van parked oan the sper grun acroass fae us. We could see everythin'. People stopped lookin' an' gathered roon them. Fur a minute ah thoat they wur gonny pull Danny oot a motor, like a magic trick. But aw they did wis gie oot torches an' whistles.

21

Mrs McCann came up tae tell ma ma that some ae the big boays had beat up auld Sandy Patterson, jist because he lived hisel' and gave the weans ginger boattles. Ma ma shook her heid an' said, 'Oh, merciful God. They're no' helpin' anybody, cerryin' oan like that.'

She forgoat tae tell me it wis bedtime. She opened the windae, even though it wis frosty, and an' told me tae listen fur a whistle 'cos when somebody blew their whistle it meant they'd found Danny.

A wee while later we smelt somethin' burnin'. Ma ma ran tae the oven, but she wis too late. Ma da's dinner wis burnt black. She started greetin'. No' loud ur anythin', jist quiet like, tae herself. Ah couldnae understaun it! She only greets at sad films, or if she hears somethin' bad. She never greets aboot burnt dinners an' stuff.

Ah didnae like her greetin' so ah showed her ma trick. Haudin' a pencil like a fag an' blowing ma breath oot the windae like smoke. She nodded an' smiled, but she wisnae lookin' at me, she wis lookin' oot at the canal.

Ah didnae really care 'cos ah wis gettin' tae stey up late.

'*God bless this earth which I lay under, holding up St Andrew's flag.*'

We never heard any whistles. We could hardly even hear the shoutin'. Jist far away. Wan time ah heard somebody shoutin' 'Mammy', an' ah thoat Danny wis back.

But ma ma leaned oot the windae an' said it wis 'Danny' they were shoutin'.

Ma da came back at eleven fur merr tea. He hud lost his gloves lookin' through the middens. His hauns wur blue wi' the cauld an' aw cut, but he didnae care. He wis tryin' tae tell ma ma somethin' in secret. Ah kin always tell. Like when it's ma birthday or Christmas or somethin'. Ah kin see his lips movin'. Ah seen somethin' aboot 'draggin' the canal' an' 'a big machine to brek the ice'. Ma ma jist sat doon an' put her heid in her hauns an' said, 'Naw. That poor wee boay.'

'Two wee mice went skating on the ice. Singing pollywally doodle all the day . . .'

Fur wans ah wis gled we lived three sterrs up. Ah could see right err tae the canal bank. They hud opened the big gates an' everybody wis there. Big lights went oan an' ah see could real frogmen, like in *Flipper* oan the telly. When the noise fae the big machine started ma ma shut the windae. She went an' sat at the fire an' kept tellin' me tae come away fae the windae. But ah wanted tae see wit wis happenin'. When ah turned roon she hud her rosary beads oot. She always gets them oot fur good luck when somethin's wrang.

Ah must huv fell asleep cos' the next thing ah remember is seein' the rosary beads burnin' oan the fire. Ah grabbed the poker an' tried tae get them oot. But ma ma jist said tae leave them an' go tae bed.

'But the ice was thin and one fell in . . .'

Peter Dolan says he seen Danny gettin' pult oot the canal. He says he came oot feet furst, an' he wis aw eaten away wi' the rats.

He's a liar, but. Ma da says Danny jist looked as if he wis sleepin'.

'Too cauld fur the rats, hen,' he said. 'Too bloody cauld . . .'

John Brady's soul'll be black noo, fur no' tellin' aboot Danny. Peter Dolan says he'll get sent tae jail!

He jist ran away an' never told anybudy when Danny fell through the ice. Went hame an' kidded on nothin' had happened. He wis too feart tae tell he hud been up the canal.

Ma ma seen Mr Brady yisterday. That's when she said, 'See whit Brady's belt an' buckle huv done?' Ma da never answered her.

Then shook her heid an' said, 'God help us aw. That poor wee boay.'

But she wis gettin' aw mixed up, 'cos she wis lookin' err at John Brady's hoose when she said it.

'*Singing, mammy, daddy, help me ah'm away.* CLOSE YOUR EYES!'

The Neighbours' Return

Michael Mail

I t was remarkable how quickly things seemed to return to normal in Kierscen. The war had been over hardly forty-eight hours before the butcher Sleider reinstalled his famous ornamental shopfront beneath the free Polish flags which grew from every building on the main street. Although everyone joked that his meat was pre-war, there wasn't a dry eye in the village. The next day, the old stamps appeared in the Post Office. The '39 face of President Moscicki beamed confidently in a range of colours despite the fact that he was dying in Switzerland. They were quickly replaced by drab yellowish ones issued by the mysterious Provisional Government. It was said that the glue tasted of vodka.

The occasional shot could still be heard in the surrounding areas, which ensured that people didn't venture too far in those first weeks. Partisans were still coming in from the forests. Some couldn't believe it wouldn't all just come rolling back as suddenly as it had rolled away.

The Russians by and large stayed away from our village. Except when they lured Wojciech's cow on to the road and it ended up making the supreme sacrifice to the 'great liberators'. They preferred the town of Liebling with its three pubs. All the pubs were owned by one man, Kasprzycki, who was said to be the first millionnaire in post-war Poland.

Someone picked up the word 'reconstruction' from the radio and it clunked round the village as if saying the word was half the task. No one was sure exactly what needed to be reconstructed. Certainly, there was the Church. All sorts of unlikely people were terrified at the thought that there wasn't place to avoid going to on a Sunday. Only two of the five walls had survived the direct hit by stray Russian shells and it became a source of pride that rebuilding began almost straight away. The Cathedral at Cracow had been used to hide most of the silverware and iconography, which were speedily returned, remaining in the town hall for the next two years.

People revelled in the rediscovered delights, soon to be lost again, of uninhibited conversation. In the absence of any form of distracting entertainment, gossip became a favoured pastime. Of course there were the war heroes whose exploits were loudly proclaimed. Like Fleveritz's son Miklos, who'd escaped to the East and came back a tank commander in the Russian army. But there were the other kind of stories, told in whispers and nods. You would think that some people would never venture into the street again. Yet everyone did, the brave and the foolish, the virtuous and the corrupt, the saviours and the sinners. Another word soon became fashionable – reconciliation. Somehow we wouldn't spend too long on who did what in the war. It was as if the act of survival itself justified absolution. The war years became almost a taboo subject. The optimists talked about the future and the pessimists about the Russians.

Then one day something happened that broke the mirage. Something happened that no one expected. Jews got off the bus.

Before the war many Jews lived in Kierscen. The Great Synagogue dominated the southern neighbourhoods where they lived. One day they were gathered together and marched out. Sometime in '43 and that was that. Soon their homes had been moved into, their businesses taken over. There wasn't a villager who hadn't benefited in some way from the discreet looting that went on after they'd gone. Furniture, cutlery, chickens, farm machinery. Everyone became richer.

No one talked about the round-up of the Jews to this day. Yet it hung over the place like a dread. Dread of the day now arrived. When some would come back.

Gershon Steinhart and his son Yozef got off the bus from Warsaw. It was the bizarrest sight. They looked normal. As if they'd been on a three-year shopping trip to the capital. Steinhart was dressed in a sombre black suit that appeared well worn. He could have been a tax inspector or an under-taker. Yozef was also in plain attire, blue trousers and a lighter blue shirt, his hair in neat waves across his forehead.

From the beginning, we had all understood the arrange-ments for the Jews. More so than the Jews themselves. The camp being built for them in Platow was well known. You couldn't miss it. A huge ugly factory on the edge of the town. Some had family who had helped with the construction. They knew its purpose from the start. Everyone did.

It was just a matter of when they would be taken. The restrictions against them began with the occupation. What type of work they could do. Where they could live. They had to wear badges to identify themselves. Then one day a third of the village disappeared into the night. We all heard the commotion, shouting, crying, many came out on to the streets to watch the spectacle. Some stayed at home and locked their doors.

Those who risked sneaking into the emptied neighbour-hood just after the Germans got the richest pickings. By the next morning it was like Christmas. The streets filled with families looking as if they'd just come back from tea with their

favourite auntie who'd decided to give them all her possessions. It was like a big jumble sale.

And then the arguments started. Some just moved straight
into the vacant houses. You could see fires lit the very next
night. It was eerie to witness, as if their ghostly owners had
returned. A huge fight broke out over the engineer Levy's
property with its prime setting at the end of main street. It was
famous for being the first house with a balcony and the Mayor
was determined no one else would get their hands on it. It was
quickly realised that there would have to be a secret meeting
to sort out the various claims being made. In a few weeks it
was all resolved and the once Jewish neighbourhood was
smoothly occupied. The Mayor got the Levy house.

There were also lots of stories about Jews hiding away
treasures. Dontiech got a whole field ploughed up ready for
planting on the basis of one rumour everyone was convinced
he'd started.

No one really thought about the end of the war. It was hard
to at the time. And of course no one thought that any Jews
would survive. Then that bus arrived from Warsaw.

Steinhart had been a grocer in the town. He wasn't someone
people knew much about. The Jews by and large kept themselves
to themselves. There was an understanding about the extent to
which the two communities could or could not mix. It had been
like that for centuries. Of course there was a lot more mixing
going on than people would have you believe. Especially among
the young. Politics got everyone talking to each other. And there
was the gambling – an indiscriminate passion. If you visited
Tinzer Lake in the summer it was clear which part of the
lakeshore was taken up by which community. But the island
in the middle was a no-man's land, common ground. It was like a
free zone where all sorts of things that would never be counten-
anced in the village went on, and not a few secret romances
were begun under the cover of its leafy terrain and permissive

ambience. Both sides knew each other well. It wasn't like there was a lot of tension. People just got on with their lives. Everyone bought their bread from old Mama Greenstein's. She was the mother of the town not just the Jewish quarter.

What shocked everyone was how well Steinhart appeared. Initially no one knew who he was. It was only when he went into the Post Office and asked if any letters had been kept for him that the story of his return got out. It chased round the town like a storm. Was he the first of many? Were they all coming back? Maybe the Jews of Kierscen had been treated differently. Maybe they were used as slave labour and had survived. What did Steinhart know?

And what about his home, all the homes, everything that had been owned by the Jews parcelled out to their grateful neighbours. There wasn't a family that hadn't benefited in some way from the bonanza. Even the priest, Father Lubomirski, suddenly procured an ornate rug for his chambers, which it was said, somewhat mischievously, had been taken from Rabbi Wilmeier's place. Would it all have to be returned?

Steinhart was now heading slowly down the main street. The way he walked suggested he wasn't trying particularly to recognise or be recognised. His face was set rigidly forward and he was holding his son Yozef's hand tightly. Yozef's look contrasted his father's. He was smiling at people. But it wasn't happy smile. It was more like a request. For a moment I thought about the huge welcome-home party they had given Miklos, Fleveritz's son, decked out in his splendid Russian uniform, beaming like he'd won the war by himself. The whole village turned out as if Miklos was everyone's son, a bit of all of us. And you felt this strange sense that he *had* somehow actually saved the town.

They were heading towards the old Jewish district. It would just be a matter of time before Steinhart would arrive at the door of what was once his home and was now lived in by the butcher Sleider. Sleider had left his former flat above his shop and had been in that house now for over two years. The assumed permanence of his occupancy was further underlined by the slaughterhouse he had built out the back.

Steinhart's journey was being discreetly monitored by all the townspeople. It was like watching a lit fuse meander towards its end. Someone said that he should be spoken to. Reasoned with. We should find out what happened to all the Jews. But no one would volunteer. Someone else said he should be arrested but no one could think why. Fleveritz said it was an official matter and the Mayor should take charge. He disappeared and we assumed he had gone off to get him.

On Praga Street, Steinhart suddenly stopped. Mrs Porwuit was walking up the street and he started talking to her. Soon he was moving on again and Mrs Porwuit was quickly pounced on and interrogated. She didn't reveal much. He'd asked about the clock tower that had stood on the street corner. It had been dismantled and taken by retreating Germans scattering grenades as they ran. She'd asked him about Mama Greenstein but he didn't know.

Steinhart reached the front of the Great Synagogue, now more a ruin than anything else. It had been the most impressive building in the village, much to the annoyance of the Catholic Church, which had successfully lobbied to have the main steeple reduced by fifteen feet to make it lower than its own. The gold lettering that had once adorned its façade had long been stripped away but the Hebrew and Polish words could still be made out: 'Let mercy roll down like waters and justice like a mighty stream.' They walked around the building and then entered through a side passage. There couldn't have been much to see but they were there for quite a while. It was being used for storage and what hadn't been taken was rotting away. Maybe they prayed.

People were now waiting for Fleveritz to come back with the Mayor. We gained a bit more intelligence from Mrs Kolchak, who'd sometimes bought food from Steinhart's store. He was a quiet man. His wife mainly served in the shop. And they had two daughters as well as the son. He was in his late forties and Yozef probably eight or nine. Someone said the Mayor was in Cracow. There was a growing sense of panic. Sleider had closed his butcher shop and rushed home.

Steinhart emerged from the Synagogue and carried on southward. Rembertow Street had been the location of the central market and would normally have been bustling with people. The quietness must have been startling for them. But he would surely have known how everything had changed. Now there were only Polish faces in these streets. Surely he didn't expect to come back and find things the same. Return to his home. Go into his kitchen and prepare hot water on the stove. Surely he knew. So what was he doing? That was the baffling thing. Was he simply going home?

They were just a few roads away. In streets that would be very familiar to Yozef. He would have played football with other boys on the rough piece of ground by Poniatowski Avenue. In the winter, he would have sledged down the steep hill on Torun Road, careful to miss the huge hole half way down that would scupper the less experienced or the careless. Now for both of them, memories would be enveloping. Walking down the same streets that they had been marched out of on that cold spring night. Into the blackness.

Finally, they arrived in front of Sleider's house. Steinhart scrutinised the outside for a moment before, incredibly, taking out a key. It seemed to fit and he turned it but he couldn't open the door. He turned the key again and you could see the door give up some of its resistance yet still it remained closed. He started knocking, then banging. There was an urgency, an aggressiveness in his manner that contrasted sharply with his careful, ponderous progress through the village. As if his mild demeanour had been corroded by the journey. Yozef looked as if he could fill the street with tears. Then suddenly, like a shock, the door opened and they were gone.

What happened to Steinhart and his son became another concluding fable straight out of the war. Lost in the haze of stories, some true, some less so. It turned out that Flever- itz's son Miklos had spent the war years working in a brothel somewhere in Soviet Asia. Soon no one was sure what really happened to them. Some said they were passing through on their way to Lublin and had caught the next bus out of town, others that they were communist agents. A few even disputed that they had actually got off the bus. No doubt their disappearance was a relief to many.

Their last sighting was the two of them standing in that doorway. Being welcomed in by Sleider. Apparently he had given them a tour of the house. One can only imagine their surprise at seeing the place almost exactly as they had left it. Then he took them out back.

No more Jews returned to Kierscen. The see-saw of Polish history swung Russian and Red. A joke circulated the village that the engineer Levy had survived the war and was now Mayor of Tel Aviv.

Souvenirs

Tom Rae

Rosie bursts into the day centre screaming she's going to give that bastard **AIDS**. She is always threatening to give people **AIDS**, as if a well-aimed spit is all it takes. She scratches too. Ask Karen, her forearms turned septic. When Rosie gets too stroppy, big Gordon usually 'forklifts' her out of the centre by the oxters, from behind of course, Rosie trying to catch him in the groin with her heels all the way.

Everyone says she is evil. Jane, the student placement, disagrees, *Rosie is always fine to me*, she insists; but then old Wully McClure'll pipe up, *Aye, but when Satan wants tae get aroon ye, fit wey dizzy go aboot it? Ah'll tell ye, quine, he shows ye aw the nice things . . . am ah no right?*

Big Gordon thinks that the travelling folk like Rosie have been destroyed by the cities; Scotland's Plains Indians he calls them.

– *Ah'll give that bastard AIDS!* She screeches like a pterodactyl as the old boys look up from their dominoes and shake their heads.

That bastard is a Fyvie bloke who turned up in the day centre last week – the usual story about the chance of work in Aberdeen, with the oil and that. Meanwhile could the centre feed him till his Giro comes through, like?

All week Rosie has courted him, fetching cups of tea and

rolling cigarettes. How is he to know the day centre is a Giro graveyard, Rosie the keeper of the cemetery gates? They left at eleven this morning to cash the Giro.

– The bastard never even bought me a drink.

– What's wrang wi ye? Asks gentle Hannah.

Hannah hears how Rosie went into the bus-station toilets to comb her hair. When she comes out, the Fyvie man is waving at her from a window of the Cruden Bay bus. There was the chance of work in Cruden Bay . . . with the oil and that.

Hannah looks relieved when Rosie gets up and goes across to the settee. She moans that it smells of piss – it does; Dan McNee's kidneys are a mess. Before sitting down she takes the medicine-yellow gloves she has just put into her anorak pocket and places them in her handbag. Always there is this touch and transfer of personal belongings.

The domino crowd begins to pack up; the Sally Army will be serving tea and sandwiches at nine. It's been a quiet night. One of the young ones has bought a second-hand video.

Now Hannah makes ready to leave. It can take her a full ten minutes to snub a fag, sort out bus fare and put her coat on: a further ten to say cheerio and tell how bad the buses are.

Soon Rosie is the only one left. She knows the centre shuts earlier tonight (it's Giroday), but still she sits slumped on the couch. It's best to let her be and get on with the clearing up.

Suddenly she is at the counter, in the mood for a chat now. That means a coffee, free of course . . . a coffee means a story, and a story deserves bus fares.

– He even tried to tak ma gloves, ken. She fusses over the mittens. I was given these by a very good lady friend, stays in Brig o Don . . . respectable ken, church-folk, twa kids, bonny kids . . . She pauses.

– Naw, nae cunt . . . nae cunt takes Rosie McPhee's gloves n lives.

Listening to Rosie is like interpreting a dream, establishing the connections between illogical leaps. A fixed point tonight seems to be these yellow mittens.

– Ah sorted thon last bastard n'll sort this wan the day. One curse from me means death, before yer next birthday, jist like the other wan.

A soft smile comes over her face.

– He used tae take me dancing . . . Ah was lost wan night, ye see, Glasga's a big place, in the streets ahin the train station they told me no tae go.

She lifts the mug of coffee in both hands and sips it like a secret chalice; smiling at some silly clandestine thought. Something angers her and she bangs down the mug.

– Aye but they nurses wurnæ any better than me. And they'd the cheek tae ask money aff ye when they ran oot by a Wednesday.

Rosie always claims to be a trained nurse; that she was sent down to Ruchill Hospital straight from a children's home in Aberdeenshire.

– Every night for a week he took me back tae the hostel in a taxi, plenty a money like . . . a toff. Always wore a blazer . . . D'ye ken John Garfield? Well he looked a bit like him, a wee snub nose n black wavy hair.

She begins to run a hand through her own hair.

– Men used tae say ah had hair like Rita Hayworth. Ah wiz always being told that at dances.

She embraces herself and sways, croaking a snatch of melody.

– *I got you . . . under my skin. I got you . . . deep in the heart of me.*

She laughs modestly.

– Miss Semple made me sing for church people when they came tae the home on Sundays.

She sips at the coffee, which is cold by now. It is after nine o'clock.

35

– N it had they big fit dae ye caw them? – she makes a face – things wi wee mirrors stuck aw ower them, big baw things hinging fae the ceiling n going roon n roon aw the time. There wiz patterns on the floor like sun hittin the water. Aw the quines fancied him. This cow kept wigglin ur arse against um aw night, goin up tae um when he went tae the bar . . . He wisnae stingy. No like that Fyvie bastard the day. Haud oan a minit.

Rosie turns and makes her way across the room to the toilet. She moves unsteadily like a baby, stiff-legged, the soles of her feet hitting the ground flatly. She sings again. A long silence follows. Maybe she is combing her Rita Hayworth hair. The sound of the toilet flushing.

Just then there's a frantic rapping on the window and a face appears. There's too much exhaust grime on the pane to make it out. A few seconds later McNee walks in. He has old Jeanie Robertson with him. This is what happens if the lights stay on past closing. Rosie comes out of the toilet clawing the air, too mechanically to be cat-like. McNee hasn't seen her yet.

– Ah got her . . . the wan wi the arse, Rosie whispers, stauning there in the toilet makin faces at hersel in the mirror. Wan scratch – rip – that wiz enough for the cow.

McNee rushes to hug her.

– ROSIE! Ma wee darlin.

Shrugging Dan off she glowers at him.

– Oh Rosie, dinna be like that.

– Let me get on wi ma story.

As usual Jeanie begins to pick tiny bits of dirt from the floor. She will ignore a crispbag, but used matches, a fallen chip – these she pursues as fussily as someone picking ouse from a black jumper.

– Ony chance o a wee cup a tea? McNee asks. It's brass monkeys oot there.

Rosie talks over him.

– Course, ah wiz worried in case Peter saw the blood oan the bitch's face. Ah didnæ want um tae think ah wiz scruff n lose um. Ye know somethin? He never tried tae push himself against ye when ye were dancing, ken fit ah mean?

– Who's Peter? asks Jeanie innocently, already emptying the contents of a palm into an ashtray.

– Ony chance o a cuppa? Ah'm bloody freezin, persists McNee.

Suddenly Rosie switches to her declamatory mode about people who have warm homes to go to and don't know what it is to spend a night on the pavement. A riot once started because Wully McClure joked what did she know about cold pavements when there was ay some idiot too drunk to ken what was creeping in to his bed.

– Who's Peter, Rosie? asks Jeanie again.

Lips pursed, disdainfully shaking her head, Rose replies.

– Peter Manwell wiz hung for murder.

– Oh, says Jeanie.

– Ah went wi Manwell.

– Ah went wi Emmanuel, shouts McNee, laughing.

– He asked me back tae his mother's hoose wan night. He said they had a farm. It wiz too late tae be let intae the nurses' hostel, that wiz why ah went wi um. He said ah could use his sister's things, her *toiletries*, ken.

She utters the word 'toiletries' as if it was significant – an authentic detail in a web of fiction?

Jeanie has found a damp cloth and goes round wiping tabletops. McNee announces that he is going for a pish. There is a knock at the door and Hannah comes in shivering. The nine o'clock bus hasn't come and the next one's not till a quarter to ten. She spots the three mugs on the counter as she makes for her usual seat beside the radiator. Rosie is mumbling to herself again.

– Ah showed that bastard the toon, kept um oot a trouble, took um tae the Post Office . . .

It is difficult to steer her back to the story. She wants to curse the Fyvie man. Now the gloves are being transferred from handbag to trouser pockets for warming up.

– He wanted ma gloves tae, she confides.

– He didn't try to steal your good yella mittens, did he, Rose? sympathises Hannah.

– **NAW**, no him! Peter Manwell did.

– Who?

– Have ye never heard of Peter Manwell, the murderer?

– Well, ah've heard of a Peter Manuel, replies Hannah. Ah could hardly no huv when ma family's from Uddingston.

– Am ah gonny get tae tell this story or what? . . . He said his mother's house was just behind some fields. It wiz a cauld night wi a full moon. Ye could mak oot the dykes and hedges. Ken the wey ye can see heids n shooders in the pictures in thon dark light?

McNee must have heard all this from the toilet because when he comes back he says that if two people are holding hands and looking up at the moon they will fall in love.

– Ah remember goin through a field wi um. It wiz that cauld the glaur wiz like rock n ma feet were sore. Ah kept stopping. Many a fella'd tried it on but no him, he didnæ touch me.

At this McNee grabs Rosie round the waist and snuggles his head into her shoulder.

– GIT! Her tone softens magnanimously as she wriggles free. Drink yer coffee, Dan.

– Here, Rosie, asks Hannah. Are you sayin you were out in a field in the middle of the night wi a murderer?

– We came tae a fence. There wiz a coo beside it. Ah wiz waitin fur um tae help me ower it when he says, See that – he's pointin at the coo, ken – Ah wance shot wannythame. Bang. Right up the nostril, right intae its stupit brain. He called me a wee slut, he told me his people never had a ferm. They never even had a gerden. Noo ah'm no sayin ah wiz as pure as Fairy

Snow, but on ma deid mother's grave, God rest her, ah believed him aboot the ferm. Ah think it wiz his posh voice. That wiz the worst thing, how his voice could change like that.
– Ye must have been terrified, Rosie.
– Aye, ah wiz terrified. He wiz going tae rape me, wizn't he?
– So ye told um if he laid a finger oan ye, ye were goin tae seg um, interrupts McNee.

He grips himself by the throat and pretends to choke. Rosie stares.
– Dan, can ye not let us hear the rest of Rosie's story?
– Ye should come doon the men's hostel some time, Hannah, she tells it there often enough.
– How would you know pissbag, says Rosie, they never let ye in for pishin the beds.

While she continues to stare at him, McNee goes into a mad act.
– Naw! . . . The evil eye! He shouts. He falls to the floor, eyes rolling and making throttling noises. Nosferatu! He lies on the floor laughing.

Rosie is quite capable of flinging an ashtray at him. He has insulted her gift: the evil eye. This time she just resumes quietly.
– Ah never conked oot, ah never conked oot. He had me by the neck wi his two hauns. There wiz nothing ah could dae, he wiz near the height of big Gordon. Ah scratched and kicked a while n wee lights started in ma heid. Ah couldnæ breathe. Then there wiz only his eyes, enjoying it. As God is my witness he had the evil eye in um tae. But ah'm travellin folk . . . ah stared n stared at um n he couldnæ staun it.

He drapped me like a wee rag doll. Aw the time a kept givin um it . . . the evil eye. Ah remember him liftin ma bag, he took oot ma hanky n fumbled aboot doon the front of his breeks wi it. N then he lit a fag . . . wannamine, that gallus filmstar wey like John Garfield. Ah thought he wiz gonny throw me wan.

Get up, he says. Ah telt um tae fuck off. But he just stood n looked at me for a while, smokin.

Rosie pauses. It is as if something is happening in her mind. McNee suddenly sits up, resting his elbows on his knees like a court jester. Hannah isn't sure what to do. She asks if Jeanie needs a bed for the night. Jeanie now rushes to clear the mugs into the sink. No one offers McNee a bed because of his kidneys.

But Rosie has not finished her story.

– He took ma gloves oot ma handbag. A nice pair they were, the matron gave me them for ma Christmas. *Just a wee souvenir*, he says. Ah got up then, cause nobody takes Rosie McPhee's things. But he's walkin away ower the field. Ah could see the wee red tip of the fag in the dark. **You are deid, Mr Manwell!** ah shouted. Ah put ah curse oan the bastard.

– Aye, and right enough Rosie, eh, he ended up hung.

This is Hannah, timid as ever, trying to restore a normal atmosphere. As she ends the story, even by the centre's standards, Rosie seems deranged. Still she stares straight ahead. It's as if her eyes are still following that glowing cigarette tip across a dark field.

– We'll have to hurry up, Jeanie, it's nearly half past. Come on, get your coat, orders Hannah. The pair of them exit, thank-youing and cheerioing all the way to the door. McNee gets up and goes over to spread himself on the couch. Rosie remains transfixed. Everything has been cleared away, there is no justification for Rosie to stay any longer. She begins to comment on how cold a night it is.

– Ah've a friend in Mastrick'll put me up – McNee, asleep on the couch, gives the moral leverage – if ah had the bus fares.

She knows there is plenty of small change in the box drawer, the tea money. It is best to count out forty pence and coax her to the door.

– Haud on, ma gloves, where's ma gloves? She pulls them out

of her pockets, a filthy comb stuck to one of them. Ah'll have tae fix ma hair, ah cannae . . .

Anything to gain a few more minutes.

– Ach youse don't care aboot the likes of us poor folk.

She staggers off along the street, jostling the walls. She stops now and again, head cocked to one side as if listening to something. Passing cars are sworn at. From a distance it looks as though she is communing with some invisible companion, but tonight she is going to make the top of the street safely. The bus stop is just around the corner.

A man coming round the opposite way almost walks into her. He looks alarmed by the bedraggled creature that confronts him. *Nae chance*, it is saying. *Nae chance, mister, nae cunt takes Rosie McPhee's gloves and lives.*

Timing

Lizbeth Gowans

T he rainstorm started. Her headache lifted at the same
time, as always. She stepped out on to the deck, high
above the street, to greet the fresh waft of wet air that set the
wind chimes going.

She loved the sound of the chimes. During the first days in
Seattle, that sound had enchanted her as she walked in the
street. Every deck in this high apartment building was hung
with Japanese lanterns, wind chimes of bamboo or Tibetan
bells and, on her first exploratory walks around the university
district, she had thought the swaying lanterns and bells the
most exotic thing, like a prelude to some slow eastern dance or
a little *kabuki* scene about to take place in front of her, the sole
watcher in the street. And now here they were, tenants in that
very building, and her on a balcony amid lanterns and chimes
of her own.

She lifted the sleeves of her kimono bathrobe and folded
them across her breast, turning her face up to the raindrops,
relishing the absence of the day-long headache.

'Hey, Ailie!' Dirk's voice and person behind her startled the
chime by the screen door. 'What're you doing out there? You
not getting ready? We're supposed to be there at eight.'

Ailie turned. 'It's the rain at last. Such a relief. The chimes
like it, too.'

He reached up with his towel to flick the bell chime on the corner of the overhang. 'Here, I'll make 'em dance for you.' Then, over-playfully, he flicked at her legs. 'Let's see *you* dance, girl. Give us a Highland fling.'

He laughed uproariously, turning the balcony into a stage for clowning, his favourite mode, which he thought endearing – and so it had been, in the locker room and at summer camp, two important sites in the making of his maleness. She smiled, curving a token arm over her head and one hand at her hip, then followed him inside.

Once in a Paris garden, in the Faubourg Saint-Germain, he *had* been endearing, when he remarked that he was a poor lumbering bear when it came to courting a pretty woman and, by way of reassurance, she had quoted to him Flaubert's famous sentence. *Human speech is like a cracked kettle on which we tap crude rhythms for bears to dance to, while we long to make music that will melt the stars.* *

That period in France, when they had met, hadn't been long enough, surely, for either of them. She wished now that she'd known more Frenchmen, for a start, absorbed more of the world away from her own culture, the way her university year abroad was supposed to be. As for Dirk, wandering in Europe had just served enough to blur his certainty about what might be expected of men towards women. It was out of that shifting perspective, a certain unsureness behind the eyes, that he had woo'd her so successfully, for she liked uncertainty in the male, as being akin to sincerity, honesty, humility, and perhaps even a wish to be enlightened by her, to be shown, as it were, the steps.

Returning with him to his native spot in the far west, she fancied the change had something to do with old ways between men and women that were just in the air here. But, if she

---

* La parole humaine est comme un chaudron fêlé où nous battons des mélodies à faire danser des ours, quand on voudrait attendrir les étoiles.

were truly honest with herself, the disharmony had sounded months before, from the moment they'd become lovers. It was, romantically, called that – 'being lovers' – but to her the term had more grace in its wording than the performance itself in which Dirk had no scrap of uncertainty. All was simplicity and mastery, with nature leading.

She lifted her hairbrush, frowning at herself in the glass. It still dismayed her that anything could be amiss and she not understand the cause and be able to put it right. She wondered if it mattered all that much, fairly sure he had no notion it might matter at all.

She took off the kimono and put on a peasant blouse and full skirt, with flat ballerina shoes. It was to be a family gathering, a pot-luck supper, everyone bringing something, at his sister's home on Windermere, one of Seattle's exclusive hill sections into which Deb and Frank had recently bought. Frank would do the salmon steaks broiled in beer on the *hibachi* and make one of Deb's huge wooden bowls of mixed green salads with much parsley in it. It was a special occasion because the visiting cousins, Mary Lou and Ern, didn't often come over from Eastern Washington and hadn't yet seen the splendid new house. Dessert would be brought by Jim and Paula, while the college kids, Barby and Rob, wanted to do the garlic bread. Dirk chose to bring the wine, several gallons of Californian that he would decant for the table as needed, a ritual he liked.

Ailie liked them all, except for Ern maybe. It wasn't dislike she felt so much as distrust of a certain look in his eye, a look that she fancied dismissed her from the moment she did not laugh at one of his anecdotal jokes that smacked, she feared, of the boot camp he was proud of having undergone, as he was proud of passing the ordeal of initiation for the fraternity of his choice. Her failure to appreciate his humour seemed to antagonise him, for he took to using the word 'European' in a particular way, with a pointed pause and a look away from her just before he said it. 'Like the blouse, Ailie. Very . . . European.' 'Superior *vino*, Dirk. Quite . . . European.'

As they drove in the rain to Windermere, Dirk grumbled, 'Why are we always late for things? I'm always ready first.'

Yes, she thought back. You are. 'We just have different timing, that's all.'

He glanced at her quickly to see if this was some kind of cheap dig at something else, but she smiled and patted his hand on the wheel. 'Sorry I wasn't ready when you were,' she murmured, taking the blame reassuringly, which she knew he thought only right in this case – and even, for all she knew, in the other.

Deb opened the door to them wearing a slim shift dress of Hawaiin design, her long black hair caught up in a coil skewered with a Japanese butterfly pin. Her colouring, like Dirk's, came from Welsh and French ancestry, but she had adopted the Orient as her preferred mode in her clothes, house interior and cooking. Doorways were hung with bead curtains, pagoda bells tinkled at the open windows of the kitchen, a collection of beautiful rice paper fans was displayed on one wall, a low Japanese table surrounded by cushions instead of chairs waited in the sunken dining room, and outside on the covered patio was a planter furnished with bonzai trees. Frank's ancestry was Swedish. Along with a small swimming-pool he'd had dug in the backyard among a stand of pines there was a birch-built sauna. To Ailie, the union of the big blond Scandinavian and the little dark 'Oriental' was a very interesting and successful partnering, which she studied anew each time she came into their presence. In turn, they seemed to be equally intrigued by Dirk's Scottish wife and, like almost everyone she met here in the north-west, had a romantic *Brigadoon*-like idea of her native land, a declared fascination with her 'lilt', and an expectation that one day she would teach them how to do a strathspey. Cultural variety, she often told herself, would teach her much, if she paid attention.

It was a wonderful dinner, as always. Americans, gifted in recipes from their multi-immigrant forebears, certainly knew how to rejoice in such fare. Ailie was still learning from a Betty Crocker *Dinner for Two* given her by Deb on her first Christmas among them. Raised on a regular diet of mince and mash – which had its own excellence, she thought – the wealth of things to do with food dazzled her.

Also, she liked the way folk here sat on at the table after eating, conversing, listening to popular music, well into the candlelit night. She'd have liked to tell Ern that this *was* European. It was a soft-spoken time, lazily relaxed, when the women touched the men's forearms as they made familial references or nudged their shoulders against the man's upper arm, showing and spreading affection. Dirk often put his arm along the back of a chair at this time, smiling at the occupant. It was as if a warm expression of gratitude in the air touched everyone at the table, prompted by the food, the wine, and the nearness of a nice known person safely married to someone else.

Tonight, cushions made for that much more intimacy round Deb's table and Ailie wondered if anyone would remark on it, hoping they would not, for she wanted everyone to be as unaware as they seemed, natural, fine, motivelessly innocent.

The music was a compilation of contemporary favourites, sung ballads mixed with early rock, some of Frank's Tiajuana Brass, some Beatles, and The Doors brought by Barby and Rob.

In a lull, Ailie looked round the gathering. 'I bet we all come from a range of musical eras here. Don't you think? Deb? Frank? Who'd you dance to when you were students?'

They looked at each other. 'The big bands. Benny Goodman.' Frank snapped his fingers.

Deb clasped her hands and leant her cheek on them. 'Ah. Dave Brubeck. I love him still.'

'Jim? Paula? How about you?'

'Well, who else? Bill Haley and the Comets, I guess. Right, Jim?'

'Yeah. And the smoochy Platters . . .'

'Oooh yes,' Mary Lou said. 'I remember dancing to them real slow at high school hops. Long before you, honey.' She reached across the table to touch Ern. '*We* danced to everything, didn't we? All the ones you've said. And then some. All the modern stuff, and old-time, the lot.'

Ern indicated Mary Lou with a wide hand, as if introducing her to an audience. 'Yeah. She's a real dancin' fool from way back. Me? I can soft-shoe shuffle, but that's it. No fancy . . . European . . . steps.'

Ailie looked to see if Dirk had anything to say in the vein, but he was helping himself to more wine, reaching over to refill Ern's glass. He saw her watching him, raised his goblet and mouthed a favourite sentiment sanctioned by Baudelaire. *Enivrez-vous*! It brought back a flavour of their French era and with it a memory, an evening in Paris.

They had been walking, hand in hand, past a little *place* outside a café where someone's *fête* was being celebrated. The jovial *père de famille* had welcomed them with outstretched arms. *Venez, les amants! Dansez avec nous, hein!* Dirk had taken her in his arms, positioned as for the waltz, and she'd prepared to be swung wonderfully round to the accordion playing '*Avec celui qu'on aime*' (a tune on everyone's lips then), for she loved to dance, especially the old-time dances that her parents and grandparents did at harvest homes in her childhood.

But with Dirk there was no marvellous dip and turn, only a stiff stepping from side to side with an accompanying rock of shoulders up and down to the music, all accomplished more or less on the one spot. It was rhythmical, yes, but had no grace, no sweep, and no scope for that exhilaration of covering the ground that left you breathless and delighted – a sort of *ivresse* indeed.

Over by the record player Deb shuffled through more records to prepare a new stack, while Frank began rolling back the carpet. 'You guys wanna dance, feel free.' Thereupon, he grasped Deb round the waist and swung her out into the middle of the parquet floor where they did a cool jive to *In the Mood*. Joined by Jim and Paula, both smooth dancers, with the ease of movement and steps that belong to long-time partners, the result was infectious. The kids began to do the latest campus craze, a sort of stretch and sway of the body while positioned on the spot, facing each other, followed by some complex arm and hip rhythms.

Ailie watched them with fascination and pleasure. Rob noticed this and, still dancing, drifted over to her and pulled her to her feet. 'Let's dance, Ailie!' She was shy, unskilled at the mode, but wanted eagerly to dance, just dance, any dance. Barby tried to get Dirk to follow suit, but he shook his head and pushed Ern forward. Having no better luck with him, she faced Mary Lou who responded with an inspired pirouette just as the band went into a change of tempo, becoming the slow *Tennessee Waltz*. Mary Lou picked up the hem of her full skirt and, with her other hand placed delicately on Barby's shoulder, the two of them waltzed exaggeratedly round and round, step perfect.

Giving up on Rob's dance with a laugh, Ailie watched the waltzers, feeling the dip and sway of it sweeping through her. She held her arms out and closed her eyes, humming in tune, swaying, longing for that wonderful whirl away into the throng of dancers under lamplit rafters to the music of accordion and fiddle.

She opened her eyes just as the waltzers circled past her and, seizing her chance, she swerved between them, grasped the nearest one by the waist and swung into the dance without interrupting the pattern. Mary Lou looked startled, then grinned brightly while they continued waltzing round for a few turns of the floor. As they passed near Ern and Dirk standing by the stairs, Ern murmured to Dirk, 'Quite a move, huh? Must be . . . European. Maybe they'll go home together.'

Mary Lou's smile and foot faltered. Soon she said that was enough for her, she needed a drink. Ailie whirled away and waltzed alone back to where she'd left her own glass. 'That was splendid,' she laughed to Dirk, patting her chest, catching her breath. 'Mary Lou's a good dancer. I haven't waltzed like that for years.' He looked at her strangely, with no answering smile. O, fiddle, she thought. He thinks I'm making a crack at *him*. So tiresome.

Later, driving home, he was silent. Ailie chose to put it down to companionable tiredness, but then remembered. 'Dirk? What did Ern mean?'

'Well, what d'you *think* he meant?'

'Don't play games. Why d'you think I'm asking?'

'Look. You just made a fool of yourself in front of my family, that's all. No. Worse. You made a fool of *me*. Think about it.'

'Because I wanted to dance? But *everyone* was dancing . . .'

'Was that what you were doing, Ailie? Just dancing round like a sweet little girl at a party? Come *on*!'

She stared at his furious profile. 'Why, yes,' she said, her voice small and puzzled, like that of the little girl he'd posited. After a moment's thought, in which she inwardly told him and Ern both to go to blazes, she turned her head away, leaning her forehead on the window. The street lights shone mistily on wet sidewalks, passers-by in couples leaned in to each other. The night's music lingered in her mind where presently a tiny waltz tune began, to which she kept time with her front teeth tapping behind her lips. The blurred colours and movement outside flowed with memory and the tune into a scene of circling couples, old and young, parents, aunts and uncles, cousins, grandfathers with children, girls with girls, boys with grannies, neighbours with other neighbours, smiling and dancing to a familiar old compilation: *Bonnie Gallawa', Sweet Rothesay Bay, Come Ower the Stream, Chairlie, Ca the Yowes, Helen of Kirkonnel* . . . Between each tune the band always played a certain bridge at the end of which you swung into the arms of a new partner to a new tune. When the new tune came, the dancers sang along with the words, for they were all old songs, and if you wanted a special one played or the band needed requests to keep them going, you waited for the bridge, which might be played twice, marking time, waiting for the call, 'Gie's *Far from Islay!* or *Braw lads!*'

All the way home Ailie could not get the tiny tune out of her head, nor could she remember the name of it or any of the words, though it was as familiar as all the others. It was only when she'd got undressed, put on her kimono again and stepped out on to the deck among the chimes to reclaim some measure of calm that was going to be needed, that it came to her. It was, of course, the bridge.

Year of the Vezzas

Chris Dolan

What is it royalty do? They *summer*, don't they? They don't go on holiday like ordinary people. They summer. Like exotic birds. Giacinta summered. Rest of the year was flat, centuries long, eventless. The town endured in its valley, like the rocks on Monte Capanne, patient, dry, waiting. Spring sun, autumn sun, a little rain, the odd wind, nothing changed it for more than a moment. There was school in the mornings, piazza in the afternoons, church Sundays and feastdays, during the holidays off down to the beach to kick a ball and swim. Sneak a look at the girls when they were in bathing. Everything as it should have, and always had, been San Piero. Until Giacinta came summering.

Giacinta was like nothing you've ever seen. White hair, white skin. White, as if she was always standing in front of the sun. But even at night you still had to screw your eyes up, the whiteness of her. It was like she might burn herself out. That's Roberto's memory of her back then – burning from the inside out. And the clothes – clothes you can't imagine. Not fancy gear, not expensive gowns or anything like that, fancy jewelry. Her mama had all that – fur coat, diamonds, the lot. Her old man wore gold rings, gold bracelet, smart suits. But Giacinta – they used to say she dressed in seaweed and flotsam. Time was when Roberto almost believed it too, imagined her getting up at dawn and going to the beach when no one was around, draping lengths of surf grass and kelp over her, frilly redweed, rockweed. Giacinta wasn't from another country. She was from another planet. First she said she was Romantica Nuova. In later summers she explained she was a Goth. Gotica. She whitened up her already-white face. Her hair should have been black to be a real Goth, but her blonde hair was too great a prize in that overbaked island. Elba. In Roberto's mind now, a roasted almond. Sweet and bitter and hot and deep. Giacinta used to wander through the town – to her parents' concern and the locals' delight – like some lost sea-sprite draped in the ocean's broken chains. Not knowing human language, washed up and stranded. An air of loneliness that had taken hours in front of the mirror and years of non-communication with parents to perfect. When he was older, Roberto would learn the word selkie. Maybe it would have helped back then. Probably not.

Giacinta and Famiglia were an annual invasion. At the end of June every year, the big, wooden doors of the house were dragged open. Like an alarm clock, sounding out across the town, breaking a long sleep, heralding summer. Every able-bodied villager would be up and dressed and down there, gawping in at the biggest and grandest house in San Piero. Right on the main square it stood, cocking its snoot at the Mayor's house and the Town Hall and the café on the three other sides. Like a sunflower, the Vezza house. Head bent and dour all year, then in July it opens up, stretches, faces the sun. The kids watched the cleaning lady start her brooming and then they'd race off together, squealing and yelping. They're coming! Down to the sea for the second event of new-born summer – the opening of the boathouse. Again, they all stood and watched, gasping at the chrome and steel glimpses of sleek motorboat. Gli Scozzesi! Motorboats are ten a penny round those parts nowadays by all accounts, but back then? It was a kind of glamour, a magic from another world.

The circus came to Portoferraio every year and the Vezzas to San Piero. The Vezzas were the bigger act. Two huge cars, Signori Alberto's and Luigi's, their wives with their fancy big hats, all of them waving, blowing their horns, the kids hanging out the car windows shooting fiery toy guns and shouting in English. Vezza cousins and second cousins twice removed and folks without a drop of Vezza in them but trying it on, all of them out in the streets welcoming the invaders, with jugs of wine and snacks and presents for the kids. And sitting at the back of one of the cars, always so still and white and strange and sad in her sea clothes, Giacinta. She would give one pale smile, fleeting, like a teardrop, a spring shower. One brief smile for Marco.

It wasn't the sun coming out that made summer in San Piero, it was the Vezzas coming home. The children were given fast rides in the motorboat; there were picnics in the orchard at the back of the grand, old house; Signor Alberto paid for a band to play at least once every year in the village square and everyone danced. There'd be trips in the cars to Portoferraio or out of town for barbecues. Dads got drunk and mums tipsy at Vezza expense; grandparents got fat. Girls dreamed of discos and shops and popstars. Lads got crazy at the sight of Giacinta.

And the way she spoke. Her Italian was fine, understandable, even with Sanpieresi expressions, but the words crisp, crackling on her lips. Like Dominici's well-fired panini. Sounds that were round and full in a Sanpiereso's mouth were smooth and flat and fragile in hers. Her Scottish accent they said. As no one, from one year to the next, ever heard any other mention of this Scotland, it might as well have been Moontalk. This Scozia; high up, near America. Annarosa and Rita were her girlfriends, and she'd stay close to them, in the street or wherever, whispering. Every boy in San Piero spent his nights imagining and discussing what on earth that whispering might have been about. But Rita and Annarosa never broke her confidence, in all those years.

The boys hoped, too, that Giacinta would take up sunbathing, so they could better ponder that strange luminous skin of hers. But she never did. She'd go to the beach with her little brothers and cousins, dressed in her weird, flesh-covering costumes. She'd play for a time with the youngsters, building sandcastles, creating little canals and moats for the tide to run through. Activities no one had ever thought of in Elba, nor undertook again until Giacinta returned. Then, suddenly, she'd strip off to a one-piece, run to the sea, splash about, tippy-toeing back on to dry sand, shaking the water from her hair and limbs like a protective veil. She'd dress again before anyone could get a proper look. Il Tornado Bianco. That's what they called her. The White Tornado. Those brief, dazzling, dashes to the sea, legs and arms and neck white hot.

Her mother was foreign and you would have expected Giacinta to be a mix of her and her father. Half north half south. But she was even fairer than her mother, not a hint of Sanpieresi in her. Not back then. Except maybe her moist, orchard-earth eyes, thick eyebrows. Her little brothers, by the end of each summer, were as ripe as dark Elba plums. Of all her family only Giacinta had that see-through skin. Lemony, like expensive lingerie. Not that Roberto ever saw much of it. She wouldn't allow it. Nor would Marco.

Signor Alberto used to joke he'd marry Giacinta off to a nice Scottish Protestant boy. Protestant boys don't spend half their lives perched on Vespas combing their hair in the reflection of café windows. But everyone knew that, really, he wanted Marco to be Giacinta's man. Big, strong – rich – Marco Ionta. The Iontas owning the best of the land around San Piero, down as far as the outskirts of Portoferraio. In that way, too, they make Robert think of royalty – powerful families marrying wisely, annexing land and wealth. Little villages in forgotten islands can have their aristocracies too. Even in this country up here, amidst the factories and cold and new towns, there can be little nobilities.

Before Jackie, Giacinta la Principessa. That's how Robert, Roberto, remembers her. Appearing each year, like the sun coming out, lighting up the whole island for a time, then vanishing again behind the clouds. Back to her home in the barely existing misty north. An ocean girl. A starlet. That's how it was. He swears on his mother's milk, that's how it was.

It exists now all right. The north. Hard and solid as a factory wall. Cold as an anvil. Robert sits there with the suitcase dragged out. The case he never really unpacked, keeps underneath the bed. Jackie knows it's there. She knows he takes it out every now and then, knows he sits wondering whether or not to empty it, once and for all after all these years. Or start packing.

Of course, it should have been Marco sitting here. What would he have made of the deal? Had he worked it out already, way back then? Robert didn't think so. He knows that Giacinta chose him over Marco Ionta. Attributes her change of heart to that day on the motorboat when big, brave Marco overplayed his hand. But maybe he knew all along that what Giacinta had to offer wasn't for him. He said later that he never wanted to leave the island and he was true to his word. He never did. He's still there. Down in the town now, in Portoferraio, with a wife and two kids. One less than Robert and Jackie.

Even if he had known the deal, Roberto, he'd have gone with Giacinta. Back then, if she'd said she really was from the moon, or from a shell-palace on the ocean floor, he'd have jumped or dived, suffocated and drowned for her. No question. When he got to this place, with its sharp, jagged name, and its endless houses and rain and work, it was still worth it.

When he realised the source of the Vezza's wealth was a couple of small, cramped restaurants making fish and fries for people to take away or sit in and eat; realised that Scotland was not like America in the movies, that the only thing Kilmarnock shared with New York were those steely Ks like flick-knives, even then, Giacinta was worth all of that. Work your butt off eleven months a year. No perks, no days off. Sundays spent doing the books, doing the stocks, scrubbing solidified lard from surfaces. So that, one month a year, you could summer. Play millionaires among the folks back home. Except they never did any more.

Maybe Marco had worked all that out, but it was unlikely. The fact of the matter was that Giacinta had made a clear and definite decision. They were out on the motorboat, the three of them. The fact Roberto was there at all, two years younger than Marco and the son of an Ionta employee, un contadino, proved that he was already in favour with Giacinta. He knew that, that summer, he looked different in her eyes. He had grown, had become thin and a little unhealthy looking, had let his hair grow long and unkempt, the way he knew she'd like. Marco, on the other hand, had had to be neat and straight and cropped for his military service.

They went out far in the fast little boat, each of them taking turns at steering, Marco and Roberto vying with each other, out-stunting one another, turning the boat at dangerous angles, skidding it across the taut blue surface of the sea. Giacinta loving every moment of it. Now he could see why. Plain little Jackie Vezza, something of an outcast back home, as wan and fair-haired as a thousand other girls in the same provincial town, has two strapping young Italian men competing for her, playing high jinks on the Mediterranean sea. She must have relished every detail to tell the girls back home. Girls who never believed her, or, if they did, sneered at her oily chip-shop men, her ramshackle town.

There was a liner on the sea that day, making its way from the Côte d'Azur to Livomo or Corsica most likely, a cruise for the genuinely rich. Marco decided he would cut across its front. He revved the engine up and sped the little boat, flat out, across the line of the approaching ship. It seemed he'd given himself too easy a dare – the massive liner didn't appear to be moving at all. But it was, and fast. Within a few moments it was clear to Giacinta and Roberto they weren't going to make it. They'd ram straight into the side of the vessel – quarter of a kilometer of sheer sheet metal, thousands of tons of blue-painted death. They shouted at Marco to change course. Could make out faces on the many decks, some of them half way towards the sky, looking down on them in their little speedboat, like a pond-skater bug darting, panicked on the top of the water. Marco did change course. In time to save them splintering head on into the liner, but not from being caught in its wash. For a moment there was calm, as they watched the waves streak out behind the ship, grow and gather pace, rush towards them. Then engulfing the little boat, throwing it around in the sea. Roberto held on to Giacinta and Marco was washed out overboard. He came to no harm, except that, by the time they moored at the island an hour later, Marco Ionta and Roberto Rossi had changed positions in relation to the great Giacinta Vezza.

Signor Alberto was not pleased at his daughter's change of heart. That was the beginning of their problems. He attended the wedding and bought them a present and, after those early arguments and fights, entire-family rages, he never again said a word against Roberto. Robert. But equally, he didn't pull his weight when they got back home. Told his brother Luigi to back off too. The two fish restaurants had been little gold-mines for years, but now, suddenly, they were competing with curry houses and pizza chains, bistros and coffee shops and fancier Italian restaurants. That'd been Robert's plan, to move upmarket. Open up a big place specialising in Elba-style seafoods and roasted vegetables. But there was no time. Every waking moment was spent trying to force the businesses they had to eke out a measly profit.

They went back to Elba the first couple of years, but could only afford a fortnight. Her parents were too frail to make the journey any more, and Uncle Luigi, widowed, moved permanently to the house in San Piero, mainly at Robert and Jackie's expense. They had to sell the motorboat, and the casa grande began to crumble, dry-rotting, around old Luigi. Things weren't the same anymore. And along came Gina, then Luigi and Alberto junior. Then poor little Tony, who left them again, pale as death from the start, hardly staying long enough to leave his mark. They'll never go back now. They're no longer Sanpieresi, Robert and Jackie. The kids never were.

But still he pulls his suitcase out every now and then and wonders. And remembers. Giacinta before she was Jackie. Burning from the inside out. Maybe tonight he'll catch a glimpse of cypresses in her eyes, a waft of seaweed about her. Maybe not. If they work hard this year, perhaps they could go south next. To Rome, perhaps, or Spain. Or perhaps by then Robert'll have given up the ghost, packed up, gone back home to San Piero.

She'll be home any minute now so he stuffs the case back in under the bed, remembering again that first, victorious kiss. Don Roberto Rossi's One Big Seduction on the night of the village concert. They'd crept away into the deep damask of an island sunset, out beyond the village, and kissed for the first time. When they had finished Roberto pulled away and declared he never wished to kiss her again. Giacinta was stung, stunned, her white face embering into pink flame. That one, single kiss, he solemnly said, would serve him for the rest of his life, and she laughed in relief and joy. Then he said he wanted to record every detail of this moment for posterity, so that they could keep it with them for the whole of their lives together. He begins to list Purple Sunset, Stars, Cypresses and Oaks, a distant band playing 'Ti Amo'. A Chill in the Midnight Air. Now she is laughing for real, a laugh full of love and wonder at their luck. Then Roberto made another list, stating out loud, one by one, all the beautiful things about her. Hair like satin, skin like silk, jewel eyes, the beautiful curve of her breasts and she pushed him away, modestly and excitedly at the same time. La Giacinta Vezza, before she was Jackie of the chip shop, Goth, sea-sprite, Moongirl, was now, and forever, all his.

Mother's Boy

Linda Cracknell

I'm waiting for Mum, like I do every night. Ben's cheek squashes pink on to the pillow next to me. Mr Brock's paw is in his mouth. His breath gurgles a bit as he sleeps. The stove hums and smoke crackles up the chimney in the middle of the bender, our home. Dad's on his bed. His cigarette smoke wafts over to me and I hear the flick of his magazine pages, the creak of the mattress as he fidgets, reaching up to the hammock above his bed to pull things down. Books or clothes. His candlelight makes the bender brighter than it is by day. If I look carefully, I can see the frame which Dad made by bending tree branches. They're a bit hidden now by all the cloths and blankets stuffed behind them. Dad said the blankets were to make it warmer – warmer than it would be with just the tarpaulin over us, or the Tarp as we call it. I make it into a game, passing lots of time while Mum's not there by searching for branches among the dark folds.

Once Dad's put his candle out, there's no difference whether my eyes are open or closed. But I don't need eyes. I lie and listen to all the cars going by on the main road to the town. It depends on which way the wind's blowing how clear they are. If it's raining, they sizzle like eggs frying on our stove. I always know when it's her coming. I know the exact signs. The way the car slows down to turn into the track. At

63

first you just hear the bumps and sucks of the puddles as she makes her way towards us, climbing towards our camping place. Then the engine sound grows, and finally, once she's past the bend, Mum's lights shine in through our only window – the one made out of see-through plastic. They cast a square of light on to the wall. It's criss-crossed, like the light from an old-fashioned lantern on a Christmas card. As she nears us, the square of light squashes and gets long. It moves up the wall, slides and curves along the whole tunnel of the ceiling. Then Mum's Lights hit the mirror. White, and getting larger.

Dad always goes to sleep before Mum comes home. And then I wait for her on my own. She works in a factory making sweeties – toffees and fudge. She calls the factory the 'Stink Tank'. To make sweeties she puts all the things like sugar and butter into this huge tank a bit like a swimming pool and they get mixed up. You smell her when she comes home. I guess it's because bits splash up when she's leaning over to stir it. It's a heavy, sweet smell that lands on you after she's walked past in the dark. I don't mind it but I think Dad does.

Dad found the mirror in a skip, said its owners didn't want it but it would do for us. Mum looked into it and screwed up her face, said she looked so old these days, that was what working nights did to you. She didn't want it. I put it at the bottom of my bed. So although as I lie there I face away from the window, I can see the reflection of Mum's Lights. She bounces home towards me. The lights put warmth in my tummy. I can go to sleep.

After the lights have slipped off the edge of the mirror, the car stops and the engine clicks off. Sometimes she doesn't come in straight away – says she likes to have a cigarette out there in the dark rather than disturbing us. And I'm usually falling asleep by the time I hear the car door slam and the flap of the Tarp as she comes in the porch. She always whispers Hi to Taff. Taff's old bones click as he wakes a bit and stretches his legs. His tail beats on the floor. Mum says it's the sheepdog in him, not happy till he has his whole flock together. Then the smoke shoots up your nostrils as she puts another log on the stove.

If she crackles when she comes in, it means she's brought us a bag of toffees. Rejects, she calls them. They taste all right, though sometimes the wrappers are more on the inside than the outside. She never eats them herself. And she pushes me away if I eat them too close to her, says the smell makes her feel sick. She doesn't want to be reminded of the Stink Tank when she's at home. One day me and Ben went to Jason Clark's house after school. We took a big bag of Rejects and we watched *Grange Hill.* When Mum came to collect us, she said she was calling us from the doorway for five minutes before we noticed her. We were staring at the TV, with toffee wrappers a mile high around us and our faces all brown. Later on Ben was sick. She didn't bring Rejects home for a while after that.

Then you hear her pull the covers back to get into bed and a few sleepy whispers with Dad as she settles next to him. Their voices are usually too soft to hear the words. But there was one time, a few weeks ago, when I heard what they were saying.

– You turning your back on me? Mum said.

Some mumbles buzzed between them, getting louder like wasps when you try and swat them. Dad did his Giant's Voice.

– You smell like a fucking crème caramel.

– All part of a night's work. One of us has to earn some money round here you know. There was a sharp creak of movement. I could picture her glaring at where his face should be in the dark.

– Yes, sweetness. There was a pause and then the snap of his jaw as he finished a yawn. I'm just not in the mood for sticky toffee pudding at four a.m.

– You . . . Jesus! The smell's not my fault. Some of us aren't on 'hot bath' terms with the local tarts.

I hadn't heard her yelp like that before. I do it when I get really cross with Ben and want to hit him but know I mustn't. But not Mum.

Dad laughed, and not long afterwards Mum jostled down as his snores started again. I didn't get to sleep for a while after that. Mum was sniffing.

While I wait, I use the heavy black torch which Dad says not to waste the batteries of. In the dark I hold it against my hands and feet. They go dark pink. I can see these red stick things inside, like a skeleton except different. I'm transparent. I don't know any other boys at school who are. Like some sort of alien. I don't think Mum knows, although she realises I'm a bit special. What would we all do without you, Jack, she said, when they were both in bed with flu and I had to keep the stove going and walk to the shop to buy food.

It must have been boring before I had the mirror. Every night now there's a boy called James who appears in it. We speak to each other in whispers so we don't wake the others. He tells me about things that no one at school knows anything about. And I don't tell anyone, not even Mum or Dad or Ben. It's our secret. I only need the torch and the mirror to make him appear. I sit in bed and shine the torch upwards from the blankets under my chin.

James says that if I concentrate hard enough, I can become anything. Like a bird, or like Robert Chatham, so I can do brilliant cartwheels. Or I could turn into a warrior and be able to beat up the big boys who say 'Crusty' at me and call Ben 'Smoky Bacon' which makes him cry. They find it funny that our clothes smell of smoke. It's just because Mum hangs them to dry on a rack above the stove. She says that was why she cut all Ben's hair off before he started school – so he wouldn't get called names. I'm not sure why she's never done that for me. She thinks I can look after myself I suppose. It didn't work for Ben anyway. They still call him names.

Sometimes I hear voices while I wait. Outside. The first time I thought it was like a whole playground of children chattering and squawking. But more beautiful. Like a playground would sound in heaven. I went outside to see what was happening. But there was nothing. There was just trees and a light sky which confused me because I thought it was night. The bender looked so small and low huddled against the wall of the ruined house for shelter. And Mum wasn't back yet. Then Dad came out to find me, said I was a pillock. It was birds. Birds. Where are they then? I asked. He said they were in the trees, go back to bed. But I had to keep asking. Why are they making so much noise? They don't sound like that during the day. He said they're just happy to be alive, which you won't be unless you get back in there fast.

Dad spent a few nights away from home around that time. Mum watched him walk off down the track. The metal buckles on his rucksack glinted off the full moon. Bloody werewolf, I heard her say at his shadow.

It was later that night I went to look for aliens. James told me that alien landings always happen at full moons. And they'd be sure to land on the hill up behind the bender. I was going to go on my own but Mum was looking a bit sad so I asked her to come too.

I walked a bit ahead of Mum. The aliens would need to see me first; they'd recognise me. I carried the big torch but I kept it turned off. Each time I looked back, I could see Mum's outline following, a tall shadow with her head bent and long hair swinging out from her shoulders. Taff ran ahead.

After I'd climbed the gate, and I was under the big oak trees, it was dead dark. I followed the rustle of Taff upwards on a kind of path I knew was there in daylight. His paws stopped and pee crackled against fallen branches. Otherwise my breath was the only thing I could sense; it formed clouds in front of my face and came out in big puffs from the climb. Looking back over my shoulder there were tree trunks and the gate patterned against the town's orange lights, and Mum climbing over the gate towards me from the moonlit field. The black shape of hills rose beyond the town. I turned upwards. Branches brushed the top of my hat and something reached up to lick at my legs. I'd lost the path. I tripped on a root and went face down. My hands were wet, and a fungus smell went up my nose. I put on the torch so I could see better. But the opposite happened. Everything disappeared, and when I looked back – no Mum. I flashed the torch below me but she wasn't there. I started calling her. Then I was stumbling back down the hill till the panting filled up my ears. I heard nothing, saw nothing, until I ran right into her. And her arms wrapped me. And Taff was jumping up at us thinking it was a game.

She laughed and said, You came back to find your poor lost Mum, hey?

We walked back down to the bender, me lighting the way with the torch and her with her arm around me, saying I was her big brave boy.

One night last week I heard those high voices again. They went on forever. And then I saw not Mum's Light but the sun, coming out properly and reflecting in the mirror at the bottom of the bed. I hadn't heard the car. And then Dad was out of bed, his vest and trousers on, stooping out of the porch without saying anything to me or Ben. I heard him chopping wood with the axe. With every chop there was another noise – like the noise the dog made when I saw it get run over on the main road. Taff, I thought. What's he doing to Taff? But when I got outside, Taff was lying there as usual and he looked up at me like he wanted me to explain something, his stomach stuck to the ground. He looked back at Dad, one ear crooked. It was daylight and the car wasn't there. Then I realised that it was Dad making the noise. Every time the axe came down the noise came out of him. When he turned towards me and Taff, his face was all ugly and looked wet. Where's Mum? I said, but he looked away and said something about visiting a friend and stared hard at the log before he split it. And Ben and me went to school but we forgot our reading books, and were still wondering where she was. I told Ben that she'd gone to have her cigarette somewhere else so she wouldn't wake us.

After school she was there as usual to meet us.

Here she comes. The car's bumping along the track. The headlights start to do their thing on our ceiling. I say bye to James, switch the torch off and lie back, watch Mum's Lights bouncing towards home. The handbrake cranks on outside and I settle down to sleep.

The flap of the Tarp jolts me back awake. Something's different. The engine's still futting in the dark outside. She's forgotten to turn it off. I clamp my eyes shut as I always do, to look like I've been asleep for hours. Taff clicks and grunts but she doesn't speak to him. The footsteps creep up to our bed, and I feel Ben' side of the mattress bounce upwards. She's carrying him somewhere, all sleep-heavy. I squint through lash fringes and see her legs by the side of the bed, Mr Brock black and white on an empty pillow. The Stink Tank smell gets stronger and I can almost feel her warm fudge chocolate breath on my cheek. I know she's bending over me. But I'm asleep Mum, just like I always am when you come home. You never need to worry about me.

Then her legs through the fringes move away and I hold my breath. Frozen in pretend sleep. Straining to listen. Flap. She's back outside. A car door squeaks and slams. Ben first of course, the Baby of the Family. Then she'll come back for me. I wait. I hear another car door shut. The engine roars, the wheels slip on mud. She's going. Then the engine stops. My breath gushes out.

But there's no 'flap' of her coming back for me. The engine restarts with a cough. Mud splatters off the tyres against the Tarp. Then the car's getting quieter as it leaves us, away down the track. I open my eyes properly. No need to pretend now. In the mirror Mum's Lights are bouncing. But they're red and they're getting smaller, closer together. They disappear into the dark around the bend and I can only just hear the engine. The car stops at the end of the track, pulls away down the main road. And then it's quiet and dark.

King of the Castle

Iain Grant

I t wasnae fair. We was there first. Weed bin there fer ages. We always played on the hill. We was playin king o the castle. Me an Bobby was kings an Mikey and Kev an Tosh they was knights; they was tryin tae get intae the castle an get us oot.

Weed bin there since teatime it was wednesday ide had sausages.

Mikey had a sord an the rest of us had sticks but it didnae matter we was only playin king o the castle cos Mikey had a sord. Usually we played war cos me an Bobby an Kev got guns an guns is better than sords but we let Mikey hae a go with his sord cos ma mam says you gottae be fair. We was bein fair an lettin Mikey play king o the castle wi his sord. It was fun but it was no as much fun as war, sept war's no as much fun when ye had tae be the germans. Someone always got tae be the germans but we always take it in turns cos ye gottae be fair.

Anyways, its oor hill we was playin on. Well, its no really a hill cos its tae wee ken. Its just a lump where the diggers hae bin buildin the new hooses an that but its a kind o a hill an its great cos its got hedges an ditches an its great fer playin war. Sometimes we tried to play footie but its tae slopey ken and the ba just runs away an gets stuck in the ditch an anyways me an Bobby's no ded keen on footie.

71

We was wearin hemlets what Mikey's dad had mek oot ae they buckets for tha tile sticky stuff ye stick tiles wi cos Mikey's dad's a tile sticker fer yer mam's bathroom an kitchen an that.

Weed bin there since teatime we was gaun tae play til half past eight Bobby had tae go hame half past eight cos Bobby's mam didnae let him stay oot late even when it was the summer holidays. Weed bin there since teatime it was mebbe seven oclock when they came an they tellt us tae beat it. Weed had trouble before when the witch lady fae number twenty-nine tellt us tae be quiet we was mekin tae much noise an that time when she tellt us off fer throwin stanes even though we wasnae.

When they came Bobby tellt em beat it you weer playin here its oor hill but they wouldnae listen. They just come on up tae the top of the hill an stood there standin. We all stoppt playin sept Mikey he was fightin some sodjers wi his sord an everyone was watchin him cos then he got killt wi a bow an arrow lookt like he got shot in the back an he shouted oot AAYYYYEEEEEEEEEE an spinnt roon an fell doon wi his legs kickin but he never dropt his sord cos ye could see it it was still stickin up.

When weed finished lookin at Mikey we all lookt at them an they lookt back at us an the big one lookt at Bobby an pusht him in the chest an said you beat it you weer playin here noo. We said thass no fair we was here first its oor hill but the big one slappt Bobby's face. For two seconds mebbe three mebbe four I think he was gaun tae hit back but then he stoppt hissel. Ye cannae hit em. Yer tellt not tae all the time by yer mam an by school so ye cannae hit em so ye dinnae.

Well we couldnae think of what tae dae then so we went hame. There's naewhere else tae play specially when ye want tae play war or play knights an ye've got tile sticky hemlets on an a sord. We stood roon fer a bit but they tellt us tae beat it an started peltin us wi mud an stanes so we legged it. Mikey was a' clairty frae the flair an Bobby'd already gone hame.

When I got hame ma mam says tae me yer back early what is it did ye get bored? an I says no mam we got kickt off oor hill an she says who was it done this tae ye an I couldnae tell her no at first anyways cos it was embarrassin. I says tae her it was just some kids an she says aye but which ones so then I had tae tell her an she laught. Lassies? she says ye got kickt off yer hill by lassies? an I says aye by lassies. That big one that Heather Syme she's really strong an dead fierce an she's slappt Bobby an nearly made him greet an I think there was mebbe tears in his eyes sept he didnae want it tae show so he turned aroon an went hame so that's why the rest of us has went hame tae. Sides there was more of them than us an that big one shes really big an she's in the year up frae me ken in Miss Docherty's class.

Then ma mam she says ye've got tae stan up fer yersel. Ye cannae let people push ye roon she says. So I says but ye always tell me ye should treat lassies wi respec an that. Be nice tae em ye always say.

Aye thass true ma mam she says but ye cannae let em push ye roon. See the morn? Ye should go back there an play on yer hill an if they come back ye should stan yer groon.

So we goes back the nex day Bobby didnae want tae at first but we made him. We said weed play war an he could be not germans even though it was his turn tae be germans. We made Mikey be germans with Kev cos Mikey got tae play wi his sord before. Mikey said he would only be german if he could be german wi his sord but we wouldnae let him cos it was silly germans got guns not sords.

Weed bin there since teatime it was thursday ide had pie Bobby heed had sausages. We was playin war an Mikey an Kev was germans and me an Bobby an Tosh was black watch cos Bobby's gramps was in the black watch though he never went near no germans Bobby said cos he was only oor age mebbe a wee bit older when there was the war.

Weed bin there since teatime it was mebbe seven oclock mebbe ten past seven when they come an tellt us tae get lost. Beat it you they said weer playin here noo

Na, I says, you beat it you weer playin here we was here first its oor hill. That tall one that Fiona she grabs my airms then that big one that Heather she slaps me in the face an she says beat it you weer playin here noo. Then she slaps Bobby tae. Bobby shouts oot ISS NO FAIR WE WAS HERE FIRST ITS OOR HILL an stamps his feet but that big one that Heather she just laughs at him an says beat it weer playin here noo an picks up a big dod o clairt an puts it in his face. Bobby looks like hees gaun tae hit her but then he stops hissel an runs off hame mebbe hees greetin I dinnae ken I cannae see.

There's naewhere else tae play so Mikey goes hame an me an Tosh an Kev stan roon fer a bit an talk aboot whas happen but naebodys got naethin much tae say ken sept its no fair we was there first its oor hill. Me an Tosh an Kev say weel all come back the morn after teatime an weel play war even if Bobby willnae come but I say I'll try mek him come. Then we couldnae think of anythin else tae dae so we a' went hame. Ma mam says did ye get kickt off yer hill again an I said aye we did an she said did ye no try tae stan yer groon like I tellt ye an I said aye we did but they was tae rough ken like that big one that Heather she slappt me then she slappt Bobby tae. Then ma mam she says why d'ye no try talkin tae them no hittin each other naeone never got naethin done by hittin big boys dinnae hit folk. I says we didnae hit naeone an she says it takes two tae tango an wouldnae lissen. Jus try talkin tae them she says an they'll lissen tae ye mebbe ye can a' play on yer hill. I says we dinnae want tae play wi nae lassies on oor hill its oor hill we was there first. Ye cannae hae the hill a' tae yersel she says ye've got tae share ye have tae be fair.

So we goes back the nex day. Me an Bobby an Mikey an Kev an Tosh we all go back tae play war. Bobby wanted tae come

Bobby said he wasnae scared o nae lassies weed hae a real war if they lassies come back again weel show them. Na, I says first we got tae talk tae them like ma mam says let them play wi us if thass what they want mebbe they just want tae play on oor hill wi us.

Weed bin there since teatime it was friday weed all had fish sept Bobby Bobby disnae like fish heed had fish fingers. We was playin war I was bein germans wi Bobby. Weed bin there since teatime it was seven oclock when they came an tellt us tae beat it. They said beat it you weer playin here noo.

Why d'ye no join in wi us says Bobby weer playin war ye can play tae weel even be the germans. We dinnae want tae play war that big one that Heather Syme she says we want tae play girls' games. Why no lets all play together I says weel join in wi yer games. Clear off she says weer playin here noo we dinnae want nae boys here. Iss no fair we was here first Bobby says. Aye an weer here noo that big one that Heather she says. Iss no fair I says an I slaps her that big one that Heather I slaps her right in the mou an she stans there a minute an then she starts tae greet. That tall one that Fiona she takes in her breath she was mortified. How could ye she says, how could ye hit her shes a lassie. Thass terrible am tellin my mam an am tellin Miss Docherty when school starts again an ye'll get in big trouble an mebbe ye'll get sent tae jail.

We didnae ken what tae dae. It wasnae fair. It was oor hill an we was there first an we wouldae let them share it wi us but they kickt us oot. We come doon off oor hill an we stood roon fer a bit an Bobby says tae me ye shouldnae hae hit that lassie ye shouldnae hit lassies then Bobby went hame. I didnae see him again till school started again.

I went back the nex day they lassies they was playin on oor hill. Nex day I went back again there wasn't naebody there I stood on the top of oor hill an I was king o the castle but it was just me on ma ain it wasn't no fun so I went back hame.

We never played war on oor hill nae more we never played king o the castle we never played there. It wasnae fair. We was there first weed bin there fer ages. It was oor hill it was oor castle we was kings of the castle but we wasn't no kings at a'.

Four weeks later two weeks after school startit again the men they come with the big digger thing an took oor hill away tae mek room fer mair hooses.

A Piece of the Moon

Wayne Price

That Wednesday I get woken by the doorbell but by the time I get to the door in my pants the doorstep's empty and all I can see is this big old white van parked a little way up the street. The van looks like a busted-up ambulance, but there aren't any signs. The driver's knocking at a door on the other side of the road from me. The van's hazard lights are going, off and on, though you can hardly tell with the sunshine being so bright.

The driver waits a while at the Robertsons' door, then pushes a slip of paper through it and moves up one. I look down and sure enough there's a yellow leaflet on the floor, blank side up. I close the door softly in case he hears and comes back.

It's too hot to get dressed so I pull all the curtains shut and go through to the kitchen. Everyone's already out to work or school, but there's a note left on the table. Wear this tie with your blazer, it says, and next to it there's one of my old man's black ties rolled up like a party horn. I get myself a glass of milk and take it through to the living room. I put the TV on and run through the stupid learning programmes like I do when I'm off school sick. I end up watching a guy at a table with a telescope, magnifying glass and microscope all in a row. He starts talking and touching them.

I go over to the window and take a look between the curtains. Bright light comes straight at me through the glass. I look up the street, squinting, but the van's long gone. By now it's about nine.

On the TV the guy and the table have gone. Instead there's these big rough scale things, like slabs. You can tell it's through a microscope. There's no voice, just violin music. I keep looking and the slabs get smaller and you get to see these tree trunks which you could guess are just hairs. The camera moves through them for a while, like they're a forest. Then, which is meant to be a surprise, you see this massive fly. It's in the middle of a bunch of hairs, stood over them like a dinosaur, except with its sucker going. It's kind of putting me off my milk, but I keep watching. Then the view gets bigger again, zooming out, and you get to see the fly sitting on a patch of skin. Then, next thing you know, the skin is part of some kid's wrist, who's sitting in a boat on the sea. It's a sunny day there, too, wherever that is. Anyway, it carries on and soon you can hardly see him, just the white boat he's in, this little dot on the blue sea. Then not even the boat. Then it goes up and you're in space, looking at the whole ocean he was on, in fact all the earth and everything, and further out past the moon and other planets and stars. It's all bullshit, but there I am, still watching.

The guy's voice comes back and I walk over and switch it off. I feel like I should be thinking about Hooper, seeing as I was meant to be one of his best friends and it's his funeral in a few hours. But the trouble with thinking about Hooper is that he stuffed himself with pills, so they cut him open, and whenever I try to think about him that's all I can think about – Hooper all opened up like a fat white fish, on some cold slab. All his guts out and everything. So for the past few days I've stopped thinking about him at all. But Jesus, I'm thinking, you should think about him now it's his funeral.

It's a problem.

I go through to the kitchen and empty out what's left of the milk. My school trousers are over the back of the chair like always, but the blazer's been hung up. I get the trousers on, then pick up the tie and pocket it. When I find the blazer I nearly pop a ball: my mother's gone and washed the armpits especially for today and she's left these big white tidemarks where she didn't rinse the soap out properly. It looks like sweat-salt, for Christ's sake. I go over to the basin and soak the stuff with the dishcloth. The rings just about disappear, but when I get the blazer on I can feel the cold wet, right up there.

Outside, the light's so bright it hurts. I walk down to the crossroads at the bottom of the street, where the buses stop. It's so hot there's sweat prickling my head just from walking the twenty yards to the corner. I stand there, sweating and itching. I don't know when the buses are due, so I just stand looking up the long empty street, watching all the heat waves ripple up off the road. I can smell the tarmac getting soft and behind me, in the house whose window I'm standing at, a phone starts ringing. A red car turns the corner at the top of the street and rolls down towards me, shimmering like a mirage.

At first I think it's slowing just to turn the corner I'm stood at, so I don't take much notice until it pulls up right in front of me. I kind of half-recognise the driver but don't know her name or anything. Anyway, it's obvious she recognises me. She gives me this big soft smile through the open window. I smile back, but I can tell it's all wrong. I sort of feel it.

You know me? she says, and just then the phone inside the house stops. Her voice comes out slow and goofy, like a little shy kid's. It suits the weird smile which keeps coming off and on the long white face she's got, but it doesn't suit anything else about her. The rest of her is pretty good.

Hi, I say. How's it going?

She laughs, pleased for some reason. I recognise you, she says, and nods while she looks me up and down. I like your long hair.

Oh. Thanks, I say. Christ, I'm thinking, and there's an awkward quiet for a while.

You remember that horse? That horse I used to ride? She nods again, like she's encouraging me.

Maybe she's pissed or stoned, I think. But really I know it's not that. Anyway, I nod back. I saw her plenty of times riding up our street, past our window on the way to the waste-ground, Sundays and plenty of evenings after school. I've never spoken to her but so what, I think, I am now, and I'm thinking that and thinking about her on her big brown horse, jigging up and down.

The smile keeps coming and going and for what feels like a long time she just sits there, inspecting me. In the end she says: I haven't seen you around for oh I don't know, ages. She kind of drawls out the word ages, like her jaw's had all the strings cut. Then there's the smile again, wandering on to her face like it's separate from the rest of her. Do you know what happened to me? she says suddenly. As suddenly as she can with her mouth the way it is.

No, I say. What?

She shifts herself in the car. I came off it, she says, and her smile gets fixed for a second.

Oh.

Backwards, she says.

I look up the road.

She's still eyeballing me. It gives me a thought, and I take a quick check on the armpits. The white rings are still faded down okay and I try to relax.

I like your hair. Are you waiting for the bus?

I turn back to her and take a good look. One of her eyes, the left one, is sort of milky looking. Apart from the milkiness,

80

they're both green. I notice her hair too. It's bunched up in little heaps over her ears and forehead, short and coppery. It's the same colour Hooper's was, which feels worrying for some reason, even in that sunlight. But she's got this nice little chin, under those wriggly lips. I think for a minute, then I get closer.

It's pretty late. It might not come, I say.

She nods back, really slowly. Do you speak French? she asks.

I must look blank, because she goes straight into counting up to ten in French, like it's an explanation.

Great, I say. It isn't what I'm thinking.

I can remember all my French. You can tell that. Quel âge est-il? That means how old are you.

I could laugh, but all of a sudden I feel like I might get somewhere if I keep playing along. Sixteen, I lie, and get a big smile of my own on.

Well, I'm eighteen. In my body, she says carefully, lifting the finger from her lap and pointing it at her throat. But not in here, she says, and brings her finger carefully up to her temple.

I take a good look at her eighteen-year-old body. She's wearing a little T-shirt and tight, faded green leggings. There are a couple of small holes in them, on the insides of her thighs, where they must rub. I can see pink shapes of skin showing through the holes. I picture her on the horse, bouncing up and down, with her legs apart. The holes will get bigger, with all the bouncing, I think.

That old doctor, he says it might take five years, she goes on. To get back to being eighteen. She plucks around at her hair a bit. I can see down the sleeve of her T-shirt when she does it: white cotton bra with tiny blue flowers. It's nice to look at. She smiles wide. Well, that's what he says, she insists, as if I'd disagreed with her or something. I couldn't remember a thing. That doctor. She makes a wet noise, like the start of a cough.

Everything seems fine to me. You seem fine, I lie.

Three months I was in a coma for, she says. She lifts up three fingers, then drops them dead onto the wheel. Didn't you hear about me? she asks. She sounds surprised.

No, I say. Though I might have. I might have forgotten.

She nods, and I figure it's about time to take a rest from staring at those holes, in case she notices, though it doesn't seem like she could notice much even if she wanted. I start wondering if anyone realises she's out in a car, driving. I wonder if she does this most days.

I look up the road. There's a kid on a racing bike coming down the street. I know him, though he doesn't notice us and just zips past. I wonder for a second why he isn't in school. Then the white van from earlier comes down the street and pulls into the kerb a little way above my door. The same guy gets out, this time without leaflets, and starts knocking his way along the road again. Just like earlier nobody answers and soon he's worked his way to my door. I get a feeling watching him knock at the house, like the door's going to open, even though there's no one home.

I couldn't remember a thing. Except my French, she says, shaking her head, wondering.

I look back down into the car, at her legs again, I'll admit. Then I shift closer and move a hand up to the roof of the car. It's hot as a radiator. I know it's a bad idea, with her eyes and brain the way they are, but I can't help thinking about getting my hand off that hot roof and right in there – getting some finger into those holes. I could lay it on her quim right now, I think, and she'd probably let me.

Then I think about the funeral and feel bad. In fact, I'm thinking about that slab again. Hooper's *dead*. You should feel *bad* I think. I even take a good look at him, on the actual slab, in my mind. But there I am, leaning against the car door, randy as hell. I go to open my mouth, but before I can speak she reaches up, actually reaches up and takes hold of my hand

and pulls it in through the window and I think Jesus she's reading my mind but she guides it up, not down, up to the back of her head. It feels cool after the hot roof.

Feel, she says.

The smile's flickering again now, like a lightbulb going wrong. I feel where she's put my hand, and under all the crispy hair there's this patch of skin or bone or something, all dry and cratered, roughed up into big crusty ridges. Jesus. I nearly gag it feels so bad. It's like a piece of the moon.

That doctor says, one knock there and I'm a gonner, she tells me dreamily.

I don't know what to say again so I just nod, fixed there.

That horse, that old horse, he had to go, she says. Then she sighs. She moves her head under my fingers, like a cat rubs against your leg.

All I can do is follow those green eyes she's got, watch them moving with her head nodding and rolling, one clear, one milky, like something got into the water there. For some reason I leave my hand on the mess at the back of her head, but in the end she reaches behind her and takes hold to lift it back out the window. I let it hang, the nerves in my fingertips still feeling everything, and then suddenly I get a picture of the fly I saw on TV, crawling on the kid's wrist, and I jerk my arm so hard my hand nearly hits her face and I'm scratching myself raw to kill the creeping feeling in the hairs. Christ! I nearly shout, my heart banging hard. Then I see the bus come down the street.

She doesn't move the car for the bus. I can see the driver leaning to stare down and mouth at her, but she's miles away; light years. I walk round the front of the car to get on. I nod and hold a hand up to where she is, but the sun's dazzling on her windscreen so I can't see if she smiles back or anything, or even notices I've gone. I step onto the bus. It's shuddering, ready to go.

The Flood

Carolyn Mack

There's nae two weys aboot it.

Ah feel a wee bit guilty aboot the whole mess.

Efter aw, it wis ma toilet leakin' that caused the flood an' brought Moira's ceilin' doon. The man fae the cooncil said it wis jist wee drips building up over time, 'til 'bang' the ceiling couldnae take it an' gave wey. Whit a mess! Who wid huv thought thae wee drips wid cause aw that damage? Ye widnae credit it.

Lucky Moira an' the weans wur oot. Ah'd never forgive masel' otherwise.

Ah like tae get alang wi' people an' no' be a nusiance. No' that Moira blames me. She's always sayin' whit a good neighbour Ah am, an' whit wid she dae withoot me?

She's left the keys wi' me tae let the workmen in. Well, wi' me being a pensioner Ah don't mind helpin' oot the neighbours. Aye an' they keep me busy Ah kin tell ye. Feedin' dugs, pittin' lights oan an' aff, keepin' an eye oan weans. Ah've done it aw! But they're always that grateful, an' Ah like tae feel useful.

Aye, it's a good wee close this an' Ah like tae keep it that wey. We've never hud any bother up here – well, except yon time last year. Terrible that wis. Ah'm gettin' too auld fur aw that cerry oan.

But that's the trouble noo, naebudy's got any respect fur age. Ah'm fae the auld school an' proud ae' it. Ah believe in lookin' efter things. Ah cannae be daen wi' aw this lettin' things slip an' slide. Ah've got standards an' Ah like tae keep tae them.

'Ye're a fighter, Jessie.' The neighbours'll say tae me. 'Ye should be takin' it easy at your age.'

But Ah like tae dae ma bit.

That's aw Ah done last year, ma bit, same as everybody else.

Well, it's always a worry when there's an empty hoose in yer close. Ye're wonderin' who the cooncil's gonny try an' dump oan ye. Druggies, young yins that party aw night, or some wee lassie wi' mair weans than she knows whit tae dae wi'. Mind you, Moira's oan her ain, but it's no' her fault. Her man ran away wi' that lassie fae the bookies. An' Ah've got tae say that Moira keeps her weans nice. Lovely wee things, never any bother. Ah kid them oan there's a big bear lives in the loft that eats wee weans who drap their sweetie papers in the close. They believe me as well! Ye should see their wee faces. Funny, so it is.

Aye Ah'm a good neighbour right enough. Ah watch oot fur everybody. That's how Ah seen whit wis gon' oan last year. Wi' the empty hoose being acroass the landin' fae me, Ah could see it aw. Ah wis the first tae know somebody wis movin' in. Ah heard people comin' up an' doon the sterrs. Ah couldnae see much through ma spyhole, mind you, an' Ah didnae want tae open ma door. Well, ye cannae be too careful being oan yir ain at ma age, no' until ye get tae know people. Anywey, Ah looked oot the windae an' there's a cooncil van parked at the close.

'Funny,' Ah thinks, 'whit wid the cooncil be daen flittin' somebody?'

It wis only wan person, Ah could tell wi' the furniture. Single bed, wan chair, a lamp, that kind a' thing. Oh aye an' a cat. Ah don't like animals in the close. Ah've written tae the cooncil aboot it before but Ah jist got a snooty letter back sayin' 'tenants are entitled to keep pets as long as they look after them and they don't cause a nuisance'.

So, Ah wisnae too happy aboot the cat, but still . . .

Anywey, efter a while Ah hud mair tae worry me than the cat.

Next morning Ah still hudnæ met the new neighbour. That's whit Ah mean aboot standards, years ago new people introduced thersel' an' asked aboot any rules and regulations in the close – washin' the sterrs, an' that. But no' noo. No' this wan.

Then, Ah hears somebody at the door acroass the landing so Ah hud a wee peep through ma spyhole.

Social workers. Ah could tell them right away. Her wi' her hair aw shaved like a man. An' his straggly an' needin' a good wash and comb. His jaikit aw ripped an' nae shame aboot it.

'Noo,' Ah thinks tae masel', 'who gets visits fae social workers, eh?'

Somebudy that no' right ur somebudy that's aw wrang. That's who. The mad an' the bad.

Ah've read in the papers aboot these folk gettin' oot ae prisons an' asylums tae live among decent people an' gettin' up tae aw sorts. Ah began tae get worried. Ah mean if this new neighbour hud problems we hud a right tae be telt aboot them. It's us that huv got tae live here no' the social workers.

The door opened an' shut that quick tae let them in Ah never saw a thing. But Ah knew they wid huv tae come oot, so Ah got a chair an' sat behind ma door. They wur in there fur an awfy long time. As soon as Ah heard the door open, Ah opened mine. But Ah wisnae quick enough. The door wis shut an' the social workers wur gon' doon the stairs.

'Excuse me,' Ah said, aw polite like. 'How's the new neighbour settling in?'

They looked at me as if Ah came fae Mars, then she looks at him an' back tae me.

'Fine.' She says.

That's aw. But Ah'm quick oan the ba'.

'Ah wis wonderin' if they wur needin' anythin'?' Ah says.

This time he spoke an' Ah didnae like the wey he sighed.

'Mr Lambie's a private person. He'd rather be left alone.' Then he says, 'Thanks all the same.'

But Ah knew by his look he didnae mean it.

Well, Ah never seen hide nor hair ae that man. He didnae even let his cat oot. Noo that's no natural. 'There's somethin' far wrang here.' Ah thought.

Ah let it lie fur a couple a' days then Ah went doon tae the housin' office. Ah told the wee lassie there that Ah wis lookin' fur information aboot a Mr Lambie an' gied her the address. But she said that information wis confidential.

'Noo whit's so bad it has tae be kept secret?' Ah asked her.

'All tenants' information is confidential,' she tells me, 'even yours.'

'Mine! Ah've nuthin' tae hide, hen. There's nuthin' confidential aboot Jessie Sanders. You can tell ma neighbours anythin' ye want!' Ah says.

But Ah couldnae get a thing oot ae her.

Oan the wey hame Ah met Moira an' the weans comin' oot the close.

'Rotten weather, Jessie, in't it?' she says tae me. 'I'll be gled when the summer's here an' Ah kin let these two oot the back tae play, they're drivin' me mad.'

Well, Ah felt Ah hud tae say somethin', cos if anythin' happened tae thae weans Ah'd never forgive masel'. So Ah says.

'Surely ye'll no' be lettin' them oot the back noo?' Ah nodded ma heid up tae his windae.

'Whit dae ye mean?' she asks.

Noo, Ah'm no' wan tae kid on Ah know things Ah don't, but Ah don't believe in makin' oot everythin's rosy in the gerden when it's no', either. So Ah jist shrugged ma shoulders, a wee warning like, an' Ah left her staunin' there.

Well, Ah'm the kind that likes visitors, but Ah wis runnin' oot ae tea bags an' chocolate biscuits! Moira hud passed oan ma wee warning tae everybudy she met. People Ah'd dinnae know wur comin' tae ma door! Want tae know whit Ah knew, ur whit Ah'd heard. Ah pit ma hauns up an' told them, Ah didnae know anythin' – no' fur sure. Jist that it seemed strange tae me that this thing wis being covered up by the housin' office. An' Ah told them, Ah've heard ae people huvin' wan social worker but two? Must have done somethin' serious tae get two.

Everybudy wis oan their guard efter that. Weans wurnæ allowed up oor close, an' the wans that live here wurnæ allowed oot thersel'. Ah wis gled people wur takin' me seriously. Ye cannae be too careful wi' weans, no' wi whit ye read in the papers these days.

An' auld folk as well, fur that matter. Ah'm no' the nervy Norah type, as Ah said tae young Alex doon the sterrs, but aw this wis beginning tae get tae me.

'It's a sad day when ye don't feel safe in yer ain hoose.' Ah telt him.

That's how Ah nearly jumped oot ma skin the next day wi' the bangin' oan ma door. Ah looked through the spyhole an' saw it wis the polis.

'No' before time!' Ah told them. But they jist looked at me.

'D'ye know anythin' aboot this?' Wan ae them says, an' he stood aside tae let me see the door acroass the landin'.

Well, Ah'm a pensioner. Whit wid Ah know aboot paintin' sweary words oan a door?

They wurnæ very nice polis. Startit askin' me a lot a' questions.

'Did ye hear anythin' last night?'

'Did ye let anybudy intae the close?'

'Did ye see anybudy hingin' aroon?'

Noo, Ah hud nothin' tae hide, but their questions wur gettin' me aw mixed up an' Ah wis gled when they went away.

Ah don't like vandalism ae any kind but Ah'll tell ye this, if anybudy hud done that tae ma door Ah wid've been oot wi' the turps right away. But no' him! Naw, he wis quite happy tae leave thae filthy words oan his door fur long enough. Nae thought fur the wee weans that wid see them.

'Ye know the sayin', if the bunnet fits, wear it.' Ah says tae auld Donald.

It wis thae two social workers that finally came an' scrubbed it aw aff.

It wis wan thing efter another then.

Ah still hudnæ set eyes oan this man when that lassie wi' the shaved heid came tae ma door wan mornin'.

Mr Lambie's cat hud gone missin' an' hud Ah seen it?

Well, Ah told her aboot the cooncil rules ae lookin' efter pets, but she jist walked away. They kind a' people ur no' interested in anybudy's rules but their ain.

Later oan Ah heard somethin' Ah've never heard in ma life. I wis frightened, Ah don't mind admittin' it. Anybudy wid huv been frightened wi' that horrible moanin' and wailin'. Ah wis too scared tae even look oot ma spyhole. The whole close wis fillin' up wi' the noise. It wis screechin' through every crack an' hole.

'He's went mad!' Ah telt the 999 operator.

It seemed like forever but at last Ah saw a polis car pulled up ootside. Ah waited fur them tae get up the sterrs before Ah opened ma door.

Well, Ah will never forget whit Ah saw fur as long as Ah live.

That poor wee cat hingin' up oan the door wi' a piece a' string roon its neck. Its mooth wis opened, an' fur a minute

Ah thought it wis snarlin' at me. But it wis deid. The polis wur bangin' oan the door, an' that wailin' wis still goin' oan. There hud never been anythin' like in this close. Ah hud tae go in an' shut ma door. Ah couldnae look at that thing hingin' there.

The noise eventually stoapped an' a wee while later the polis came roon the doors askin' the same questions as the last time. Noo, Ah don't like tellin' people their joabs, but Ah wis surprised that they wur lookin' fur anybudy else in connection wi' this incident. Ah told them aboot the noise an' suggested that mibbe he snapped an' done it hisel'. But the young yins think ye're senile if ye're over fifty. They jist looked at me an' said the 'noise' wis the 'poor' man finding his cat.

Quite a few ae the neighbours agreed wi' me, mind you. They wur angry at the polis treatin' them as suspects, an' they wur fed up livin' in fear ae their lives.

'It's terrible,' Ah said tae wee Annie. 'First a cat. Whit's he gonny dae next?'

Well, Ah don't claim tae be psychic ur nuthin' but fur a horrible time we thought we knew the answer tae that wan. Lucky it turned oot tae be a false alarm.

Moira's wee Sarah went missin'. She wis only seven an' hudnæ came hame fae school. The young yins went roon the streets lookin' fur her. But we aw hud wan thought in oor minds. Finally young Alex an' some ae the other men hud enough.

They chapped his door but got nae answer. He should've known when he heard the bangin' that somethin' wis up. But he didnae even bother. It wis his ain fault. If somebudy disnae answer their door, an' ye know they're in, well, ye think they've got somethin' tae hide don't ye? So, whit else could the men dae? They kicked the door in.

Aye, an' him as well.

Noo, Ah don't like violence but, as Ah told the polis an' thae social workers, when a wean's in danger ye don't hesitate.

'Except nobody was in danger.' The skinheid says tae me.

Aye, the thing turned oot awright in the end. Wee Sarah hud gone tae a pal's hoose efter school and hud furgoat the time. Well, weans don't think, dae thae? We wur jist gled she wis awright.

Oh aye, an' the social workers took Mr Lambie away. Back tae the hospital where he hud come fae.

Forty-five years he lived there. Ah think it wis a liberty fur them social workers tae drag him oot ae somewhere he's lived fur so long. If they hud let us know we could huv kept a wee eye oan him. Still, he'll be better aff back there, among his ain folk that know him an' ur used tae his wee weys.

Ah said that tae the social workers but they wurnae too pleased. Their wee experiment hudnae worked an' they wur lookin' fur somebudy tae blame! The wee skinheid lassie says tae me.

'There's "do-gooders" and "good-doers" ', Mrs Sanders. You should learn the difference.'

Cheeky wee besom!

Anywey, things got back tae normal at last. Until Moira's ceiling came doon, that is. Ah still cannae believe thae wee drips caused aw that damage.

Ye widnae credit it.

The Worm Eater

Alan Bissett

A m searchn th grund fur th – wurms wurms wurms wriggly wurms tht play lke babeez jst blow the srface, tappn th grass lke BIG JIM shwd me, tappn n listnin wi ma big eerz doon cloze tay the grund. Am heern um doon thair, whisprin, panickin. Am wundrn if thy ken um here.

Boof – is hoat th day! Suns roastn! Wurms mst be gaspn fur drink z me. Taptapn. Makum hink sraining haha.

A wee blun wurm poaks z heed ootfay th grund, wavn lke wan thay snakes tht gits played moozk bi Pakis. Heez lookn fur me, Eetum, BIG ME, bt e canny fun me coz am sabig an heez sawee. The coastz cleer, wurm dcidez, n eez punk, shiny, loang, loang bodys cming ootfay th grund an am grabbn th wee basturt fore hekn run.

Heez wriggln roon n roon n roon tween ma fngers. Sfunny moovmens, an allaff loud! Bt a noaf goat teet it fore he gts away, so a put thwee hing int m mooth. *Pop!*

Mmmmmooooommmmm! Swrigglinwrigglinwrigglinin- there. Proberly hinks sin the grund still. Am swallown all down lke Mammyz Good Laddie, lke spag-bol it Mam makes it goaz doon. Sluvley. Wan mair.

Taptaptap. Tap. Tap. Taptapit goes. Wan wurm. Two. Freefourfivesix Oyabeeza! Am grabbn aw erra place. Mmmmmm. Ooooommmmmm. Nnnmmmm.

Omph!

Ga . . .

My hands chaff on the low-slung wall as I lift my legs to the other side, panting slightly in the heat. The grass, unfortunately, isn't any cooler here, and I search my imagination for the feeling of stepping into a cold bath, or dew on my bare calves. An eternal spring of hope, my imagination. Does me less good these days.

This bone-dry wall (I run my fingers down its uneven crevices) must have been here for a thousand years. As old as I feel. Weak clouds wrap the Campsies like a papyrus death-shroud, promising rain, but never delivering. Green stretches thinly to the horizon, broken only by lines of rock and a clump of houses that could have been dropped by a sun-weary giant. I begin to wish we'd lived back then – cattle for currency, stones for comfort – until I realise they would have burned us.

I look back the way I've come, my footsteps absent in the long, dry grass (which strangely upsets me a little). Our caravan is supposed to be white. Shit is whiter. Smells nicer, too. It looks from here like a cigarette box thrown from a car window. In the darkness underneath its rotted chassis, milk-crates and half-bricks form a village for Ronnie's dolls, one of them – Lucille – discarded at his will. But even she is privy to what I am not – the owner of that shiny, red Merc out front. I suppose things like this are not me and Ronnie's business. Mam knows best.

Brushing stone-dust from my knees, a familiar rasp alerts me: Ronnie is on all fours in the centre of the field, retching the grass yellow. I run to him, on his back now, grinning, drool reeling from his teeth.

'Leslie, Leslie, ah dund baad!' he chuckles, wide-eyed, and I notice the bile-coated worms, struggling to sink back to the earth through a glistening layer.

'Big Jim taught me a way to fish frum,' he says, dipping his finger into the pool to flick a worm here and there. 'Tap the grund, see? Worms thinks raining and they all come up. See? Eetum fooled um! Eetum fooled um!' He sucks on his fingers and grins his pride expansively, showing stomach-stained gums. I have to look away: at the caravan, at the hills, anywhere but Ronnie's mouth.

'Stop saying that "Eetum" word,' I chide, trying to summon fondness from somewhere. Dad's last gift to me – a description of Ronnie as 'a twenty-year old foetus' – stays, though he has gone. 'Your name is Ronald. Only bad boys call you Eetum.'

'Eetum! Eetum! Eetum!' he sings, slapping his hands in the puddle of sick, making the worms dance and writhe. 'I Eetum! I Eetum all up!'

'Stop it!' I snap, grabbing wrists that continue to flap and flail. 'Ronald. Say it: *Ron-ald.*'

Last week, the village post office had been arena to a host of baseball caps, bikes and skateboards, all chanting:

> Who ate all the worms?
> Who ate all the worms?
> *You daft bastard! You daft bastard!*
> You ate all the worms!

Ronnie had cheered enthusiastically, confusing their sadistic smiles with a birthday party that shifted seats in his head from long ago. He'd had to be dragged, reluctant, from the reach of those hands, that pointed home like bayonets, firing:

> Eat-*um*! Eat-*um*! Eat-*um*!

It was a new identity for his foggy mind to cloak itself in, making him single-purpose worm-hunter in deed and title. This had come with Dad's advice on luring them out;

dispensed, no doubt, before he'd loped off, fishing bag swinging from his shoulder, leaving Mam and me to pick the worms from the caravan. It was probably when Dad was here last week that he showed Ronnie the trick of dissolving slugs in salt. Mam had been infuriated when there'd been no salt for the dinner; in fact, she had cried for an hour over it.

I stare past two fields to that shiny, red car again. It waits there like a thirsty dog for its owner – the owner I have not yet seen. Only Mam ever greets these infrequent callers. In the caravan. Alone.

She's been a nightmare since Dad's visit last month, all mood-swings and tears. She interrupted my exam revision today, although I suppose there's nothing unusual about that. No, it's the recent tremors in her voice that concern me most.

'Take your brother for a walk, Leslie, there's a dear. More people coming to see me about . . .' (she'd hesitated, stubbing out her fag) '. . . benefits.'

'Okay, Mam,' I'd replied, pretending not to notice the uneasy tic at the corner of her eye, nor the ashtray: full now; empty twenty minutes before.

Am still feeln wee bt seek. Still taste wurms in ma mooth. No nice. Alook upit Leslie, tryin ta say *stumick, stumick, Leslie! Sair! Sair!* bit Leslie no wull lookt Eetum. Leslie lookn backat hoose. Funny look. Keeps lookan. Whitcha lookan at Les?

That car, Les says. Whose that car, Ronnie?

Eetum lookan where Les lookan. Big ridwan. Dinny ken.

Wellv ye seen anybdy rive? Les says. Naw says Eetum. Jis BIG JIM BIG JIM bit canny mine when, mibbe lasweek, mibbe thisweek, canny mine.

Mon says Les, walkn back house, owner wallsn feels. Mon lis see, she says. Quiet but, beelike Spiderman dead quiet an that. Creepup house. Like Spiderman ges me cited though, bt Leslie says shhhhh Ronnie. Eetum shhh.

Owera wall. Shhh. Owera feel. Shhh. Gttn closa. Bigrid car. Shiny. See hoose moovin wee bit like whn Mammy diz kleenin. Kin see ma dolly unnera hoose – Picta Fine Time Taleave Me Lucille – na go ta gettur. Leslie says no. Shhhh. Me an Leslie shhhh uptay hoose.

Eatit hen, sumbdy sayn, Eatit hen, assgood, assgood, fuckin eatat hing.

Uptay windae.

Big moon. Big moon wi wee broon hole. Whissit? Oh! Smammy's bum! Haha. Mammy's bum. Haha! Shhhh.

Eatat fuckin hing. Kin see leggies. Mans leggies. Him sayn eatat fuckin hing. Whis . . . ? Whissat hing? Sat . . . ? Sata . . . ?

Mam!

Mam's eetina mannies wurm! Mam eetina wurm like Eetum dae! Mannies wurm! Mannies wurm! Look Les, look Les! HAHA! Eetum! Eetum! Eetum! Eetum! Eetat fuckinhing! HAHA!

Mhmm? Bu- Les? Wherewe goan, Leslie?

Lesl-*eeeeee*?!

A surf of white noise roars in my ears as the time I wet my knickers in primary school surges back to me, the time my first-year class threw bugs at my hair and called me 'Nitty', all the bad things, awful memories, rearing up from the grass to taunt me here, now, and I run and run, the relentless sun battering at me like a disapproving god, losing Ronnie's hand as he falls in the grass, howling, and I keep running, keep running, from what, I do not know, to where, I know even less, but all I do know is *I CAN'T fucking TAKE this any-more!!!!*

But I have to take it. Ronnie is screaming behind me.

I stop – breathless, overheating. Mam looks cartoonish and comical with her dressing-gown flapping across the field behind her. It's not comical enough to slow the tears though; not so hot they'll evaporate before she gets here.

'Why?' is all I can say once she reaches me. Not: *you slut*, or *get away from me*; or *I'll never forgive you for this*. Just: 'Why?'

We stand there baking in the dry grass, listening to the whisper of a faint wind, my sobs, and Ronnie, whining in the next field like a broken radio.

'Eet*aaaaatfackinhiiiing!*' he roars, infant-like, 'Me no *un-nerstaaaaaaan!*'

'Why?' I say again.

'Yer dad came to see me last week, Leslie,' she whispers. 'He's gawin abroad. No leavin us wi a penny. Nae maintenance, nuthin'.'

'He can't do that, Mam,' I try to tell her. 'We have rights. We're his children.' But even as I say this it dries on my tongue, and truth spirits it away to old, sun-hammered hills. It's Dad we're talking about.

'Leslie, hen, we're gypsies,' she breathes eventually. 'Tinks. Scum. Hameless. Naebody's gawin tae help us. Nae lawyer's gawin tae come near us.' Her hand, cracked and weary, touches my hair. 'Yer faither *kens* eh kin git away wi it; could've goat away wi it a long time ago.'

'But *why*?' I sob again, 'I don't . . . understand.' It hurts me to say these words. I sound too much like Ronnie: stupid, uncomprehending.

'Well . . .' Mam shrugs, 'ah dinnae hink eh reckons ehs dealin wi humans anymair. Tae him wur like they animals in the zoo whit ye sponsor.'

'But . . . but you don't have to . . .'

Mam suddenly grabs my cheeks with her hands. Her face is like blasted rock near the base of a cliff. 'The wey ye *look* at me, hen, wi they brainy eyes eh yours. Ah kin *see* the disappointment in yer face. Believe me, this isnae the life ah wantit for any eh us. An when Jim telt me that . . . ah thoaght: naw, ah'll

98

no let the lassie doon this time! Ah'll git that fuckin money somehow!' She shakes my face with rage, then clasps me once again. In the distance a tractor roars across Ronnie's cries. 'It's aw for you, Leslie, do ye no see that? Aw so you kin go awa tae college an dae mair wi yer life than yer mam ivir did, hear me?'

'I hear you, Mam.'

'But for noo . . . aw we've goat is each ither, ma lassie. An *ah've* goat tae help yese if naebidy else will.'

'You don't have to do . . . what you're doing, Mam,' I mumble to her shoulder. 'I can get a job. I can . . .'

'It's the only wey, hen,' she says softly. 'Noo jist let me dae it. Ye'll be helpin me oot mair by playin wi yer brither an lettin me get oan wi it. We'll show yer faither we're no animals in the zoo.'

We both look in silence at Ronnie on all fours. He looks like a wounded dog dragging back to its owner – trailing hurt like futile limbs.

Mam tries to smile: toothy, old, unconvincing. 'You jist take care eh him, eh? An ye kin git me fags ivery noo and again an aw, ye wee bastart.'

I smile too, despite myself.

'Are we going to move again?'

She sighs. 'Mibbe. Might need tae. Depends how much yon punter opens ehs mooth in the village.' She knows what I am thinking. Always has. A symbiosis that makes me fear I'll turn out just like her. 'Next school ye kin dae yer exams, hen, ah promise. Then the college. Ye ken ye'll make it, eh? Ye ken ye'll get away?'

'Aye, Mam,' I say. Then I hug her closer and wipe my eyes. We break. I fear it may be the last time I hug my mother like that, with sincerity. Emotions evaporate in the heat. I cannot look at her as we part, for fear I see my future.

'Come on, pal!' I make myself shout, trekking back across the field. 'Come on I'll take you on that walk.'

Mam goes back, but her-customer's gone: sped as quickly as Big Jim did.

The hills take the last of my tears; I have nothing left to cry. All I want is to merely exist here on the skin of the Earth, like rock. But Mam will move us on. Nothing ever changes: neither this land nor the dispossessed that wander across its back, place to place, every place the same. Wherever we arrive, whichever hopeful new town, they'll still look at us like we're devils, still stare at us in the back pews of the chapel as the priest berates the enemy, an enemy happily encapsulated by a slut, her child, and an idiot. So we'll move somewhere else to keep Ronnie from harm, and in that place too I'll raise my head from the ground – blinking, hopeful, parched skin aching for rain . . .

Devoured. Hopes and all.

Vomited back up to crawl somewhere else.

Ronnie plays on the verge below me now, giggling in his own little private world. He catches me looking at him and hides his mucky hands. He's been tapping false hopes into the ground again. 'Kinna, Les?' he beams, 'Kinna tapfurum, kinna tapfurum?'

'You were sick last time, Ronnie,' I remind him, though I know he'll do it anyway. 'On you go then. But please – don't eat them.'

Taptaptaptap, goes me. Taptaptapcomes thwurms. Here thy come, up fae th grund, twistin, turnin, lookn fur th rain. No rain, wurmz! No rain, just Eetum! HAHA.

The Magic Word

Kate Thomson

10.41

A man is entertaining the crowd that has gathered around him just outside Princes Square. I can see him through the gaps between the bystanders, keeping a diabolo moving to and fro along a length of rope as easily as his well-practised patter holds the audience's attention.

Hey, what's this? A glint in the light. Storing coins in your ears again?

Tsk, I've told you they're safer in your piggybank.

I glance away, but can't keep my eyes from returning: the conjurer has attracted the attention of a child who has stepped away from the crowd towards him.

– How high? I hear the conjurer challenging the child to guess, – How high do you think I can throw this and still catch it?

The child's voice, not used to professional presentation, is lost in the background sounds of shoppers, but the face glows with excitement, with belief.

Another trick.

Do another one. Pleease.

10.43

I walk on, ducking away from the crowds into Fraser's. Inside the doorway I pause, letting the restful, clinical atmosphere of the cosmetics hall seep a little way into my skin. Clinique,

Givenchy, Elizabeth Arden, Guerlain, a woman could remake herself a million times over in here, assisted by the soothing voices and the soft hands of the white-clad sales girls.

I move further in, to the perfume counter. It takes me six minutes to decide what I want, making my selection from the bottles on display, and distracting the smiling assistant with questions about one brand while I slip a half-empty bottle of another into my right pocket.

Do I have anything in my hands?

Anything at all, now?

I sniff at the bottle in my visible hand, frown and replace it on the counter, telling the assistant I'll think about it.

10.50

I walk out via a different doorway and dodge the taxis across Argyle Street to the St. Enoch Centre. At the entrance, I spray my wrists and my throat, then drop the superfluous bottle into the first bin inside.

10.53

The crowds are starting to build, window shoppers and baby buggies cluttering my path. I stride through them into The Body Shop, slowing down as soon as I reach the entrance – I don't want to look too purposeful.

An assistant waylays me, but I deflect her with a – Just browsing – and she smiles, nods and moves further away. I pick up the cosmetics idly, smearing some on the back of my hand as though considering the colours. I don't look at the assistant again, but when a voice in my head says NOW, NOW my body knows just what to do.

Close your eyes and say prestidigitation.

Giggle. A stutter of p's.

I move away from the cosmetics, study a bottle of sensual aromatherapy massage oil, then move out of the doorway. I have £30 worth of make-up in my coat pockets and no one saw my hands move.

11.08

I sit on the hard stone by the fountains to transfer the cosmetics from my pockets into my bag, peeling off the covers, smudging my finger into the eyeshadow so it looks old, so there's nothing to say it hasn't been mine for weeks.

11.12

I drop the waste on to the floor and move on. I have enough time not to need to rush, so I window shop several stores, taking my time, choosing carefully: I want to look my best.

Close your eyes and say prestidigitation, and I'll disappear.
A squeal, just in case he really could. Prestip – Prestick.

11.17

I walk into the store that contains the skirt I think will suit me, that I think he would like on me. I pick it up in two sizes, slide one into the other, replace the now superfluous coat-hanger on the rack and walk to the changing rooms.

11.21

Swishing the curtain closed behind me I try on the clothes. The first one fits so I slip it off and reach into the zipped compartment of my bag for my pliers. I frown with effort at the plastic and metal bugging device that doesn't want to come off and pinch harder until I feel the snap beneath my fingers and the pieces slide apart. I kick against the carpet, but there are no loose edges so I tip the stool in the corner of the cubicle on to its side and hide the bits beneath it.

11.27

There is no assistant at the door when I put the spare skirt on the discard rack and stride out, my latest acquisition rolled in the corner of the bag bouncing against my hip.

Daddy's press-studs for years as matches, cards, coins, watches vanished.
Show me how, show me how.

103

11.44

It takes longer than expected to find a suitable top to complete the outfit. The racks are crowded, in the middle of a sale, other shoppers crushing around me so I take a chance, sliding the item I require off the hanger and into my bag in a single, smooth movement whilst apparently just browsing through, shuffling clothing from one end of the rack to the other.

Prestidigitation.

By the time I could say the word, my hands were as deft as his.

My bag is fastened before I move away, leafing through some of the other displays before strolling out.

11.49

I ascend the escalators and walk along the gallery to the car park exit, to the toilets.

11.52

The third cubicle I try has a working lock. I fasten it behind me, hang up my jacket, unfasten my jeans and shrug them down past my hips. I step out of my shoes and jeans, then back into my shoes – too difficult to be worth the bother to acquire, I just keep my own. I check the pockets as though putting them in for a wash, then fold them: back pocket to back pocket, legs in thirds. Placing them on the floor I pull my T-shirt over my head, fold it shoulder to shoulder, arms across, hem to neck and leave it on top of the jeans.

I put the lid down on the toilet and put my bag on top, taking out what I want to change into and putting them on, biting through the plastic tags that got left behind, smoothing the skirt against my hips, tugging at the top, frowning down, hoping it all looks as good together as I thought it would when it was apart. I pick out my make-up bag, fold my jacket and shove it into the bag, tug the lock back.

The cracked, stained tile floor provides a focus for my eyes until I'm close enough to the mirror that I can't see the whole picture – I don't want to know until it's all done – I don't want to spoil the magic.

Leaning over the sink, the porcelain pressing comfortingly against my hips, I begin by smoothing foundation over my skin: forehead, nose, cheeks, chin then down my neck to blend it into my own slightly paler skin tone. Face powder follows, and two complimentary shades of eyeshadow, one of which exactly matches the colour of the top I selected. Eyeliner and mascara follow, making the eyes that look back from the mirror larger, brighter. Lipstick completes the look, two coats and a sheen of gloss over the top. The only thing left to do is to reach to the back of my head, pull out the band that's been holding my hair back in a girlish ponytail, and shake the blonde strands around my ears, loosening the look with my fingertips.

Prestidigitation.

Don't open your eyes. No peeking.

12.19

I step back from the mirror – Ta-Daa!!

It is a new woman who stares back at me. Her eyes are smoky and her lips glisten as though she's just eaten something sticky and sweet. I don't recognise her for a moment, then I move and see myself for a fraction of a second. I have become an optical illusion – focus one way and it's me, focus the other way and it's a glamorous young lady. I wonder which one he'll see, if he'll recognise either of us.

12.22

I tip the make-up into the bin beneath the hand-dryer since I won't be needing it any more. Then the new woman and I sling the roomy bag over our shoulder and leave, shaking our hair back and tilting our head up to face the world.

12.31

Ignoring the conjurer who is still working outside, we push through the swing doors into Princes Square, heading to the lifts at the back. No one joins us and we slide silently to the rooftop level.

12.32

The waitress smiles, asking if it's just one for lunch. I tell her I'm expecting someone, and that I'd like to sit out on the balcony where there's a view.

She smiles, says of course and walks ahead.

12.34

I order a glass of wine and light up my first cigarette of the day. When I started I thought it would make me look grown up, sophisticated. It didn't, it just made me sick. But I thought I was doing something wrong, so I persisted, thinking the sophistication was just around the corner, thinking it would all suddenly snap into place. It never has.

12.37

I look down at all the people I can see on the lower levels, watching for the one face I know I'll recognise.

12.41

Another cigarette. The waitress returns, asking if I want to order, or would I prefer to wait? I tell her I'll wait. I wish I'd brought a book. Waiting makes me nervous.

A blink of my eye and he was gone.

Prestidigitation.

12.49

The lipstick is coming off, scarlet against the brown of the filter as I stub it out. I won't smoke any more, don't want to spoil the look I went to such trouble to create.

12.51

12.55

No, thanks, I'll wait.

12.57

12.59

1.01

1.03

Prestidigitation.
Prestidigitation. Prestidigitation. Prestidigitation.
1.04
Maybe it was supposed to be a different word to bring things
back.
Noitatigiditserp.
1.06
1.07
1.08

I get up and walk to the till to pay for my wine. My face is tugging down and I can't help it. It's only the thought of the mascara that's saving me from worse.

The waitress smiles sympathetically as she changes my note into coins – Stood you up, has he? Forget about him – you're worth better than that.

I nod. Smile to show I know that, even though it makes the tugging worse.

Inside the lift I rest my head against the brass panel. When I straighten up the face is distorted, but it looks like me again. I don't know where the glamorous young lady has gone. I close my eyes, pressed tight shut, but it makes no difference.

Life's Small Miracles

Lynda McDonald

In the monumental scheme of things, would it go down as The Day The Crumshaws Prepared For Immortality or, conversely, The Day That Brownie Died? How the latter would always make them laugh! The unusualness of having the whole family together round the table made Marjorie Crumshaw think of butterfly cakes, cosy things she'd never actually made. Over the years the children had brought home slightly bruised-winged versions in tupperware containers from school. But unless you had actually cut that neat circle, bisected it into two perfect semicircles and arranged it to give the illusion the cake was going to fly, it wasn't the same. It would go down on her list of things to do before she died.

It was quite a long list now, kept in a notebook called wide feint (which seemed appropriate) in her bedside drawer beside the Aspros and black silk eye mask. Remembrances of black patent shoes, snow-white socks and the distinctive roundness of small boys' knees gave her a feeling of tenderness as she looked upon her assembled family. She kept these joyful memories compartmentalised in an area of her brain only she knew existed. In here dwelt the soft silent toys of her babyhood (all named, no sharp edges), hidden dens of her childhood, lost loves of her teens and all the unused superlative adjectives of her later life.

She surveyed the family with which she was blessed. One bit non-existent fingernails, while one made irritating shredding noises with an emery board prior to painting her nails gang-rene shades. Nail particles floated on to the tablecloth forming a pointillist picture of a dust flower. One rubbed his chin in his daily quest to find a beard, while her 'baby' wondered how Batman would handle family gatherings. She wondered when the secret army of inches had invaded their bodies and made them grow so big, so loftily remote, speaking a language further removed from her now than their babytalk.

Arthur was going to cough to call them to order. The dread brought travelling heat to her body. She saw his neck as if in X ray, with phlegm rising and falling; and her lips pursed involuntarily in distaste. He did this in cafes, combining it with a twitch of the head to indicate something of which he didn't approve. Specks of soup on a waitress's apron – well, we can always guess the soup of the day she thought, but never said. A twitch in her direction meant crumbs on her front. Rolls in cafes, she believed, were made up of millions more atoms than those from supermarkets. Smaller ones too.

Six of them round the table. 'All is safely gathered in', she reflected, forgetting the strange 'ere' and its following winter storms. A sudden silence. It was as if they had all been superimposed upon the perpetual but imperceptible noises of the room. She believed each room had its own noise identity. You could probably be led into any room in your house and know where you were just by listening to its noises and particular silences. They pinpointed the bottomless silence as coming from the gerbil cage. Brownie the gerbil had died as she had contemplated storms and harvests. He had reaped the whirlwind of her thoughts and gone under.

'We come to bury Brownie not to praise him,' said Mal-colm, her A-level son piercing the shocked silence.

'We might as well,' said Cheryl, her eldest, oh beautiful

dancing child of light. Metamorphosed. Gothic. Alien. 'There's nothing else happening.'

Arthur's Statement must wait until the youngest had been soothed and a trainer box lined with a team football sock. No, the wool would not make Brownie itch. The funeral was scheduled for the next morning for it was raining and Brownie had come from the desert and would not like to be wet. Yes, he may lie in his casket over night on the microwave whose ping would stir him no more. No he would not become irradiated.

Arthur must strive again for order. At least the budgie looked well. How he, the head of the family, had agonised and pondered over a plan. He had made a list. It was not his customary list of masonry nails and fusewire, but had more of an ethereal quality to it. She must not look at his throat. Pressed her hands to her ears to blank out the noise and brought the sea rushing through the tube she remembered was called Eustachian like the heroine of the Hardy novel. Seaside holidays shunted through the tube and into her brain. Sandcastles with turrets that rose and moats that sank. Salmon sandwiches with powdery bones.

It had passed. She removed her hands and the sea sounds disappeared. Suck.

'We approach the Millennium,' Arthur said using an un-characteristic and ennobling sort of tense, 'and we as a family must celebrate the uniqueness of it lest it slip away like any other year.' He was not usually given to loftiness. His use of speech was prosaic with only a modicum of adverbs for emphasis. She therefore knew he was committed.

'Disney,' said the subdued youngest, thinking of a rodent less temporal.

'More pocket money,' reasoned Marcia, the next, who had dreams not of ballet shoes, but one day hoped to become a leading light at the Inland Revenue.

'A year out – travelling the world,' said Malcolm, the next, who would never eat, wash, wear any clean garment or rise from a sleeping bag if she did not travel with him.

'My own flat.' Cheryl. This pierced her heart.

She sighed and turned it into a hasty cough. They may make choices, but it was all preordained. As had been Scarborough or, when Arthur began to trust, Benidorm. Their suitcases then had contained less the lightsome clothes of assured sunshine and the newly coined genre of airport reading, than medicines against every eventuality that foreign travel might thrust upon them. She wanted to tell him they were not pioneers – explorers in a strange uncharted land – that people had trod the coast of Spain in safety before. That his delicately coloured lunchtime lettuce had really come not from dark lands of ice and snow, where photosynthesis was not an option, but from Spain, where it had blanched and bleached in endless sunshine. He had decided, and she prepared herself for their reactions, the long equation that ended in *esprit de corps*, but first had to go through the processes of disappoint-ment plus resignation plus interest plus enthusiasm plus competitiveness =, before then.

'I call it the CRUMSHAW TIME CAPSULE,' Arthur was saying gravely.

The doorbell rang. The relief overwhelmed her. She was prepared to embrace the sartorially elegant Jehovah's Witness clones to her bosom or surround herself with double glazing or have every knife in the cutlery drawer sharpened. Most particularly, she would welcome flight with the Gallic onion seller from Sutton Coldfield.

Far away Mary Lou Kominsky is waking up to sunshine. Her brain makes that instantaneous leap through the coolness of the air conditioning, the dark room, the thick blinds and tinted windows of the apartment. New York. July. It must be hot. Malc stirs. She kisses his shoulder. Swings out of bed to make coffee. Opens the blind in the tiny kitchen. The shaded sun forever on the outside looking in. A long way down, a couple Saturday-strolling, clutch their deli bags of breakfast bagels and latte in polystyrene cups. She watches them turn down 35th, glad these strangers are together. Picks up *The Times* you need a crane for all the supplements these days. Fills the perc. Scans to see what's happening in Britain (to Marjorie). Warms croissants 5 seconds. Sets out tray with polyunsaturate glue for Malc's health, blueberry jam from the Maine trip. Drops flakes down the front of her nightie and watches Malc's face wrinkle as he laughs, losing ten years. Decide to lunch in Greenwich Village to plan holidays/leave the apartment/buy in the Catskills/retire to Seattle/New England/Florida. To joke that lunch is a very moving experience.

Long letters and little exchanges of words had crossed the Atlantic since the American exchange teacher had come to Marjorie's primary school and taken back a hesitant letter from Marjorie Michaels to exotic Brooklyn, New York New York, whose name sounded almost rural, a place of hedgerow birds and brambles. It had been answered by Mary Lou Esterhazy aged ten and two-thirds and thus began the long distant friendship that meant Marjorie began to baffle everyone with 'sneakers' and 'popsicles' while far away Mary Lou would dance in 'plimsolls' and drink thin tea. Both would try out their new spelling acquisitions in school and wonder at the strangeness of things that they lost marks for.

Over thirty years of letters now, the archives of their lives. Babies for one . . . I'm writing this at 2am, the baby across my shoulder . . . The baby is teething . . . Another night-time epistle . . . If it doesn't make sense, blame exhaustion. Exotic holidays for the other (Britain 'soon') . . . doing the vineyards in Napa and Sonoma – see wavy handwriting! . . . This year the frescoes in Florence – the acoustic echo of scratchy pen on postcard . . . you should have seen Malc on the camel in Turkey . . . you'll probably find sand in the bottom of the envelope. Marjorie was a mother through and through. Mary Lou had become a teacher with no children of her own. 'I'm tenth grade teacher,' she had written; and Marjorie had wondered how long to reach first.

What are you guys doing for the Millennium? Marjorie had asked in her last letter echoing Mary Lou's usual address. Somehow that neutered noun always seemed to stand out from the page, as if g and u and y and s, were hieroglyphs from another land with an uncrackable code. If she'd ever written f and u and c and k down, she would not have felt more bold. Mary Lou and Malc would ponder the question over a glass of ruby-red Chianti that smelled of warm terracotta earth.

Brown. Marjorie cleared away the remains of the shepherd's pie. She wanted to make food that left rainbows of colour on the plate not brown, though even brown could shine. Wet soil, parched soil, the brown of the tortoiseshell butterfly, the temporarily submerged coppery brown of her daughter's hair. Poor Brownie's pale shimmering sandiness. She looked over at the microwave – wished the box would oscillate to show that Brownie wanted to play. It was the most still item in the room. Alone with the washing up, she found herself singing 'All things bright and beautiful, all creatures great and small.' Brownie. A tear came into her eye, whether for the fragile exiled creature or her long-lost primary school, she didn't know. She looked at the pinboard on which the Millennium Plan of the Crumshaws had been posted.

Arthur intended to bury a Time Capsule. Everyone had to list suggestions as to inclusions, on the blank sheet of paper. Days went by before suggestions began to replace disdain. They actually conversed at the table again. Each wanted to stake a claim to a proportion of the, as yet, unsized Time Capsule. This was Arthur's department and he was taking a short course at evening class in the art of welding. After he had learned his personal aptitude for this skill, he would know what size he could tackle.

'Err on the small side,' he had said.

'Ere, err,' she mouthed to herself making banana shapes.

'Perfume,' said one.

'Stay out of my room,' said Cheryl.

'Household gadgets,' said the Tax Inspector. 'Women will be too liberated to use them.'

'One of mum's meringues,' said the smallest. 'They're best.'

'It will have fossilised into an ammonite when they find it,' Marjorie said brightly. 'How clever.'

'I only meant they could eat it,' said the youngest, most sensitive, feeling an uncharacteristic slight, then recovering . . . 'Can I put my name and address in so I can get a pen friend like you did?', and her heart swelled, not wanting to explain the difference between finite and infinite time to him, so inappropriate when he was enjoying his spaghetti hoops.

'Mum hasn't put anything yet,' they said, as if implying that even a one-celled domestic organism could surely contribute something to posterity.

'I'm working on it.'

The list had grown to include a spirit level, a matchbox car, a defunct Sony Walkman, a Spice Girls' CD, a calculator and a never used fountain pen.

Arthur wandered in in his Darth Vader protective welding mask and made a great ceremonial of raising the visor and reading the list from time to time, nodding his head. And God saw that it was good thought Marjorie. Only Marjorie didn't think it was good.

'There's nothing personal here,' she said. 'It should be a record of *our* family. We must *write* something about ourselves.'

'Like a diary? I could tell them about Brownie, in case gerbils get extinct,' said the youngest, whose grasp of time scales seemed suddenly to have improved by leaps and bounds.

'I'll write about what we do at school.'

'I could explain office procedures,' suggested Arthur; and Marjorie saw away aeons into time, little green men being wiped out with highly contagious boredom.

Mary Lou's last letter had been written during a weekend trip to Kennebunkport. She had asked, *Have you told them about your poems? Gee – what a coup for your Time Capsule.*

(Gee, no I haven't, Marjorie had said to herself.)

'I didn't realise Arthur was such an imaginative guy,' said Malc over scallops.

'You'd have thought of it too if we weren't ten floors up at home,' laughed Mary Lou, winding linguine.

'Well, *we'll* write a thrilling love story on bright, white paper, then tear it into little pieces and scatter the fragments all over Manhattan. Everyone will make new friends running around trying to put the pieces together to find the ending.'

'They'd blow further here,' said Mary Lou.

'Mum.'

'Mmm?' She could sense the unrest in her family for her sin of omission. Helpful suggestions were impending like the squalls of the Shipping Forecast:

'You could put in a typical shopping list?' (of metaphors? alliteration? onomatopoeia?).

'Have you got a secret diary?' (the haiku of my life).

'Dad's love letters?' ('Your mother makes a cracking dumpling stew' – iambic pentameter).

'Your old school report?' (doggerel).

'Your secret dreams?' (a sonnet).

'I'm putting in a book of poems,' Marjorie replied.

'Whose poems?' (a chorus).

'*My* poems.' (Caesura.) 'Mary Lou's read them over the years, Malc's got a publishing friend who liked the idea of poems from the Old Country, so he kind of took them on.' She stopped, sensing bewilderment.

'What does that mean?'

'They've been published in New York. They're about to be launched over here.'

'*Launched?*' they said in unison.

'People are actually buying them?'

'They're . . . well . . . on the bestseller lists there, so I thought they might qualify for the Time Capsule.'

'It's possible,' said Arthur in his new self-important voice. 'Does it have a name, this book of poetry?' He pushed up his visor, though it was already up as far as it would go. Marjorie definitely looked flushed – she might be coming down with a cold.

'Well,' said Marjorie Crumshaw, 'My idea for it was *Home Thoughts From Abroad.*'

'That sounds suitable,' said Arthur.

'Only they said someone had already done that, so it's called *Renaissance.*'

Arthur rolled the title around his mouth as if it were an unwelcome pip. 'It's not way out, is it?' He had once seen a Rap poet on TV.

'Oh no,' said Marjorie, 'just ordinary things.' She crumpled into her apron pocket the *New York Times* review which called her, not plain Marjorie Crumshaw, but Euterpe. She'd been thrilled when Volume 5 of Arthur Mee's told her that Eut Erpe was a goddess, not a sibling of Wyatt's.

'Has it got animals?' asked the youngest. 'Is Brownie in it?'

'Will you make pots of money?' asked her younger daughter making mental calculations.

'Cool. If you have to go to New York to sign things, can I come?' said her elder son.

'Are we in it?' asked her beautiful daughter removing her nose ring, bored with its discomfort now it no longer provoked.

'How could I start a new era without you?' she said, the veins in her head beginning to throb with tension/excitement/anticipation.

But it was Arthur who had the last word, for, at that moment, the trainer box fell off the microwave and Brownie leaped out hale and hearty. Fright was soon superseded by unprecedented delight.

'Our Millennium Miracle,' said Arthur feeling Resurrection easier to comprehend at that moment than *Renaissance*.

So they could all leave the kitchen then, laughing. Relieved and released, leaving Marjorie feeling as if she were in suspension somewhere.

She sat down at the kitchen table and scored through an item from her list in the little feint notebook, smiling as she did so. She pressed the smooth mug of tea against her cheek. At the same moment its warmth revived her, a champagne cork popped in New York New York. Far away in her brave new world, people toasted the absent Marjorie Crumshaw and her poems of domestic joy. She turned. Was someone calling her? Did someone want something? She half rose. No, how silly. She was quite alone in the darkening kitchen . . .

. . . until the youngest came in with his hands full of glittering dandelions.

Blue

Rachel Seiffert

T he boy arrives early. He is a young man, really; older
than he looks. Soft down on his upper lip, no bum on his
legs. He has come for the keys, a wad of crumpled notes in his
pocket. The neighbour takes him across the landing, keen to
get the matter over with. The boy looks the flat over,
unhurried, but he's excited about something. It shows in
his skin. The flat is a shell with curtains. In the kitchen the
cupboards hang off the walls.

– *You square with Malky?*

The boy nods, the neighbour leaves.

Kenny hadn't planned to stay in the flat until he'd done it
up, but now he's here he doesn't want to leave. He lays his
blankets on the floor, takes the curtains off the window and
wraps himself up in a warm corner. Streetlights flood the
room, the long, bright shape of the window all along one wall.
Kenny lies, eyes wide open in his scratchy cosy curtain nest.

He spends his first two days scrubbing the place down. The
kitchen floor makes him retch; the stink of the muck in the
corners where the hot soapy water has soaked in. He pours
neat bleach in a bucket and sets to work. His fingers itch all
night, but the clean floor in the morning inspires him to scrub
the walls and the window frames, too. That afternoon he goes
round friends and family for donations. His granny gives him

119

an old washing machine, and he gets a fridge and a cooker cheap from a friend of his brother.

Kenny's dad brings the whole lot over in a borrowed van, and they haul everything up the stairs together. Between appliances they drink cans of lager in the kitchen and watch telly on the portable that Kenny's mum gave him. Her own one from the kitchen. At midnight, they decide to plumb in the washing machine and give it a trial run with the curtains. Kenny's dad leaves after the cycle finishes, too far gone to drive the van.

The third night Kenny sleeps soundly. The windows are open and his brother's sleeping bag undone, night air on his skin.

In the morning, Kenny climbs up through the attic on to the roof. He spreads his curtains out to dry, half-bricks on each corner. He's not too steady on the sloping tiles, but he enjoys the height and the sun. He looks out over the city for a while, tracing the path of the river, identifying landmarks. Kenny's never lived so close to the centre before. *What you doing?* A girl stands by the chimney, same red hair as the neighbour across the hall. The sun is behind her head, so Kenny can't look at her straight. *What you doing?* Minding my own. *What you doing with the curtains?* Feathering my nest. *What?* Never mind. She shifts from one foot to the other, Kenny ignores her. She turns on her heel and goes.

Kenny lies back down again, glad to be left alone. He allows himself a mid-morning kip to make up for his short night.

A couple of days' work gives him enough money for some paint and a mattress. He finds some chairs to go with the table he hauled out of a skip, and buys some pots and pans with his Giro. Kenny has enough stuff in the flat now to live quite comfortably. Part of him misses the emptiness, the adventure of making do, but he doesn't think Maria would like it. He needs some rugs for the floor. He has been here for two weeks.

He calls her, but she knows already. Someone told some-one, who told someone else, who told her sister, who told her yesterday. Maria is difficult to talk to this evening and Kenny can't think straight. He can hear her sipping her tea, tapping her rings on the mug, and his money is running out. He invites her round, giving her directions over the pips. Kenny hangs up and can't remember if she said she was coming or not.

The bulb in the bathroom has gone, so he has his bath in the dark. He can hear the people downstairs arguing, even when he puts his head underwater. They keep going until his bath gets cold. He puts the fire on when he gets into bed, and wakes up in the night with a dry mouth and gummy eyes. The people downstairs are shouting again, but Kenny drops off before they finish their row.

The day is endless. Kenny has the TV on for company. He buys some food to cook for tea and a bottle of wine, but then he remembers that Maria might not want to drink, so he goes out again and buys some orange, just in case, and some candles, which he fixes into a clean ashtray. He sits on the bed for a long time and then goes out to buy a newspaper, but he can't concentrate. He smokes too much, and opens all the windows to get rid of the smell. He tries to have an afternoon nap, but watches TV instead. He doesn't want to cook until she comes, but he's starving. He runs out to the shops to get some crisps. The light is going out of the day, and Kenny worries that she has come and gone while he was out.

When the buzzer goes he doesn't get up immediately. He stands next to the entry phone and counts to ten, and then he answers.

– *It's me.*

– OK.

Maria takes a while to get up the stairs. When she gets to the second floor, Kenny can watch her over the banister. He hasn't seen her for over a month and she's showing now.

121

Skinny woman with a big belly. She is walking like his sister did when she was pregnant, only her back is still straight and her legs look good. She pauses on the landing and looks up.

– Do you want a hand?

– *I'm OK.*

When she gets to the top floor, she stands in front of him for a couple of seconds to get her breath and he doesn't know what to do.

– *Can I come in, then?*

Kenny is proud of the flat, clean and bright with its improvised furniture. He shows her everything, lingering in the kitchen with its washing machine, hurrying through the bedroom with its double bed. Maria is quiet, nodding, non-committal. Kenny wants her to smile at him and say nice things like it's good to have a gas cooker.

– *I'm starving.*

He makes her a cup of tea, and she sits in the kitchen while he cooks. He asks after her family and she smiles while she answers, but she's not being friendly. There are long silences between them, and Kenny tries to look busy with the food. He sets the table and she sits with her hands folded on her belly. Then he opens the wine but says she can have orange if she wants, and she says a glass of water will do.

– *I didn't ask you to do any of this, you know?*

– No, I know.

This throws him a bit, but Maria is more relaxed now and they eat. Kenny has some wine and feels a bit better.

– I wanted to do it.

Maria nods but she looks out of the window. He thinks she might be laughing at him, but the moment passes. He spoons the peaches out of the can into bowls and they both help themselves to ice cream. She has a sip or two of his wine without asking, and then she picks the can up from the side and spoons more ice cream into the leftover syrup and eats it from the can, leaning back in her chair. She tells him about work and friends, and he tells her about family, and neither of them mentions the flat or the baby.

She says she wants to watch TV, but when she sees that there is only the double bed to sit on, she changes her mind. They stand in the narrow hallway, both embarrassed and then Maria says she wants to go home.

Kenny helps her into the cab. Maria looks like a kid on the back seat. A kid with a pillow stuffed up her jumper. She smiles at him and then she's off.

Kenny lies in the bath and can't cry. He brings the candles in to the bathroom, dripping water through the flat. He drinks the rest of the wine, rolls a damp joint that is a job to smoke but is just the trick, and he can forget it all until the morning.

It's Sunday and he goes to his mum's for dinner. He eats a lot and helps his dad wash up, then he falls asleep on the sofa watching the sport. His mum asks if he wants to stay over, but he's too old to be sleeping in bunk beds so he goes back to the flat. He buys lagers on the way and drinks a skinful so he can forget it all for a little bit longer.

Kenny spends a day in bed. He goes to sign on. He does a day's work for his brother-in-law, who gives him a sofa and some paint. He repaints all the doors in the flat, and starts on the skirting boards. Then he phones Maria.

She sounds happy to hear from him and they chat for a while about this and that, and then Maria says she'd like to come over tomorrow night. Kenny says fine, and then they say goodbye and he's back in the flat before he knows it. He sits in the kitchen and stares at the TV.

It's late when he wakes up. He has a bath and cleans the windows. He doesn't want to sit around waiting like the last time, so he goes for a walk in a park, which is something he would never normally do. Then he gets a bus across the centre of the city, sitting on the top deck. On the way back, he gets off at the river and walks across one of the bridges. It's late afternoon when he gets to the other side and he realises he has no money left to buy anything for dinner. He gets a bus to his mum's to borrow a tenner till he gets his Giro. She's hurt because he's in a hurry, so he promises to come for Sunday lunch.

When he gets back, Maria is sitting on the step outside the block, but she's not annoyed. She was early, thought she'd wait a bit. She looks relieved.

They cook dinner together and eat in the kitchen, not saying very much, but feeling quite cosy. It gets dark and they wash up together, and then Maria says she would really like some chocolate.

She is lying on the bed when he comes back. He throws the sweets on the mattress and sits down next to her. She has a sip of his lager and eats her chocolates and they watch a film together and she falls asleep. He stares at her belly and her breasts and her legs for a long time and then he covers her up and goes to sleep on the sofa. He hears her get up and go to the toilet, but she doesn't come into the living room, so he doesn't go back into the bedroom.

She stays for breakfast and helps him finish the skirting boards, but after lunch she goes home. Kenny washes up and then he has a bath and he thinks about Maria. About all the times they slept together before, and how he doesn't know if sleeping together now would be a good idea or not, but he wants to all the same and he hopes she does, too. He's already been in the flat for a month.

It's Saturday and he's got no money, so he spends the day in bed half watching telly, mostly thinking about Maria. He needs to pay the rent soon. He needs some money for food and fags and bus fares. When the baby comes he'll need ten times more. He does some maths on the back of an envelope and it all adds up to needing a job. He'll ask his brother-in-law tomorrow.

His brother-in-law says he'll ask his boss, but he can't promise anything. His sister tells him to look in the paper like everyone else and his dad tells her to be quiet. She is for a minute or two and they all eat, but then she says that Kenny shouldn't have got Maria pregnant in the first place, if he doesn't have a job, and Kenny's dad swears at her. Kenny's mum leaves the room and Kenny's dad gets angry and Kenny's brother-in-law just carries on eating and Kenny thinks that would be me if I was married to Maria and sitting in a family row. He has to pay the rent, and he owes his mum a tenner, and he knows she worries, and he has to chew every mouthful twenty times to distract himself from throwing the dishes around the room. Sprouts in the shag pile, gravy on the walls.

Kenny's dad comes round and takes him in to work. Only there's nothing for him to do and Kenny thinks his dad is probably paying him out of his own pocket which is like taking five tenners off his mum and giving her one back. After the second day he tells his dad he's got some other work. Kenny's dad knows he's lying, and Kenny knows that he knows.

Kenny goes to sign on. He pays the rent, gives his dad a tenner for his mum, gets a bag of fifties for the meter and buys a week's worth of bread and beans. He gets a paper every morning and takes a pile of tens to the phone box to call for jobs but there's nothing doing. It rains a fair bit that week and Kenny wishes he had a phone so Maria could call and it wouldn't be up to him to swallow his lump of pride every time. He holds out over the weekend, and then on Sunday night the buzzer goes.

Kenny goes down this time and keeps Maria company up the stairs. She's a bit bigger again and she looks good, even in the damp stairwell.

They settle down on the bed quite quickly and turn the TV on but leave the light off. The room gets darker and they get under the duvet where it is warm and Kenny feels Maria's legs next to his, her belly pressed against his ribs. They share a can of lager and stay like that until it gets late and they're both sleepy. Maria slips to the edge of the mattress and takes off her trousers and socks. She leaves her knickers on but takes off her bra under her T-shirt. Then she gets back under the duvet. Kenny kicks off his jeans and turns the telly off. The room is quiet and dark and neither of them moves for a while. Kenny really needs to pee now, but maybe Maria will fall asleep while he's-out of the room. He puts a hand on her arm. She breathes steadily and doesn't move. Kenny gets up quietly and goes to the bathroom.

He pees in the dark and brushes his teeth and decides to talk to her in the morning.

Maria rolls over when he gets under the duvet and puts a hand on his stomach. He touches her fingers and then strokes her arm, and then he rolls over and strokes her back. He can't see her in the dark, but he knows her eyes are open. He kisses her and she puts her hands on his chest. Kenny takes his T-shirt off and then he takes hers off, too. She is uncomfortable, but he thinks she's beautiful.

He isn't sleepy. He wonders if it was the right thing to do. She doesn't say anything, but lies very still next to him. After a while, she rolls on to her side and goes to sleep. A little later, she rolls over again, putting her back to him. After that, Kenny goes to sleep, too.

In the morning he cooks breakfast and they eat in bed. Kenny reads the paper while Maria has a bath. His brother comes round with the paint and an eighth. They whisper in the narrow hall so Maria won't hear. Kenny's brother smiles, pats him on the elbow and says he'll leave them to it.

Maria gets back into bed to read the paper and Kenny makes a start on the bathroom. She comes in after a while with a cup of tea for him and he asks her if she likes the colour. She nods, shrugs.

– What colour shall we do the big room?

– *Blue.*

– If it's a boy.

– *Yeah. Whatever.*

She comes back in a bit later with her coat on. The paint smell is making her a bit sick, thought she'd go for a walk, buy a pint of milk.

Kenny doesn't turn the lights on when it gets dark and he doesn't cook himself any dinner. He just lies in the bed and waits. He can't cry and he can't sleep. He lies very still and smokes his brother's eighth.

At the end of the week Kenny cashes his Giro and paints the living room blue.

He goes to the phone box and calls his brother to see if he can stay over. He rings his mum and says he won't come for Sunday lunch, but he'll see her soon. Early evening, Kenny hands the keys back and walks out of the estate on to the main road.

The Earth is Slowing Down . . .

David Millar

I began to feel this psychic claustrophobia about six or seven months ago: this sense that my life was being crushed by Space and Time. My routines have formed ruts and these ruts, these weals in Time, have become so deep that, soon, I'll only be able to stand on a box and peer out over the top at what my life could have been.

My small acts of will consist of going to *this* baker's shop instead of *that* baker's shop, driving to Safeway in the city instead of going to Shop Local in the town.

In the Safeway coffee shop, I engage strangers in conversation like a small child starved of affection and attention. The glow from these raids on other people's consciousness decays like radiation and I warm myself at them until they burn out.

Middle Brother follows me through to the kitchen, where I'm washing the last of the dishes before carefully wrapping them up in the day before yesterday's news and packing them into the removal firm's big cardboard cases.

He starts straight in; no preliminaries.

It's a hell ay a lot tae leave tae Mither. He takes a packet of cheap cigarettes from his pocket, extracts one and lights it with the silver lighter we gave him for his thirty-fifth birthday. He doesn't ask my permission to smoke and he doesn't offer me one, although he's well aware that I've taken it up again. He takes a couple of short pecks at the cigarette and says:

'Ye're his wife.'

'And you're his brother. And his mother's his mother.'

I scour the bottom of a pan which has a brown sludge of burnt milk coating it. I do this energetically, trying to convey to Middle Brother that I really don't need or want this conversation, that time is short and I have a lot of things I must do.

'It's jist that everyone's . . . Everyone's a bit puzzled. They dinnay understand why. I ken ye best. And *I* dinnay understand why.' I hear his lungs whistle as he exhales.

I let the pan drop back into the lukewarm water and put my hands on the edge of the metal sink. I look straight ahead at the tea-towel I've blue-tacked to the wall: it's white with brightly coloured vegetables printed on it. Each has a little label beside it, with its Latin name etched in tiny italic script. I wonder when my taste became so garish. I look down at my hands my say, 'Because the Universe is expanding. The Earth is slowing down. My one and only life is accelerating to its end.'

They've had a family conference and voted to send Middle Brother round. There are four brothers and three sisters and I've never fully understood why he came to be called Middle Brother: he's really the second oldest. You'd think that the third oldest had an equal right to be Middle Brother. But no. The rest of them are called by their given names: Eddie, Middle Brother, Gavin, Kenneth, Daphne, Helen and Frances.

I was told years ago, and I've been told again and again, at birthdays, christenings, weddings, anniversaries and funerals, why Middle Brother became Middle Brother. There are always variations in the story.

I don't think families always realise that their knots and tangles, the internecine guerilla warfare that goes on inside them are sometimes about as interesting as an Icelandic Saga to outsiders. Unless you're a gossip of course; but I suppose we all have a need to live vicariously a little.

And I'm probably being unfair to Icelandic Sagas. I suppose Icelandic Sagas are analogous to Family Sagas: full of myths and legends subtly smelted and shaped through the generations.

So, I can't now remember just why Middle Brother became Middle Brother in the first place. Anyway, it solved the problem of what to call the last born of the family. Middle Brother's Christian name is Kenneth. But everyone had called him Middle Brother (shortened to Mid) for so long that his name had become vacant and they filled the empty slot with the family's last-born child. So, there are two male children called Kenneth in the family: the second oldest male and the youngest male.

Sometimes, when I've less than nothing better to think about, I wonder if this is legal.

'Whit's the Universe tae dae with anything?' he asks.

'Do you want some tea?' I say, 'I was just going to make some.'

'Aye, that'd be fine.'

I remove two mugs from their hooks. One is an East Stirling supporter's mug (Eddie's; from the days when he cared about football; from the days when he cared about *anything*) and the other is about the star sign Capricorn. I flick the switch on the kettle, dump teabags in the mugs and spoon in sugar. Three spoons in the Stirling mug and a generous half in the Capricorn.

'I wonder where this came from?'

'Whit?' I've startled Middle Brother from some deep ruminations. He looks flushed and guilty.

'This mug. *I'm* not Capricorn and neither's Eddie.'

'Whit's Capricorn again?' he asks as if he's really interested. I peer at the mug.

'Mmm, December the twenty-second to January the twentieth, according to this.' He thinks.

'Helen's the only Capricorn in the family. Mebbe she left it here.' As the words come from his mouth, he must realise what a fatuous explanation this is and he grins awkwardly at me.

The kettle boils and I make our tea. I hand Middle Brother the East Stirling supporter's mug and say: 'Shall we go through?'

The kitchen is off the living room and I follow Middle Brother through the connecting door. I take my mug over to the window, rest my back against the glass and watch as he goes over to the fireplace, where Eddie is sitting in his wheelchair watching the television.

'Whit like Eddie?' Middle Brother says.

Eddie turns his head, smiles the guileless smile that everyone loves and says: 'Aye, I thought aboot the Escort. But the Sierra's got mair weight tae it. Ken? On balance I'd probably go fur the Sierra.' He turns his head away and stares deep into the fire. I smile at Middle Brother and move my shoulders slightly to indicate understanding, pity, sympathy and resignation. All the things I've recently started feeling for myself.

One winter night five years ago, the road between the city and the town had a tarmac of black ice laid down on it.

One winter night five years ago, Eddie and his three brothers went into the city for a night out. Eddie usually made an effort not to drive if he was drinking. His sister, Daphne, worked a night shift at the biscuit factory in the city and the plan was that the four of them would drive in, leave the car in a place where Daphne could find it and let her drive it home. Eddie and the others would get a taxi back.

One winter night five years ago, Eddie and his three brothers were driving home from the city when the car slid from the road and ended up with its nose hanging over the edge of an almost perpendicular ravine which led down to a gleaming, iced-over river. Mid told me later that he'd always remember the car's headlights being reflected back up at them by the hard, mirrored surface of the water.

The four of them were told they were lucky to be alive; they were told that, if the car had tipped over, they would have been smashed on the ice and rocks, or drowned in the freezing river. The three brothers had minor, niggling injuries. Eddie had a few bumps and bruises on his body. The real damage was above the neck.

His face looked as if someone had punched him with an old-fashioned flat-iron. But it was in his head, behind his strangely distorted face, that all the serious injury had taken place. He couldn't walk, although there was no apparent *physical* reason why not. He could talk, but nothing he said made sense. Oh, it was logical enough, grammatical and internally consistent. But it never had anything to do with whatever his interlocutor was talking to him about.

I spent thirty evenings at the hospital, sitting tense and hunched in a chair parked tight beside Eddie's bed, trying to talk to him about me and his family, our friends, his friends and my friends, the town, politics and the weather. Each evening I descended from trying to make conversation with Eddie to throwing the odd monosyllable at him, while he sat, propped up by plump pillows, and talked airily about nothing at all.

He's quieter now.

'He eyewis wanted a Sierra. I wish I could tell him thit they dinnay mak them anymair.'

I hear Mid sighing but I've turned away, to look moodily out of the window and take small, intermittent sips from my scalding tea.

Mid says something.

'Sorry, I wasn't listening.' Turning round.

'I said, it cannay be easy for ye.'

'It isn't. Did he always want a Sierra? I don't remember.'

'When we were younger. Mebbe afore he met ye.'

'I can't remember what he used to be like. I can't remember what *we* used to be like. He was in a wheelchair when we went up the aisle. Surely. Wasn't he?

'I've been feeling like that for a while now. I've been feeling that this has always been my life.

'Up, light the fire, give Eddie his breakfast, take him for a walk, make lunch, go to the day centre, shop while Eddie's there. Pick him up, cook the dinner while Eddie's having a nap. Light the fire, give him his dinner, watch telly till nine, put Eddie to bed, get the fire ready for the morning, then go to bed myself because I'm exhausted.'

Where is it that we learn to look moodily out of windows anyway? Television? Books? Films? By imitation? Everyone seems to do it: stare through the glass and go into a trance. Say, when interrupted: 'Sorry, I wasn't listening.'

I could have said to Mid: 'Then I go to bed because I'm numbed and bored by the routine. In bed, I read. Journalists and authors send me their reports about what's happening on the rest of the planet. I sometimes masturbate just to prove to myself that I'm still alive and to damp down my sex nerves. To show that someone still cares. Then the sleeping pills cut in. Otherwise, I'd lie awake all night dreaming of escape, other lives, accidents and murder.'

Mid walks away from Eddie and joins me at the window. Now *he* looks moodily out.

'I had a hellish row wi' Mither. She thinks ye're jist bein' selfish.'

'She's always thought that. The lot of you've always thought that. Selfish, cold and snobbish.'

'Naw.' Mid says, turning from the window to face me.

'Yes. Helen told me that at Daphne's wedding.'

'She'd be drunk.'

'In vino veritas.'

'Ach, that's nonsense. Ye say a' kindsay things if ye're pissed. Some true. Some a lottay rubbish.'

'Your mother's never liked me. That's why she stopped coming to help me with him.

'Now I'm going to do the worst thing anyone could do to her Eddie. Abandon him.'

'Ye're no abandoning him!'

'Leaving to get on with my own life. Abandoning him. It's all one to her.'

'She's fae a different generation. Ye get married and ye stick tae each ither through thick and thin. She's eyewis on at me. She never forgets thit I've been divorced twice. Different generation.' He shrugs.

'But she's still wanting to take him?'

'Aye. She says she's nae choice.'

'He'd get a place at Marylee.'

'She'd never let him go there.'

'They're better equipped to care for him there.'

'Mebbe. Aye. I'm sure they are. But she says thit naebody fae *her* femily's going tae ane ay thae places. That's whit she cries it. "Ane ay *thae* places". I think she thinks it's some kinday mental institution. She'd tak him even if she wis on her death bed.'

'It's a lot of work. And she's not getting any younger. She won't have any time to herself.'

'She says wirk keeps her young. I've telt her she winnay hae as much time for the grandchildren an' a' that. But she says ye dinnay turn yer own awey when they need help.' He shrugs again. 'The rest ay us'll muck in. Ye dinnay need tae worry.'

I start crying for some reason and he closes the distance between us and puts his arms round me. I've forgotten how small and chunky he is. I stiffen and wriggle my way out of the encirclement.

'Don't,' I say. 'We shouldn't. It was a bad idea.'

About two years ago, Middle Brother and I went to bed together. It was the night of some family celebration, someone's birthday I think. Eddie's mother took him overnight. At that time, she'd still do this now and then, to let me get out if she thought I needed 'taking out of myself'.

The three sisters, the three remaining brothers and me went for a Chinese then spent two or three hours in Gavin's local in the High Street. There was a lot of collusion among the members of the family to get me rat-arsed, which they managed easily enough. I've never had much of a head for alcohol and they made sure that someone was buying a round every fifteen minutes or so.

Daphne, Helen and Frances teased me about picking up a man. It would've been easy enough, but most of Gavin's pals looked like they'd need a guide book to find their way around a female body. It wasn't until late the next day that I realised how bizarre this was: my sisters-in-law trying to get me off with some guy while their brother, my husband, was being spoon-fed his supper at his mother's house. *Had* they been joking? But all the innuendo and the sex talk must've got me thinking at some level or other.

It suddenly became eleven o' clock and, probably using up my last milligram of rational thought, I decided that I'd better get home somehow, before I threw up. I stood up to go, assuring everyone that I'd be all right while four pairs of hands jackknifed and levered me into my coat.

Then, I *did* throw up. Over the table, several drinks, half-empty packets of crisps and two or three ashtrays. I stood there, swaying, back and forward, back and forward, trying to identify the slithery bits of food in the mess, too tired and drunk to do this, too tired and drunk to move. Mid got up, put on his jacket, took me by the elbow and helped me thread my way through the tables and chairs to the door.

He took me home and made me a cup of strong coffee. Over the next hour, we talked in a disjointed, fragmented way. I sobered up enough to swab the taste of vomit from my mouth with peppermint toothpaste and take Mid to bed with me.

It was disastrous. Not from a mechanical point of view. But Mid seemed to think that I was suffering from a female equivalent of male sexual frustration. He thought I needed release from banked-up sexual torment, as men seem to do, when I really needed to be kissed and cuddled and stroked as if I were a cat.

Afterwards . . . Afterwards, we lay there feeling guilty; Eddie might as well have been sitting by the side of the bed, watching.

And we never did it again.

'I'm no tryin' tae . . . We baith ken that was a mistake.' Mid moves away from me. He moves a deliberate foot and a half away, so that I can't misunderstand. He reaches into a pocket and produces a tatty, half-used packet of tissues.

'I've jist got rid of a cold,' he says, as he hands me the packet. I pull one out and blow my nose. I try to give him the packet back. He shakes his head.

'Jist keep them.'

'Thanks.'

'D'ye need a hand wi' packing?'

'No. I'm leaving most of the heavy stuff. Furniture, that

kind of thing. I'm just taking the pine chest and the dresser in the kitchen. My mother gave them to me years ago. Apart from that, it's just all the personal stuff that's accumulated over the years. I doubt if it'll even make up a van-load.'

'I'd better be going,' he says.

He tells Eddie that he'll see him later, but Eddie's chuckling at some day-time quiz show, even though nobody's said anything funny. Mid shrugs and I escort him to the door.

'Whit're ye goin' tae dae wi' yersel'?' he says, standing on the threshold.

'Stay with my sister for a while. Think.'

'Well. Good luck.'

'Thanks.'

'If ye change yer mind . . .'

'I won't.'

He walks down the steps and turns.

'Drop in afore ye go.'

'I'll try.' But we both know I won't. I'll hand Eddie's care over to his mother and go.

Mid walks down to the gate, turns again. Gives me a wave and a smile.

I wave back and a surge of feeling washes through me. Like pins and needles but more intense. Like walking over someone's grave but more intense. I've only experienced it when elderly relatives are about to die.

A feeling that Mid is fading, that he will never appear in my life again and a part of me is going, is dying, with him.

Painting the Family Pet

Sarah Salway

A strange woman comes to my door one day in early March. It's a prosperous area so we often have people selling things door-to-door – dusters, make-up, frozen foods – but she doesn't look like a professional saleswoman. She hasn't got the patter either. She just smiles awkwardly and thrusts a card in my hand: 'Amy Turner. Pet Portraits Undertaken.'

I run my fingernail along the cheap gold edge of the card and look at her, waiting for an explanation.

'I'll paint any animal in the comfort of your own home,' Amy Turner says. 'Wouldn't you like a unique portrait of your loved one? I've had experience of dogs, cats, parrots, prize bulls . . .'

'Prize bulls!' I can't help looking up and down the quiet suburban street. The thought of any of my neighbours keeping bulls makes me smile. Amy looks cross, and I realise I've interrupted her sales pitch.

'I don't have any animals,' I say as we look past each other. She must be wishing some little cat or dog would come running down the hall to give the game away, and it is the first chance I've had to sniff the air outside. It is one of those spring mornings when you wake up and find winter's gone. Even the camellia in the garden opposite has flowered overnight, vulgar pink blossoms which look shocking against the quiet greens and greys.

'Why are you still in your dressing gown?' Amy says eventually, turning her attention back to me. 'It's nearly lunchtime. Are you ill?'

'I'm fine,' I lie. I'm not going to tell a stranger I've just been sick in the toilet upstairs and would still be sticking my fingers down my throat if the doorbell hadn't rung. But now I'm not sure what to do next. Amy is still standing there. She doesn't seem to think that not having a pet is a good enough excuse.

'I'm starving,' she says and I smile politely, nodding the way you do before you say goodbye.

'No,' she puts her foot in the door. 'I'm really starving. I've had nothing to eat for two days and no one has any sodding pets for me to paint. I need some food or I'll faint, right here on your doorstep.'

Amy stands by the fridge playing with my poetry magnets while I make her a chocolate-spread sandwich. I brush past her to get the butter but really I want to see what she has written.

WOMAN RUBS

SILKY SLOWLY

PINK BUBBLES GLOW

COOL HEART

BLUELY MUSIC

I used to write proper poems to Dan once upon a time. When we were first married, I would tape them to the fridge door on scraps torn out of a spiral-bound notebook. But then he bought me this expensive set of magnetic words and I couldn't write any more. Even my poetry had been turned into something only he had the power to give me. I play with the words in their little glass box sometimes but I've lost confidence in my ability to use them in the proper sequence. I'm disappointed that Amy isn't even trying to make sense.

'Aren't you eating?' she asks as she nibbles round the edge of the sandwich. She is so delicate, her tongue curling upwards to lick the crumbs off her upper lip. If she'd really been starving, wouldn't she have crammed the whole thing in at once?

I go to the fridge and open the door, pretending I'm looking for something so I don't have to answer her question. I can feel her come up behind me but I stay there, memorising the names of all the food as if I'm about to take an exam.

'Do you always keep such a lot of food?' Amy asks.

'Do you always ask so many questions?' I say quickly, but Amy just laughs. She's standing so close I can smell the chocolate on her breath.

'I could paint that,' she says, pointing at the fridge. It's one of these tall American models. I dream about it sometimes, a huge monster standing in the corner of the room with its mouth constantly open and I'm this tiny little figure, exhausting myself in my efforts to keep it satisfied.

'Why would I want a picture of a fridge?' I ask.

'Because you seem to like looking inside it.' Amy shrugs and goes back to her sandwich.

'But I can just do that, can't I?' I persist. 'It's not like an animal or something that could die or get old or change.'

'I could paint the door of the fridge with what's inside. Exactly as it is now.' Amy sounds as if she's explaining something to a slightly dim child. 'Then you won't need to keep opening it and wasting electricity.'

There are so many reasons why this doesn't make sense that

I look at Amy standing in my kitchen and I don't have the energy to argue.

'I'll start tomorrow,' Amy says, studying her fingernails before she starts to gnaw at a cuticle with more enthusiasm than she showed the sandwich.

When Dan comes home, he goes straight to the fridge.

'Good day, Helen?' he asks, slurping from the can and wiping off the moisture from his top lip. He stands in the kitchen doorway, staring at me.

He does this all the time. I've learnt not to mind, although recently he's taken to creeping up on me so I don't know how long he's been there. It's not too bad during the day but I find it hard to go to sleep at night, knowing he'll be looking. I prefer it when I've time to arrange myself, like now, legs underneath me, skirt fanning round my body, arms resting on the back of the sofa, gaze averted.

I nod, but I can't help wondering if he messed up the fridge when he got his beer.

'Whatdayadotoday?' Dan comes to sit down next to me, and I can feel his weight upset the balance of the sofa. This is how he talks, so fast that all the words run into one. He does everything on the gallop; always has done. 'Dan needs to slow down and look at the finer details of his life,' his primary teacher said in her report one year. It's a comment Dan wants to frame and stick up on the toilet wall.

'I'm thinking of getting a pet,' I say, folding my body under the arm he's holding out behind me.

'A pet.' Dan pretends to be shocked, but then he sees I'm serious. 'No, baby, you don't want to do that. Animals take up too much of your time.'

'It would give us something to talk about,' I say.

'We talk enough,' says Dan. 'I'm not coming home tired from work and discussing what the hamster's been up to.'

'No pets then?'
'No pets.'

We eat out, although I know Dan's seen how much food there is in the house. Dan orders rare steak for both of us and after he's finished his, he leans over and spears the half of mine that's left with his fork. A drop of blood falls on the white tablecloth, about three inches away from the vase of plastic yellow flowers that sits between us.

'No point in wasting good food,' he says, and I excuse myself to be sick in the ladies. To waste good food.

Dan watches me make my way back to the table, past the thick wooden bar counter and the fake palm trees. He's fingering the bill that sits in the shallow bronze bowl in front of him. Dan's not a mean man, but I wonder if he's thinking the same as me. Do you have to pay for food that doesn't actually leave the premises?

The next morning I wake up feeling excited, not sure why. I wonder what I've been dreaming about and then I remember Amy. And then I remember Dan. Dan eats breakfast. I rush downstairs, barefoot, to check the fridge. If he's finished the milk, it could spoil the picture.

I lie down on the sofa so I can watch Amy paint. It's taking longer than she thought because she has to keep opening the door to check on the proportions.

'Why don't you buy one of those Polaroid cameras?' I ask. 'Then you could just paint from the pictures.'

'Do you think I'd be doing this if I could afford a camera?' she says.

I don't even listen to the words because I suddenly realise something. Amy answers every question with another question. The fact that I can anticipate Amy's behaviour pleases me. She is no longer a stranger.

143

Because Amy's in the kitchen anyway, she makes us both coffee every time she needs a break. She brings over the two steaming mugs and sits next to me on the sofa.

'So if I wasn't here, what would you be doing?' she says.

It's like a test. I wonder if there is a right answer she'd like me to say but then give up.

'I'd probably just be sitting here,' I say.

Amy shakes her head. She fizzes with so much energy that I'm scared to touch her in case I get a shock. I like it when she sits next to me because we balance each other out. I can feel her body physically relax as her aura meets mine in the middle. It's different with Dan because his energy takes over until I'm colonised, diminished. Amy is more unfocused, so mine beats hers every time.

Two hours later, I start to notice that Amy is looking at the clock almost as often as me.

'It's lunchtime,' she says blandly.

'So it is,' I say, handing over the decision to her.

'We'll spoil the picture if we eat anything from the fridge.' She runs her fingers through her short red hair, looking worried. 'Shall I nip out and get something from the shop?' Amy's already putting her jacket on so I stay still. I've wrapped the duvet round me now, my head just popping out at the top.

'Surprise me,' I shout as the door shuts behind her so softly I know she's left the snib up so as not to disturb me.

'Did you look at my painting?' Amy asks when she comes back and I shake my head.

'You've not moved all morning,' she says. 'Not many people can keep that still. Animals, now. That's a different story.'

She hands me first a spoon and then a small glass jar.

'Baby food!' I hold it in my hand as if it's a precious object, and whisper my thanks so quietly I'm not sure Amy hears. However, she slips in when I hold the end of the duvet up for her to get under and we spoon smooth organic carrots into our mouths like two baby birds in our feathered nest. I can feel the purée worm its way down my throat.

'I knew I was right about you.' She looks triumphant as she holds out her hand for my dirty jar and spoon.

When Dan comes back that night, I say nothing as he heads for the fridge.

'So what's going on?' he asks, coming straight back into the sitting room. It takes me a moment to realise what's different about him and then I realise he's not got a drink in his hand.

'I'm having the fridge painted,' I say and he comes over to give me a hug, holding me so tight that I feel the breath forcibly expelled through my mouth.

'My wife, the one and only Helen,' he says as if he's announcing me to a room of strangers. 'No one else but you would do this.'

'It wasn't my idea,' I say quickly, but he's back in the kitchen, shaking his head and staring at the fridge. From his smile, I suspect that he's already thinking of the story he'll tell the people at work the next morning. 'Just guess what Helen's done now . . .'

We go back to the same restaurant and I tell him about Amy while he eats both steaks. I embroider wildly on all the stories she's told me that day and he laughs so much that he doesn't notice I'm not eating anything. This time, he pays the bill straight away and we leave hand in hand.

Amy and I experiment with our lunches. She prefers the leek and potato purée while I move towards country parsnip. The day before she finishes the painting, we celebrate with a fruits of the forest dessert, taking it in turns to dip our spoons into the jar.

'What will you do when you finish here?' I ask.

'I'm not fussy. I'll paint anything so long as I get paid,' she says, looking at me oddly. 'Will you miss me?'

'I'll have your painting to remember you by.' I try to think what I could give Amy, but she seems to move through life without the need for possessions. Dan's sorting out the payment anyway. They've started to have coffee together in the mornings before I get out of bed. I can hear their laughter come up the stairs, curling under the bedroom door like a tendril of smoke. I'm pleased Dan has someone to let his energy off on to. He's got so bouncy from all the steak he's been eating.

Dan and I are positively vivacious as the waiter shows us to our normal table. I tell him which animal I think Amy prefers to paint – cats – and he says I'm wrong. She likes dogs best. We talk about Amy all evening and when we let ourselves back into the house, we're still laughing.

'Whisky?' Dan asks and goes to get the Laphroaig. I stand in the kitchen and stare at the fridge door. Amy is a real artist. The chicken breasts look as if you could reach out and pick them up, she's even got the little crumbs of toast Dan always leaves in the butter and the curl on the yoghurt lid is exactly right.

'It's better than I thought it would be,' Dan says, handing me a glass. I swirl the liquid round and round the glass, pressing my nose in as if I can taste the peat better that way.

'Will you buy me a camera to give Amy?' I ask. 'Then she won't have to spend such a long time in other people's houses. She can do the painting at home.'

'I think living in other people's houses is what Amy likes,'

Dan says. 'Amy's a natural observer.' And then he laughs so loudly that I'm forced to give in and ask him what's funny.

As Dan reaches into the cupboard and pulls out the picture, I remember Amy's words about how she would paint anything if she got paid. She's flattered me. My hair's not as long or as thick as she's made it and there's something attractive about the wistful way I'm looking just slightly off the canvas.

'It's a joke,' Dan says, when I don't laugh.

I know it is. It's Dan's joke. The one he always makes when people ask me what I do. He tells them he stops me from doing anything because he finds me so restful to look at. 'In the same way some people keep a goldfish to calm them down,' he says.

He must have told Amy this because she's painted me swimming round a glass bowl. I hold the picture closer to my eyes to try and make out if the shadow at one side is another person or not. I guess I'm hoping Amy's painted herself in the water with me.

Dan must be aware he's gone too far this time. 'It's nothing personal,' he says. 'Amy's not like you. She has to earn her own bread and butter. Come on, Helen, we've all got to eat.'

After Dan goes to bed, I draw up a chair and sit in front of the fridge for a long time. Then I spend some time opening and shutting the door. Amy's painting is like a piece of tracing paper laid over the real thing. She's even managed to get the light just right. I stand in front of the open fridge as if I'm warming myself and turn round to look at the spot where I normally sit and keep her company.

I start with the yoghurts and then move on to the cheese, cutting it up into small pieces. While the chicken and bacon are cooking, I tear up lettuce leaves and hold them above my lips as if I'm sucking on peeled grapes. The butter I force down in one, washing it through with two pints of milk. I find some chocolate at the back and eat one chunk after each raw egg as a reward. Every ten minutes, I open one of Dan's beers and toast the distorted face I see in the bowl of the spoon I'm using as my weapon. I save the ice cubes until last, biting and crunching them between my teeth until I can feel the ice splinter and crack. I open my mouth and icicles fall round me on to the floor.

When the fridge is empty, I let the door swing shut and lean up against the painted front for support. Then, slowly and deliberately feeling my way with both hands, I reach into the cupboard under the sink and bring out the bundle of super-market bags I keep there. I fill each one with good food and leave them in as straight a line as I can manage for Amy and Dan to find in the morning.

Harmonious Fist

Mitchell Miller

M am used to wrap the linen on my hands for me, stretching it tight, curving the strips over the knuckles, looping the material under the fingers, snagging it by the thumb. I like it bound tight, I felt solid and dangerous, hands that were numbed, painless yet painful. I do it myself now, now I'm grown up. My left fist is already set, my hands are so trussed they can only pinch at things. It means I always have trouble getting my right tight enough, being no lefthander. I am over over-clumsy when it comes to drawing the linen under the palm and it always seems to slacken.

But when I was starting, when I was twelve, Mam would wrap me. Both my hands would be stretched out from me, while she looped linen around my finger roots, and pulled it tight into the skin, wrapping my paws right well. You could feel the blood stop flowing. The first few times I greeted, it was sore, and my hands itched, and felt divvi. 'You'll be glad I did it tight after ye've given a few skelps.' Uncomforted, I'd then pick down the wagon steps. Dad would be found outside, and he'd smile and deek down at my fists. As I held them out, clenched, he'd inspect them, his misshapen left brow, where a bare knuckle sliced straight into him, jerked up and down as he looked over my weapons. His big brown hands took my wee ones and he stroked them with his thumb.

149

A fist, assembled properly, thumb tucked just right, and aimed at the proper spot, can kill. It can take away sight. If you stand just right, feet placed well and you go in behind it, you are a force of evil. A Selkirk doctor told me I was a pugilist, which is a foreign word for a fist-fighter. I liked the word and said it back to myself. But Dad, when he heard said, no, I am not a fist-fighter, a pugilist, I am a Boxer, which is more like being an artist. But for me, I like having a trade with a foreign name.

My teeth, a jerk back, and a thumb bracing the cloth finally gets some tightness into the right fist, and I tuck in the spit-soggy end of linen. I put up, and draw in behind my guard, feeling with pleasure the weight of my punchers. My feet almost naturally sort themselves out. Boxing or 'pugilisting' is all in the feet: 'feet and fists a good mill make' my grandad said. He left out ducking, and knowing when to follow through with your elbow and take the other one's eye, of course. I shift feet and as usual the whole floor shifts as well, a small tip back then forward. A quiet 'eee' comes from some-where in the wood of the wagon. I have heard wood strain itself all of my life, whether it's the pops and whistles as the wood cools down after a hot day, or the whimpers of fear when God whips up the winds and frightens the hell out of us, making our home sway like a pissant, Dad fouling the air with bad language while he and Joe argue about how to rope the wagon down proper . . .

I push out seven punches, one after the other, three jabs, a hook, and uppercut and a hook, but every time, jerking back just before I put a dent in Mam's wood panels, or knock a shelf and break some of the Good China. When a mill involves pulling punches as often as possible, then practising in the wagon is good. But the last hook hits off a panel, putting a big oval dent right in the middle of the brown slab of wood.

Nanty fuckin palari!

Mam will see that.

So she will!

My fingers suss out the dip. This piece of wood is polished almost every day. Mam will clip my ear right off. Dad, Joe and then Me, we all fought over many mills to pay and to keep Mammie's wee world of wood, her kingdom of order, thrift and cleanliness, for this to be a wee scratch. My fingers tell me I have committed a big sin. I actually smile to myself. I don't sin nearly as often as I'd like.

I need to go outside and draw some paani. As the Shows are open, there are a lot of men around and I'm near naked. So I put on Dad's coat, his fusty leather thing, and my custom made, short and thin petticoat, as sewn by Auntie Amy. It's a cool day outside, but dry, and the wagons don't seem to have many folk around them, as most of the shows are doing their afternoon pitches and all the punters are there to watch. Our Joe will be boxing some local flattie lad, I can just see our tent, the tip showing over the Hall of Mirrors. My cousin's wagon is a few feet away, and by its shoogling and shaking I can suss Ellen is changing, probably having a wee barney with her corset. She'll probably call me in to help her in a bit. I hear muffled swearing, and curses against the Almighty. There's no one around, but I make it quick. Toes grip the narrow steps that Dad *still* hasn't widened after three years of being ordered to by Mam. But I'm good at going down now. The water can is farther from the steps than it should be, so I have to lean a fair bit. The wrapped hands are mighty weapons but hold buckets awkwardly, and the water can lurches a bit as I timm the paani out. I don't want to tip it too far in case the whole can goes over and we lose some, so I just do it in wee spits, just tipping the can enough. In about three or four of these my bucket's full. I leave the bucket by the bottom step. I'm glad to get back inside, as the wood is freezing my bare feet.

The wagon walls hum along to the sound of the Shows, as

organs started to strike up with the coming of the afternoon. I could hear Big Uncle Sammy's organ playing 'Auld Lang Syne' far too early, that being saved for closing time usually. Wooden walls pick up the sound of the music, but our wagon, at least, never got the tune right.

Ellen said she's going with her purple dress, so I'm going with my yellow, so as to stick out better. I hate the yellow one, the skirt is too long, and flaps against my legs when I'm dancing about between punches. I like my green one, but Mam and Dad won't let me wear that. Mam says green is bad luck, which is true I suppose, and Dad hates it for the reason I like it, in that it's short in the shirt, which makes me faster, but he says its too short in the leg, and as it's men who watch the show mostly, he doesn't want them ogling his daughter. Dad can be a right divvi.

I can tell it is Ellen coming up the steps, as one step is louder than the other, Ellen steps harder on her left than on the right. She opens the door. My back is to her, laces trailing down to my backside.

'Tie up the back, will ye?'

Her fingers are bound too, so she's fairly clumsy, but she gets it done tight enough.

'Where's Auntie Moira?'

'Mindin the joint. Our Janey's not home yet.'

'You're fallin today.'

'What? It's your turn to fall this first show.'

'You're fallin on all of them.'

'How is that then? It's you, your turn and why all the Shows?'

'Aye but, I bruised my side last gaff. It's mortal sore, Cathy.'

I am not happy at this. But I bite the tongue. Dad and Uncle David don't take kindly to real barneys on gaff day. I think Ellen can sense this gets to me, she knows how seriously I can take it – I don't like losing, even when it's arranged.

'Here, we'll have a bevvy the night in ma wagon. Mam'll be out and Dad and Jimmy don't care. Dad'll be at the pub till it shuts. Come over, it's ages since we've had a good drink.'

Ellen is talking sense. I think of the whisky Dad bought a few weeks ago. He won't be taking it out for a good while yet, I can brik enough to replace it. I beckon.

'Deek.'

She follows me to the drawer below the bunk, two of us pressed close, the wagon becoming very narrow with the two of us. The wagon groans with the weight of two of us on nearly the same spot. I dig through a couple of tin boxes, where my grannie's, great grannie's, and my great great grannie's, and my great great great grannie's jewelry is stored, their wealth, now ours, stored in wee cases, never worn. Just behind them is something better, a paper-wrapped bottle.

'Here, see this.'

'Oh AYE! Oh yes!'

'Take it over now and stash it, Dad doesn't know it's being borrowed.'

'Ye chawrin this?'

'I'm buyin him another one.'

'Yer terrible.'

She takes the whisky, goes out and across to her wagon.

There is a gauntlet of mud between the wagons and the Showground, whipped up by our horses, engines and the feet of many punters. With water buckets in one hand and gloves and cloths in the other we walk carefully.

Before Uncle David came in with us I never fought for the flatties. Dad fought barefist for most of his time, but my brother Joe had sense: he only ever boxed Queensberry way, and with gloves on him. I sparred with Joe when I was a wee girl. That was the last time I ever boxed and hit someone in the mush. When Ellen and me started up as an intervening act between Joe's bouts, Dad and Uncle David made sure we never hit on the face. Being men, they thought they were helpful, but all that means is that we hit each other on the boobs more, which can be much sorer than a bleeding nose. My right breast still hurts from a jab Ellen never pulled properly. It's aching a bit now, but I'm more concerned with getting over the sucking muck, which pulls at my lace-up boots and is turning the hem of my dress brown, I'm trying, like a divvi, to hitch it up with my elbows, and am probably going to lose balance and fall over. Ellen is swearing behind me.

We make it, and we go in by the back flap of the tent. Dad has only just started to look for us, which means we've got here in time to avoid him chuvvyin us too much. As soon as he sees us he goes into the patter about the fight to the men and boys who are watching. He's already drawn a crowd inside the tent from the first mill. Joe is wiping himself down, and Mam is in, tending a fresh cut. Her cousin must be minding the joint. Mam leaves Joe to hold the cloth to his cut and comes to my corner. She's to act as 'second'. I climb into the ring and look about. There is the familiar sight of row upon row of bunnets. Big crowd, a lot of punters. We've had a good pitch this afternoon. Mam might actually let Dad have some money tonight for the pub.

Dad describes us as 'Devilish Dames' and 'Fighting Fillies'. Ellen and myself stare at each other, as if we hate the sight of each other, which some days is true. I am rankled at being the one to fall down. I don't know why, it's all money in the end. But I don't like losing, especially when I know I can put more wallops together than Ellen can, and get hit less. I'm keen to start, I realise, and I've started dancing from foot to foot, a bull about to put its head down and tilt at something. The bunnets in the crowd like that, a couple cheer, a man shouts 'Let's see mair o yer dancin legs, hen! Hitch em up.' Dad is throwing him a look of death. I'm still sore in the breasts, I should have mentioned to Ellen to go for the belly, not the bosom today. Not that the cow would pay that any heed, of course.

Dad has finished talking rubbish, so we go to our corners for the fight to start. Usually Ellen and me are attended to by our wee sisters, but as Janey is away at the school down the road for her lessons, her being a clever girl, Mam does me tonight. Ellen's wee sister, Josie, is tying up her gloves, and Mam is tying mine. We have the buckets by the side, to wipe us down, to make it resemble a real fight. The bunnets' faces are slearer to me. There are very few toffs in tonight. We've got ourselves a right rabble in, mainly farm hands, shop-keepers, howf-loiterers and a bunch of Irish navvies from the canal works. My mam, as usual, picks now to ask me stupid questions.

'Tatties?'

'Eh?'

'Did ye peel them?'

'Aw nanty. Forgot.'

'Yer always forgettin. What a gerl ye are. Just when am I supposed to do them, eh?'

'I'll do them after this show. I'll nip in.'

'Ye can mind the joint. I'll do them.'

'I'll do it, a says!'

'I'll do them.'

Duveleste!

Dad rings the bell.

I move to the centre slow and easy, my guard lazy, stepping two marks forward, then half a one back each time. Ellen is doing much the same. My back pleat whips around at the back of my neck, lashing at the bare skin on my collarbone. I'm starting to dance, trick is to keep on the hop. Once three paces separate us, matters are more serious, and we both tighten up, my fists come up in front of my face, I can just peer over them.

I bounce from side to side. I don't want to take a fall tonight.

We have eye contact, her peepers are really all that I can see. She sticks a fist out, to see what happens. It taps on to my gloves. I tighten up at that, then lash out smartly, nearly clipping her in the corsets. She's moving around to her left, and I go to mine. We describe the slow spin of a wheel on the canvas. She punches at my chest and I soak her effort with my gloves. The Irish navvies are shouting in their thick Ulster tones. The Scottish watchers give a few murmurs, and the lad who shouted earlier yells, 'C' moan, hen, gie her a skelp!'

Anything you say, pal.

I stop bouncing for just a wee bit and stand still and steady and reach out for her corsets and get her, but I don't pull the punch quite right, and I see her eyes widen and her chin set itself. I feel glad I didn't pull it properly and it was a real punch. Ellen will get me for it, and she looks straight at me as she puts a bruise on my right shoulder. I grind my teeth. It's painful, but inside I'm whooping. I give Ellen a good tap on the collar and I can see it gets to her, revenge is drawn on her face.

Dad steps between us a moment, his big shoulders blocking our sight of each other, the deformed brow scowling.

'Hi! Calm it, for fuck's sake. Stop actin it. Tap each other, that's all. I've warned ye about it before, both o' yiz.'

Happily, Ellen has not taken a blind bit of notice. Not only does she not pull the next punch, but she goes right for my boobs, knowing how sore that can be. The pain is shouted down by my excitement, and I wink at her. I'm grateful she is on my side. I go for her breasts, but catch her shoulder instead.

The round wears on and the bunnets get louder and louder. There's whistles, applause and cheers. But Dad's face gets darker and redder. He looks at the crowd with disgust and surprise. Angry with the bunnets he is, but he's mental at me. It's lucky I'm a grown girl or I swear he'd have me over his knee and be beltin me right now. But I just concentrate on my guard and work away at hers for the rest of the round. We've both scored a few skelps on each other.

The bell goes just as I take her in the side belly. Her eyes goggle. I got her a good one and she feels her side as she goes to her corner. We'll really need to be wiped down. There is blue murder on Dad's face, but it's Ellen he goes to give hell to. I get to be told off by Mam.

'What are yez DOIN? Yer out there brawlin like a pair o' bloody Glasga tarts on the street!'

'We're boxin, Mammy.'

'Yer goin bloody radgie! It's pretend!'

'Flatties like it.'

Mam looks at the clapping, approving crowd, waiting for the next round with complete contempt.

'That lot of toerags and nyucks would! Bloody men don't know any better, they've got no breedin or upbringin any of them! Don't you be thinkin ye'll lower yerself to that level, my dear, of pleasin the likes of that or I'll kick yer arse for ye, and ye'll be in no way to do any more of yer boxin. Now stop actin it, the pair o' yez. Never, ever have I seen the like . . .'

Bell.

Dad glares at each of us, a warning clear in his eyes. Ellen winks at me, and I get her scheme. Save it for the third and last. So in the second, we jump about a fair bit, and pull every punch. This subdues the bunnets. A few boo. They are clearly disappointed.

Bell.

Dad's scowl is now his customary frown. Mam is satisfied.

'I'll make up stovies with the tatties, eh?'

'Aye, sounds fine, Mam.'

'See love, it's not nice barneyin like that. 'Specially with all those men watchin.'

I say nothing. I am working out how much whisky money I can brik from the takings this week without Mam catching me.

Bell. Last time.

The bunnets are made much happier almost straight away. We both lash at each other, on the collarbones, fairly hard, and both are tipped back, no hint of a pulled punch in sight. But I'm mindful that Dad will not let a full round of real boxing go on for the full time. He'll stop it, so I'm going to go and floor this mozzy.

The last person I boxed on the face was Joe, who's been at the side of the ring laughing into his hand at all this. I was a wee girl then and I feel young again now, as Ellen's left cheek puffs and flattens on either side of my leather fist. She reels back, the left cheek already scarlet. A sneaky tap from my boot, on her right foot, and it goes out from under her; she's falling.

I can hear the navvies cheer loudly, one shouting, 'Fair play to ye, darlin!'

Mostly I can hear my own panting, each breath sucked deep into my bruised chest, my feet hopping here and there, fists by my thighs, dancing over my victim like a mighty Sioux. I have never felt so fine. Ellen has just crumbled. She falls right on her arse, arms snapping out behind her to stop her brains hitting the floor as well. She grits her teeth and both eyes water as her thigh settles down.

The bunnets are cheering and whooping. I can feel Dad take my arm and raise it. There. That's the fight over.

I don't know what kind of face he's wearing. I don't look at him.

Tears streaming, Ellen looks straight up at me.

I look right back at her.

Her face cracks. Her red cheek and the paler one curve outward, lips curl upwards. Her teeth are bared, the shoulders are shaking with her chuckles. 'I'm knockin yer bloody teeth out next time.'

I let the laugh out too. Later on the pair of us will drain the whisky bottle until we taste the glass.

Unfortunate Shortbread

Eric White

Among the tiny office clutter of books, cabinets, reams of paper and towers of vending-machine cups lurked two figures seated by a desk, attempting a conversation. Although the topics ranged from wives to Godzilla films, one of the participants was trying to sell to the other. Unfortunately the topic of monster films had driven the conversation down a blind alley, especially as the potential buyer had progressed to acting out Godzilla scenes and laughing uncontrollably.

Directing conversations was not Dougie Wilson's strong point, a major factor in his recent sales record of two crates of haggis in the last three weeks. Businessmen enjoyed talking with him, but they rarely bought what he offered, partly because Dougie himself wasn't terribly impressed by the goods – Scottish cuisine, supposedly tailored towards the oriental market. Today, however, he had come prepared with a novelty item, an invention that Mr Kawasaki wouldn't find anywhere else. Happy to let his customer indulge in some Godzilla mother-in-law impersonations, he allowed his mind to drift back to the previous week and the happy accident that had led to his discovery.

Having promised his despairing supervisors that he had a revolutionary idea up his sleeve (one of them had pointed out he was wearing a tank top), Dougie had returned home in a panic. His understanding wife, Daisy, her empathy deriving from being constantly misunderstood herself, had sat him down in the living room and gently, but firmly, ensured he discussed the problem rationally with the aid of a cup of brandy with a nip of herbal tea in it. By the time he'd finished speaking, he noticed a sly smile creeping over her face and realised how she intended to address the problem.

'I still don't understand the Japanese being suddenly obsessed by our cuisine. They've always found it pretty revolting in the past.'

Dougie nodded, the alcohol seeming to have made his body heavier as he sank into the armchair. 'Independence, Daisy. It's given Scotland a different lease of life and a brand new profile around the globe. Mr Kawasaki even told me they like Fran and Anna.'

'. . . ?'

'Yes, apparently they feature quite heavily in their cinema. It all started with the Godzilla versus Fran and Anna blockbuster at the end of the decade. Quite frightening really.' His mind conjured up a picture that made him sniff the dregs of his mug suspiciously. 'That tea was helluva good. Any more?'

She smirked at his eager expression. 'Maybe later.' She wandered off slowly, her pace increasing as she reached the door. She was back within seconds, a cardboard box in her hands.

'I see,' he said, hiding the sense of dread that the sight of the box had induced, 'we consult the fortune cards.'

Her smile widened as she scurried over and placed the opened box on the arm of his chair.

'They've never failed me yet. By following their advice I've gained a degree in Occult Sciences, met and married you, had a son and helped you with your career.'

Dougie had less faith in the cards, especially as his wife kept them locked in a secret hideaway to ensure the magic remained uncorrupted. She'd created the cards following her discovery that the keyboard player of her teenage idols revealed in an interview that he used random 'strategy' cards to direct his decisions. Upon each card, supposedly cut from a special papyrus that Dougie preferred not to ask about, was a message or instruction similar to the directives used by the musician. Although Daisy consulted them regularly, Dougie had only used them twice and he couldn't see how either message had benefited him. Daisy had seen events differently however, explaining how the advice had brought him a job and a better hairstyle. It was this lengthy explanation that had put him off using the cards again but now, sedated with alcohol, he decided he had nothing to lose and picked a card from the middle of the pile.

'*The solution is closer than you think,*' he read.

'Now that could be interpreted in a number of ways if we put our minds to it,' said Daisy, her tone that of a schoolmistress. Dougie was saved from the rigours of interpreting by the intrusion of his son, Marvin, and some truncheon-shaped piece of dough he carried on a tray.

'Marvin is the solution!' whooped Daisy. 'The fruit of your loins will point you in the right direction.'

The podgy figure ignored this outburst and waddled soggy underpants fashion towards his father, trapping him against the armchair and shoving the tray forward into Dougie's face.

'I made these for you and Mummy,' yapped Marvin, his mouth stretching wide open with each syllable. Dougie observed his son had recently partaken one of the truncheons himself.

'There's your answer!' screeched Daisy.

'Eat one now!'

Dougie noted the boy's determined expression and picked one of the truncheons up, marvelling at the oversized holes (gouged out by a pencil rather than a fork) and feeling relieved that they didn't smell of plasticine or play dough. He risked a bite and swallowed quickly before his taste buds got to work.

'. . . eeliciouss,' he spluttered, his throat protesting as the dry crumbs poured down.

'Beautiful, Marvin.' He turned to Daisy, his face red, eyes watering. 'Tea!' he coughed.

It was whilst Daisy was away attending to his beverage that he realised just how close the solution was. As he recovered from his coughing fit, he saw that the fortune card had fallen on to a truncheon of shortbread and cut it open, embedding itself within the slit. Half of the message now protruded from the biscuit, reminding Dougie of a fortune cookie.

'Fortune shortbread,' he muttered, 'could that be the solution?'

With Marvin engrossed by the six o'clock cartoons there was no one to answer his question. Consequently Dougie selected another card, forgetting Daisy's golden rule about one card per consultation. The card told him to '*Have faith in your judgement*', causing him to spring from the chair and send Marvin into tears as his work flew into the air and on to the carpet, where it was trampled upon.

'I've done it!' he shrieked. 'Eureka!'

Daisy arrived in time to see him ruffling the sobbing child's mop of hair whilst punching the air in delight, a stick of shortbread protruding from his mouth like a cigar.

'Very good, dear. And perhaps for your next trick you can find out what's the matter with Marvin.'

'What? Oh . . . er, yes.' He hauled the infant towards him and gave him a bear hug, earning instant forgiveness. His actions over the next few days weren't to be forgiven quite so easily however . . .

The dishonesty of what followed made him squirm quite visibly, enough to distract Mr Kawasaki from his one-sided discussion and bring him, rather ashamedly, back to reality. 'I apologise, Mr Wilson, I did not mean to disturb you.'

'That's alright,' Dougie heard himself say. 'Perhaps I should show you the novelty product I mentioned over the phone. I've got samples stored in the microwave behind these cups.'

He rose, carefully negotiated the room's obstacles to the towers of cups, which he promptly binned, and clicked open the door of the uncovered oven, brushing away a cobweb in the same movement. He then removed a silver tray of freshly baked shortbread, a fortune protruding from each biscuit.

'Fortune shortie!' exclaimed Mr Kawasaki. 'How very novel. May I sample this speciality?'

Dougie was happy to oblige him, his hopes rising as the taste of his great grandmother's secret recipe provoked a reaction that reminded him of the businessman's monster impressions.

'To your liking?'

Mr Kawasaki was already reaching for a second when Dougie pointed out the paper fortune on the tray. Smiling apologetically, he snatched up the card and read its message. '*You will become that which you most admire*,' he chuckled. 'A nice idea.'

The second biscuit was in his mouth before Dougie could comment. He was about to congratulate himself when he caught a glimpse of the fortune, large wobbly letters in red crayon. He felt ice cubes of disbelief crystallise in his chest and the image of the businessman began to blur as he remembered the owner of the red crayon. In a panic he snatched a biscuit for himself and pulled the fortune out with his teeth. An infantile drawing of a man with a very runny nose (one that had taken the best part of Marvin's green crayon) looked back at him.

Four days earlier, but two days after his discovery, Dougie had stolen for the first time in his life. With Daisy spending the weekend at her mother's cottage on Arran, Dougie had been able to take her not-so-secretly hidden fortune-card paper, substituting it with varnished sandpaper. Then, working long into the night, he'd carefully furnished the cards with cryptic but beautifully written fortunes. He'd got quite good at some of the descriptions and was still writing when Marvin, having bounced out of bed to watch his dawn cartoons, decided to investigate.

'That's Mummy's paper,' he said accusingly. 'Her extra special paper.'

At this moment he looked uncannily like Daisy and Dougie suffered an unpleasant few moments as the idea that she was watching his betrayal through her son emerged. Rationality cleared his panic, allowing him to store his guilt to the back of his mind as he explained the situation.

'We'll be rich, son,' he insisted, wincing as Marvin, toying with the anglepoise lamp, turned interrogator and shone the light into his eyes. Marvin's expression demanded a better answer and this was where Dougie had the idea of letting Marvin join in, allowing him to copy the adult as he wrote out ideas of his own. When the infant became bored with writing, he began drawing the fortunes. Dougie only really turned his attention to him about a quarter of an hour after drawing had lost its appeal and given way to infant lavatorial-style sketches. He sniggered at the first two and frowned at the next, shaking his head. It wasn't until he noticed how little of the brown crayon remained that the first worries surfaced in his mind.

'I mixed the papers up,' he winced, remembering how tiredness had affected him afterwards, as he'd filled the first batch of shortbread.

'I'm sorry?' Mr Kawasaki was discarding his second fortune, '*Yoo will ete lots of biskitts*' and reaching for a third piece. The fact that the message was in red crayon didn't concern him.

'Oh nothing,' lied Dougie, hurriedly switching his gaze to the writing protruding from Mr Kawasaki's latest victim before flashing a temporary smile. As the businessman continued to look puzzled he decided to risk a little truth. 'It appears my six-year-old son has added a few messages of his own,' he chortled, forcing laughter that hurt him. 'There's one of his on the table.'

'Indeed,' was the reply Dougie should have heard, but it was lost in an avalanche of crumbs as Mr Kawasaki demolished the biscuit and its fortune before snatching two more pieces of shortbread. With a blissful expression on his face he reached into his inside pocket producing his cheque book.

'My company will buy as much as you can produce, Mr Wilson,' he spluttered, 'and if you'd care to name your price I'd like to purchase some for myself.'

Dougie did hear the words but they didn't provoke nearly as much reaction as the brown crayon drawing that dangled from Mr Kawasaki's mouth. He appeared to develop zoom-lens vision, his view consuming every detail of the incontinent figure in the drawing.

'This shortbread is addictive,' gasped the businessman, patting his already ample belly, before throwing the opened cheque book on to the desk. Several more biscuits were consumed before he stood up suddenly, his forehead beaded with sweat as his body shuddered. 'Perhaps I should visit the men's room whilst I consider our deal.' He closed his eyes and eased his body upwards and forwards without his feet having to shift position. In a higher pitched voice he said, 'Complete the cheque as you feel appropriate. I shall be back to sign it in a minute.'

With his body maintaining its strange position he waddled out of the room. Dougie watched him go before digging out a handkerchief from one of the desk drawers and attending to his suddenly runny nose. He found himself wondering what lurked in the remaining biscuits and promptly removed two more fortune cards. '*For now the hermit's way is best*,' he read on the first card. On the other was a Marvin interpretation of a phone with a few wavy lines to indicate it was ringing. 'Well, that seems harmless enough.'

An office phone screech muffled by reams of statistical printouts decided otherwise.

'Go away,' he muttered, the hermit advice suddenly quite appealing. The caller seemed anxious to speak to him, however, and he decided to answer it before someone else did.

'Please be a wrong number,' he groaned as he turfed the ancient statistics away and picked up the receiver.

'You've abused the cards!' shrieked Daisy. 'Marvin's told me everything and I'm absolutely horrified. How could you be so stupid?'

'Hello, dear,' mumbled Dougie. 'I thought I'd do what the cards suggested.'

'You've opened the magic up to corruptive influences. You must return the fortune cards to a safe place before they can do any more harm.'

'Harm?' gulped Dougie, the ice cubes now trickling into the pit of his stomach. 'How did you know about that?'

There was an electronic shriek that might've been Marvin, followed by the sound of Daisy roaring at him.

'Thanks to your bright idea, Marvin has used the cards to insert himself into the television. I searched the house high and low for him before I noticed him on the screen helping Jerry beat up Tom. I've already had several angry phone calls from the BBC.'

'Can't you get him out?'

'Your son now exists as a series of television-screen pixels. How the hell am I supposed to get him out?' She paused as an electronic burbling distracted her. 'Yes, I know it's a glove puppet. Marvin, put it back.'

A rather hideous screeching suggested that Marvin had just been disillusioned in a big way.

'I'm not surprised Geoffrey's angry. Now put it back!'

Dougie heard her launch into a scathing attack and switched his ears off for the five minutes it would take up. In that time he tried desperately to think of a solution. In doing so he remembered the original suggestion the cards had presented to him and waited for the attack to die down so that he could offer that.

'Perhaps if you make a card that says *"Everything will be as it was before"*, then Marvin will get out.'

The stunned silence that followed told him that he was either a genius or had just said the worst thing imaginable. It turned out to be the latter and furious speeches about corruption and abuse of magic burnt a hole in his left ear for the next five minutes. Such was the intensity of her anger that he didn't notice the wailing stampede going on outside his office as twenty-nine typists decided to leave early. Nor did he turn around as the reason for their departure entered his office. It was only when Mr Kawasaki spoke in a much deeper voice than usual that he realised where his problems really lay.

'You haven't filled in the cheque, I see,' growled a voice like gravel. 'Why is that?'

The angry buzz from the telephone receiver faded to a hiss as the large shadow passed over him.

'Mr Kawasaki?'

There was a pause as the shadow-caster considered this. 'Once upon a time the answer to your question would have been yes. However, I now appear to have become that which I most admire . . . in the words of your fortune ticket. Therefore I am no longer Mr Kawasaki.'

'Ah,' Dougie replaced the receiver and clasped his hands in prayer.

'Indeed,' rasped the entity formerly known as Mr Kawasaki. 'I'm afraid I shall have to renege on our business agreement.'

'I understand.'

'Your biscuits no longer appeal. The crumbs irritate my fins.'

Dougie began the first gradual movements of the action that would, if unhindered, allow him to curl up into a very tight ball.

'There is one thing you have that stimulates my appetite however.'

The movement stopped and Dougie, in an action that defied logic, sneaked a look at the creature. Something resembling a man dressed in very bad monster costume smiled back.

'Believe it or not, that which I most admired was a man dressed up as Godzilla. As a child however, I did not think it was a costume.'

'Oh.'

'There is no man inside. The body is me.'

Dougie tried desperately to curl up into a ball again, but a claw tapped him on the shoulder and hot breath prickled the back of his neck.

'I did say there was something you have that will satisfy my hunger?' said 'Godzilla'. 'In my new form I appear to have developed an irresistible craving for those haggises in orange sauce you tried to sell me two weeks ago. I would be very happy if you . . .'

Dougie didn't hear any more. In his head he was drawing up plans of living the hermit's life down a twenty-foot hole in Cramond Island. There he would be free of Godzillas, sons in television sets and wretched fortune cards. And perhaps there he could hide from the horrible suspicion that he had just gone mad.

Yellow Man Walking

David Kilby

I am where I should not be: at a time when I should be pursuing another activity. I am in the midst of a fraud and the soul-searching is painful.

An old boss once told me that skiving was harder work than working. He was right. He delivered this small parcel of truth when my car was in my driveway and I was at the kitchen table drinking coffee and failing to complete the quick crossword in *The Guardian*. He pressed my doorbell and I shat myself when I saw his deformed shape through the frosted glass of my parents' front door. I should have been in Paisley selling typewriters.

He gave me a lecture on skiving.

'These are the golden rules,' he said seated at my parents' kitchen table. He mentally completed my crossword. 'The first is don't get caught. The second is never involve anyone else from the same company. If they get caught, they'll take you down with them. Thirdly, only do it when you're on target. Then all you'll get from your boss is a wry smile, not a final warning. You've only broken two out of three. Next time you're out.'

I followed him out, pulling on my jacket, and headed off to try and sell calculators that cost £250 and weighed almost a hundredweight to Paisley scrap merchants. Later that month I did what was to become my usual and resigned before they sacked me.

I've never been on target in my life – only in jobs where luck has come my way, usually when I start a job. People say that you make your own luck, but I used to steal other people's. I would often scoop up the droppings of the previous incumbent.

I would most likely last about eighteen months or two years. Then I would move on, explaining to all and sundry that that was what happened to salesmen. Jobs were easier to come by when I was younger, because jobs were easier to come by and I was younger. Now it is different. I have grown chubbier and greyer and I am not so attractive at the interview. I can say the right things: like working harder not smarter and adopting a vertical approach to markets having a structured sales situation. But it is hard to be enigmatic and chubby. It is hard when your stomach hangs over your belt, and you can't get a proper parting in your grey hair; and your suit shines and the crotch of your trousers reaches between your knees; and the twenty-six-year-old recruitment consultant with the neatly coiffed hair and the suit that cost more than your car is listening to your well-known phrases or sayings and thinking, 'Thank god my dad made it while he was young,' and 'Where am I going out to tonight?'

So it's all about forcing myself. Each day there is a regular journey through a mangle, knowing that the only relief will come when I slap on to the washroom floor at the end of the day. I can now keep a job for four years. I've been selling cable for four years and two months. I am plagued by recidivism.

My name is Dave and I am a skiver. Despite all the pain that is going to come my way, and I am not as adept as I used to be at avoiding the bullets of dismissal, I cannot tell you how much I am enjoying this moment. I am in my home, illegally drinking coffee and a company with five thousand employees which is quoted on the New York stock exchange is paying me wages. It is better than being on drugs. Think of your best time on heroin and then multiply it by a thousand. My wife is at her office answering her telephone. My son is attending his lectures at the university and then he will go to the library where he will study. And I am drinking my fourth cup of coffee and I have just completed the large *Guardian* crossword. My car is hidden in my garage, which I had built many years ago. My garage has no windows.

I can't keep this up forever. It will soon become obvious in my sales figures that I am not selling. But for the moment, for this small instant, before the caffeine kicks in and I start to worry, I am in heaven.

Yesterday I told my manager forty-three lies. He was querying the slump in sales and I told him about the forty-three doors I had knocked. I told him about the rejection, the pensioners who would not let me across the doorstep because they had their life savings in jars, about the minister who didn't watch television and he only had four sets in the house, about the young woman who came to the door in her dressing-gown and allowed her left breast to fall out, about the number of people who were just not interested, and so on. Anyway, it was all lies. Forty-three of them. If he phones up anyone of them, he'll find out. He could be phoning right now. But I'll not worry about that.

'It's not that I'm not working,' I said.

I could have won the Oscar for best supporting liar.

I'm into day five of the skive. I get the feeling it is going to be terminal. I've decided to start planting job-changing seeds in Frances' fertile brain. She's heard the bit about the company not doing so well and folk down south getting the bullet. In a few days, I'll tell her it's worse than we thought.

In a few days, it'll get harder to lie when I meet my manager in the evening and I have to tell him why I am not selling.

He'll have guessed I'm not working. It'll be the story about how I am going through a bad time and it's not a good patch and I'm finding it difficult to motivate myself. He'll tell me to push myself on but he'll appreciate my honesty. That'll last for a few days more, then he'll get me in to have a hard look at my figures. Then he'll start laying down a target that I'll have to meet and if I don't I'll be on a warning. So he'll set another and if I don't meet that I'll be on a bigger warning. Then he'll set a final target and I'll be out. The choreography of failure. I've got about six weeks to get another job. And I'll only be forty-eight.

It must happen because my skiving habits have set in. I can't do without three cups of coffee in the morning. The *Guardian* crossword is now one of life's necessities. I would rather finish it than get a sale. The radio's always turned up loud so that I can hear it from most rooms in the house. I'm a words man. Gave up music in my early twenties. Interviews, discussions, *Woman's Hour*, all that. I've taken to looking out the bedroom window. Seeing what is going on outside and listening to the radio. It is warmer than work. I stand back so no one can see me. About ten o'clock each morning, just after *Woman's Hour* starts, during the interview of the famous woman, my Yellow Man walks out.

The front door of his house is opened by his wife who manages to remain hidden. Like me, she stands back from her window. Like me, she seems ashamed. He falters down eight steps to the red chips which I watched him lay some months ago. I have counted the steps, so he must have.

Slow piddling steps and he doesn't even crunch the red chips. His stick almost falls from his hand. He used to carry his stick to ward off ruffians, he once told me. But there were never any ruffians on the stairs to his front door. He had paid too much for his house. As he reached the end of his drive, the twitching curtains failed to conceal the pained look of his wife.

She did not like his neighbours to see him so close to his death. She did not wish his yellow to upset them.

The Yellow Man adjusted his footing to cope with the firmer ground of the pavement. He set himself against the slight incline of the small hill. I wondered where the hell he thought he was going, but he had some goal in mind. He wore about three sweaters, a coat such as we used to throw on our childhood beds before the duvet revolution, a wide-brimmed hat and a scarf. Was there still money in millinery? He wore all this in the warmest August since records began. One man's summer is another man's winter. He trod this street in slippers with zips.

I watched as one foot moved and then the other. The stick was used as Ian Carmichael would punt a boat on the Cam. The curtains radiated concern as a new neighbour passed by the cancer stick. Like a clockwork doll, finally winding down, he raised a smile and doffed his hat at the young lady. The small daughter stared silently. He returned his hat and started his journey again. He did not see the little girl being scolded for turning her head and glaring at him. His steps and movements were slower and even I could see they were painful. His grimaces were almost invisible.

On previous days he had reached his small summit and disappeared over the other side. Many minutes of panic were caused on both sides of the road until his safety was signalled by the jarring movements of the brim of his hat. But today he only achieved the top of his hill. He stood for a moment and looked over the other side. We both watched his looking. The red sandstone bungalows and the tarmacadam roads were his masterpieces. He looked for the longest few seconds of his life and mine. His yellow lined face gazed sadly over what was left of his British Empire. I could see him trying to breathe in some fresh air. He moved forward and leant on his stick and his head swivelled like some old-fashioned camera. Then he executed the slowest pirouette in the world and started the descent.

As he faltered down the hill, he looked at every flower, every blade of grass, every brick in every wall as his eyes inhaled every colour, every form and shape. He reached the driveway and slowly floated over those red chips.

He stood at the bottom of his eight stairs. He looked at the bottom step and scanned his eyes to the top. His hat made his head look pivoted. He gazed at the steps silently. His yellow creased face looked sadly upon the steps. His left arm started flapping. His wife put her hand to her mouth. He shook as if his puppet strings were beginning to loosen. He looked to his right and his left.

I did not really know the Yellow Man. We had not lived there long, we moved down from a better house. Our fights prevented us from smiling at the neighbours. Our shouting and not knowing if we had been heard constructed an embarrassing barrier. We could not pretend to be nice to each other, why bother with them? Other people were foreign to us. There was no vitriol in their language. Their sentences were not constructed with the barbed wire that no one would cross to discover their true meaning. Bloody words.

I looked to the top of the hill, to the end of the Yellow Man's last walk and saw a red saloon of the variety favoured by many companies for their middle management. The sort favoured by my company. There was a registration number that I recognised, and a baldy head. The bastard was spying on me. My manager sat in his car staring down at my house.

The Yellow Man's movements caught my eye. His arms were trying to fly and his stick fell across the bottom three stairs. He swayed from left to right and then forward. He sprawled across the bottom three steps beside his cane. His hat fell on to the red chips and his yellow face pressed into the grey stone of the step. He tried to mouth some stupid yell. His wife stepped back from the curtain her mouth opened and her eyes widened. Aside from that she made no movement. She watched as his arms made scrambling motions underneath his body. He could not push himself up. I stared at her and nodded my head as if that gesture would start her on his rescue. But she did not waver, except to wipe a tear from her eye. I heard the Yellow Man cry. It was a silly weak noise that had dying all the way through it.

The baldy head in the red Mondeo sat on the hill waiting to catch me. It would be the bullet. They were trying to lose people. His eyes were on my house, trying to see through my curtains. It was too late to phone in sick.

The old woman was still playing statues. The Yellow Man waved his arms more slowly now, beached on the steps.

There was nothing to him except the smell of decay. I stood him up and he squeaked his thanks. I put my hands under his elbows and helped him up the stairs. His face was the colour of pus and what had once been a good head of hair was now a skullcap of grey. He teeth smiled when he wasn't smiling. His arms were skinny and plagued with brown spots. They moved like a skeleton draped in snakeskin.

His eyes were yellow and they stared at me. His words came slowly and quietly as if they were the last guests to leave a funeral. Small sounding words of thanks floated from his brown lips. He could count his final steps. He would never walk to the top of the hill again.

She was at the door to greet him and pull him into his hallway. She mouthed the word 'cancer' at me and closed the door.

As I walked across the street I gave baldy the fingers.

I got fixed up not long after the funeral.

Selling insurance.

Body, remember . . .

Morgan Downie

As he sleeps I watch over him, the pale shape of his facial bones against the pillow, the dark sucking of his mouth. He is retreating from life while above him the dust performs faint arabesques in the fading sunlight. I try to still the unconscious tremor in my fingers, shivering, cold sweat, the early morning memory of blood, dark clots against the harsh porcelain white. I sip some more Maalox, wince at the anticipated pain. I am hiding, here among the dying.

Shift's start. I am sparkling, chilled champagne in the park, summer sun on the hot touch of grass. Today nothing can touch me, I am immune. Tony is waiting at the station. He jerks a thumb over his shoulder towards the nearest isolation room.

'Hey, Scottish, new blood in departure.'

I roll my eyes. 'Let me guess, today's special, just for a change because we both know it's a personal favourite of yours and mine, we have ruled out PCP? TB?'

'Too easy.' He taps a set of medical notes. 'No, something just a little bit different. A boy-girl, a transsexual.'

'Really?' I am curious.

He grabs his crotch. 'Think he's got a dick?'

'What age?'

'Twenty-four.'

I shake my head. 'Too young.'

Tony reaches for his wallet. 'I have ten says he doesn't.'

He comes to us septic, infected left breast prosthesis, subsequently removed. In addition he has all the usual suspects, the tuberculosis, the PCP, the tell-tale scabbing on his legs, which, if he lives long enough, may even turn out to be KS. Some may bet on horses, others on cards, here we bet on acronyms, putting our money down with a fatal certainty. If he has a white-cell count we neither know nor care. HIV, the virus, is rarely if ever mentioned, too commonplace. Here everyone is infected. His name is Antonio Maldonado, he likes to be called Juanita, but to us he is the infected site, the pretty boy and he is worth ten dollars.

I dress his wound, angry, red, the flesh dying. We are pouring antibiotics into him like a leaking bucket. He turns his head away.

'Am I hurting you?'

'No,' he says, his voice cracked with pain. 'You're very gentle.'

And then, as I finish. 'Thank you.'

I wash his hair. I buy shampoo and conditioner, the hospital-issue glop resembling nothing so much as viscous toilet bleach. These small gestures allow me to believe I am still capable of caring. I let him smell the bottle before I start. Jamaican blend, coconut and mango.

'Have you ever been?' he asks.

'Oh sure,' I say. 'They love white boys down there.'

This is how I met Antonio called Juanita. We smile when we remember him. What he looked like before, we could not know. He had no photographs of himself, nothing to indicate a past existence. In this place the only history that counts is of disease. By the time he reached us there was only the faintest trace of a former litheness in his wasted limbs, his hair a matted, dyed thatch, his nail varnish chipped and broken. I could only imagine him in the photographs of his magazines as he held them up to me.

'Don't you think she's beautiful?'

And I would cut the pictures out for him so that he could decorate his room with images of impossible white women and dream of what might have been, denying the changes in his body as his skin slackened and his implants sagged, the budget for his hormones superfluous to his treatment requirements.

In the ward Antonio is rare as ambergris among the junkie flotsam cluttering the beds. Gays are scarce enough. We cluster them in the four-bedded rooms, deliberately, consciously, keeping them for ourselves, the regulars, the survivors, easy to deal with, glad of our presence. Tony says in the old days there were more but not now. Disease ate through their community like a brushfire. They were annihilated. Now we are kept busy with a never ending supply of junkies, casualties, bitter and angry, bottom of the pile with no way to go but down, and this is where I am, the white man, the killer. We are careful around them, fearful that they will see through us, see through the burnt-out quality of the years into our desires, the fuel that keeps us running. Even the wreckage in the corridors, brains rotten with CMV, tied to chairs, jerking, twitching, do they scent last night's late drinking on me as I pass, leeching out of my skin on a haze of vodka?

'Hey, hey, hey. Can I have something for the pain, man?'

'What am I? A fucking pharmacy? Wait your time.'

This is the floorshow, this is our day.

I can escape briefly into Antonio's room, the departure lounge, the last stop. Normally we keep the gomers here, the persistent vegetative states, but he slipped by on the pressure for beds. The TV in here is paid for by the staff. We share our quiet time with the dead. I also use it as my recovery area.

'Why is your skin that colour?'

My head feels bruised. Muddled, I uncurl myself from the chair. 'What?'

'Your skin, why is it so red? Have you got a fever?'

'No, I've been in the sun.'

'Do all your people do that?'

He has never left the city, never seen the sea except for the river, never stood next to the ocean, never seen a mountain. I paint imaginary landscapes for him, recalling a rose-tinted country from the never-never land of memory, creating an idealised future in which he becomes feminine once more and I am his guide and in this collusion perhaps I too am healed.

Emergency buzzer. Running. I clamp the mask on the bearded face. Tony on the chest, grinning, practised. The bed soaking with blood.

'Shit, where the fuck did this blood come from?'

Chaotic arrival of doctors. Flatline. Adrenaline. Shock. Security outside keeping the relatives at bay. Finally the anaesthetist and I can leave. The security guy has someone pinned against the wall by the throat.

'Don't you think you're being just a little excessive?'

Inwardly I am groaning, the paperwork forecast is high.

The man in the bed is still dead. His eyes look away from us, away from the ruin of his body. The doctors make the most of his remaining presence.

'Does anybody else want to try intubating?'

I whisper in the resident's ear. 'I really think it's time to leave now.'

Leaning on the bed I do not notice the discarded syringe; the needle goes straight through my hand. Of course it is full of blood, the whole junkie spectrum, HIV, hepatitis B and C, syphilis and on and on.

'Fuck.'

In staff health, after my immunoglobulins, they offer me a prophylactic course of AZT. I laugh. 'You are joking, right?'

On the death certificate they write it up as heart failure, but in reality the man's brother pulled out his central line and left him to bleed to death. We say nothing. Who could blame him?

Juanita is so thin now I can lift him from his bed to the chair with no assistance. His heart beats against my chest like that of a frightened bird. I brush what is left of his hair, do what I can with make-up. He has no visitors.

'Juanita,' I say. 'Have you got any family you want us to contact?'

He turns his face away. 'They rejected me. For the way that I am, you know?'

'What about friends?'

He looks at me wearily. 'Dead. All dead. You, this place, it's all I have left.'

Tony takes a Polaroid of the two of us, which I sit on the table beside his bed. He continues to take his medication without complaint. I move the bed so that he can see the sky. I spend as much time with him as I can.

'His lungs aren't getting any better,' says Tony.

I agree. His chest X-rays are a sequence of deterioration, shrinkage, white-out.

'Have you thought about a DNR order?' He lets the question hang in the air.

'No,' I say. 'Not my responsibility. That's a medical decision.'

'He likes you. You should tell him.'

And here in this place so familiar I am suddenly alone.

'Thanks,' I say. 'Thanks a lot.'

So I speak to him, I tell him his poor prognosis, I outline his options, I tell him there are places he can go where the care will be better, where there will be more staff, where he won't be here. And he says. 'What are you asking me to do? Do you want me just to give up? Because I am sick, because I am tired? I am not going to run and hide, I am not going to throw it all away. I cannot.'

He looks at me. 'Life is precious.'

I say nothing.

He is started on oxygen. He hates the mask and even in his sleep pulls it off. We do not discuss altering the course of his treatment. We wait.

On the last day he says to me, 'Why do you stay?'

And I say, 'Where would I go?

He smiles, 'You have a choice.'

'Do I?' I sit on the edge of his bed. 'I can't imagine any other way to live. On the outside no one understands.'

'Why should they,' he says. 'They have their lives to live. It's you who stays, drinks too much, makes a martyr of yourself.'

'I don't think of myself as a martyr.' I start to laugh. 'Maybe I don't have the imagination to do anything else. Maybe this is all I was made for.'

He smiles. 'Martyrs aren't made, they, they make themselves, they choose.'

'Like you?'

'You think I'd choose this?' He waves his hand over his wasted body. 'Do you know what I think?'

'I know you're going to tell me.'

'I think it is love that keeps you here, a stubborn love perhaps, a love that you do not recognise, but love nonetheless. Why else would you stay? Why else would you continue to care? You may hide the truth from yourself but it is there for all to see.'

In the lifetime of my career, among many such moments, this is my epiphany.

'Thank you.'

As I walk out the door he waves.

Shift's end.

This is my goodbye.

Antonio called, Juanita died that night. He was discovered by an agency nurse he had never met. As was his wish, he underwent the full resuscitation procedure but without success. Time of death was 02.43. Cause of death was noted as sepsis secondary to wound infection. I was at home, drinking chilled vodka into the darkness. I allowed myself one dream. In the dream Juanita is sleeping. I am watching over him. His hand is in mine. As I watch, I notice the pattern of his breathing slow. He is smiling. Gradually each breath takes longer than the other, becomes irregular. Stops.

I wait until he releases fully his hold upon what was him and then I open the window to let him go. It is a spring day, just after rain. I kiss his cheek.

Stillness.

This is what he leaves in his passing.

Tony is waiting at the station as I arrive the following day. 'Hey, Scottish, come and look at the fat fuck we admitted this morning.'

I peer round the door at the man mountain and grimace. 'How much?'

Tony frowns. 'I don't know, three seventy, maybe three eighty.'

I reach for my wallet. 'I've got ten says he's not a pound under four hundred.'

It goes on.

Life is precious.

Glossary

AZT   Azothioprine – routine medication for HIV patients.
CMV   Cytomegalovirus.
DNR   Do not resuscitate.
KS   Kaposi's sarcoma.
PCP   Pneumocystis – common marker infection in HIV.
TB   Tuberculosis – common marker infection in HIV.

The End of History

Gavin Bowd

As ever, she was up before dawn. She noticed how her flesh creased and bulged modestly over her abdomen as she left the sheets. Beneath the shower, age's folds seemed less pernicious, and her soapy hands wanted to rub away all their influence. Then she dressed, ate a roll and drank some coffee, left food for the sleeping cat, and went out of the flat.

As ever, the tram picked her up at the Stassfurter Strasse. It was her favourite driver at the wheel and they exchanged bleary greetings. The tram was full of people, standing and seated, heavy in their overcoats. Their eyes were all concentrated on a point that each had chosen. All carried expressions of solemn expectation. Someone passed the time in the dense text of a novel. A girl varied the angle of her reflection in the window, in pursuit of maximum beauty. None of the men were particularly attractive: their veined and puffy faces suffered the further affliction of strip-lighting.

Once she'd known a man. A soldier. He'd crossed her in the town square on May Day. Down by the river, where no fish dared swim, he'd liberated her from her shirt of the Free German Youth, and broken his way into her entrails. And she'd known the commonality of flesh, in furtive spasms, in hotels and behind bushes, in the shadow of the Red Army barracks. Until, brutalised by beer and vodka, he'd sworn undying allegiance to his wife.

In the receding darkness, she could make out few signs of the new freedoms. Camel cigarettes and Coca- Cola expressed their witticisms on flaking walls. A travel agency predicted sun and sex. But the town had not lost its familiarity, as Trabants and Wartburgs expelled into the air a new day's quota of sulphurous fumes.

The tram now approached the chemical works. Its fumes embalmed the countryside in a yellow haze. The river bubbled like a basin full of dishwater. On descending, their throats were seized by the rasping air. She would work eight hours, dutifully doing the tasks of lower management.

Later that day, she walked across the town square. A clock with several faces told the time in Hanoi, Moscow, Algiers and Havana. Its hands were out of synch, and no one had thought to repair it. She stopped at the new pizzeria, and ate a pizza with mozzarella, black olives and pepperoni. She bought provisions for herself and the cat, then walked home past the new shops. A sign promised the opening of Liberty.

At home, you could watch the television without fear of denunciation to the secret police. Game shows offered the chance of a life of fortune. You could watch the futurist moral struggles of *Star Trek* dubbed in German.

The cat paid no attention to the flickering television screen. Snug in her lap, it remained oblivious to the airwaves' bombardment of drama, merchandise and sex. Occasionally, terrible dreams electrified its face, and sent claws shooting from an outstretched paw.

She took to bed, with a glass of water. Before sleep took her, her hands strayed over her belly. Nerve-end upon nerve-end, the arid loop of solitary touch. No sharing with another. No proclamation of intimacy to others.

Once she'd known a man in upper management. An

engineer whose trained intellect fulfilled the Plan. Who took her in his car, in her flat, one day in his office. Whose ambition could dispense with her presence, which took him to cities, to the international friendships of Bulgarian, Czech and Polish beauty.

One day she took another tram-line. She didn't recognise the driver. The line would pass by the soda works. It had few employees now, and many of the seats were spare. Eventually, she arrived, on time, at the gates of the workplace.

She took her orders and dispensed a subset of orders. She watched over the array of chimneys and pipes that produced their wealth. The sun was a wide, diffuse spot in the haze, and could be stared at with impunity. It hung over the obscure humps of the Harz Mountains, now reduced to frontierless innocence. Her fingers were stiff with writing and typing, her back and buttocks sore from stretching and sitting: Her hand ran down to her newly-shaved calf. Across its stubbled softness ran blue veins.

Once she'd known a man in the Party. Who'd loved her as patriot and worker. Whose keen eyes and eager hands had applied their power. Whose moments of nudity scattered belongings and schedules. Whose comings and goings were watched and whispered upon. Until discipline diverted his eyes and pulled up his zip.

One day, the chemical works closed. The sun burned freely through the clouds, and you could no longer set your eyes upon it. Throats were less sore and swollen, shoes less dusty, and people could wander all day, across the town square, past the shop-windows, across the river, where swans now glided imperiously. Rough grass and rabbits colonised the factory site. The air was filled by new birds who nested in the ruins of the Red Army barracks.

She took one of the new buses that followed a circular route which lasted approximately half an hour. Past the idle, newlyjeaned young, the sultry and hated, mini-skirted Vietnamese, to estates on the edge of town, where walls carried the hieroglyphs of tags and the occasional anti-Nazi slogan. Past the paper mill, the soda works, the college and the hospital. Then the bus looped back to the centre, where the old and middle-aged wandered, and the young struck poses. She got down from the bus and thanked the driver.

Once she had been in the Pioneers and spent weeks in summer camp. They'd set up tents in the mountain forests or by the hundreds of lakes in the East. Rowed, ran and played, learned the names of animals and trees, giggled behind the back of the ideology teacher. Watched each other grow, until they bled and warped. Sitting in the twilight, feeling ridiculous in blouses of the Free German Youth, they could dream of adventure within their borders, of the man that would tear up their red neckerchief.

At home, the cat nuzzled into a sunlit patch on the rug. She stared at the bright triangle of light that intersected the living-room wall. It highlighted the crack running down the plaster for about a metre. Up in the top corner was an old spider's web. A fly passed by, then bounced against the window pane. Outside, the treetop was swaying on its axis, its leaves were shouting in the wind.

Norway Maple Leaves

Sheena Charleston

T he nurse used her eyes like diagnostic implements, levelling mine with cold stares of satisfied contempt. She was bothered by my suitcase. It was far too big to remain on the ward. She said that it made me look like I was going on a luxury cruise. She told me that the operation, though major surgery, was routine and had been done thousands of times before. My suitcase would have to be collected by a relative as soon as possible. There simply wasn't the space for it. If all the patients had brought as much stuff as I had, there would be no room to do the operations. Four elderly ladies occupied my ward. Sleeping like hairy maggots encapsulated in tubular blankets. Snowdrift white and blow-holing like whales through lax lips comfortable without teeth. If sleep comes from a sleep factory, I thought that it must be these four who produce it for us all. The intakes and exhales expertly annunciated.

I sat on the edge of my hospital bed for an hour before unpacking.

Archaeologists would have unpacked the Ice Man's pannier but storms had already teased apart the tethered branches. Contents had spilled the slowest spill ever recorded in history.

It took me a while to fill up my locker. The door squeaked, snapping loudly like cracked glass, awakening the ladies from their meeting of sleep. The frailest, whispering words too big to swallow, mashing gums through puckerings, a word like gruesome. Then a radiant smile became her and she listed wistfully back to sleep. Her lips frilling into rosettes. I apologised, my mattress creaking and crinkling like frozen ice.

As well as arrows, daggers and an axe, the Ice Man had chosen to take his ember box and a stone talisman. The corpse was lifted from its grave wearing nothing but one right shoe. The ice had removed his trousers. The shoe was made of grass.

In the morning, I was given a consent form which I was to sign after formally understanding that they would remove all of my large bowel.

None of his clothing was of woven material.

My blood was taken. The shower room was smelly. Mould sucked up the cracks. I experimented with disgust by imagining someone actually eating it. The fittings were loose. I thought of old ladies' bodies standing under the same steamy water with their demented arguments, horny feet and flakey skin hovering, hovering. Frail, bony buttocks and resistance to the obvious directions of nurses. I uncapped the bottle of detergent that I had smuggled in and tipped it neat over my belly. It spiralled down my legs like pee and burned. It would protect me from flesh eating microbes. The surgeon's blade would slice me open in two hours' time.

The Ice Man wore a bracelet of fungi with antibacterial qualities. He would fight back with his flinty dagger. Cut and thrust. A kiss of sultry snowflakes melting into his wind-blown hair, gypsy-man beard, his laughing gap-tooth insults held impertinent by echoes for future avalanches.

The sheet-white theatre gown unravelled down to my toes. It made me feel thin and giddy. The garb of a ghastly countenance like a religious martyr ready to be hoisted up into knots of cruelty. Gifted to mankind.

The breakfast-trolley nurse served the old ladies bowls of

awkward porridge. I wasn't allowed to eat or drink but even if I had, I felt too squeamish with nerves. I went and lay on my hospital bed and waited. The Ice Man had enjoyed birch-tar chewing gum before he lay his head against the stone. A nurse brought pre-op medication in a plastic cup. Three thousand years before Jesus sipped wine in Galilee, the ice man reached his hand out to grasp the twentieth century as if hailing the kinder of the Four Horses of the Apocalypse. Pre-op pills tasting of gullibility and wisdom. Slowly, the ward became absolutely riveting. Suddenly I was moving. A porter and nurse wheeling me down shafts of light and darkness, flickering, flickering.

For a second I dreamed that the Ice Man told me that his name was not Otzi but was Ptakchmylol. He spelled it in the ice for me.

Snow cradled him like a lover. Organising him out of his own limbs. Animating him free of stiff death. The infinite patience of one millimetre each thousand years, turning him over in his sleep without disturbing him. Keeping him. Hidden from theft in the snow skirts like a nunnery keeps its reliquary of balsa bones. Snow wrapping and rewrapping the skull as if it were a vase to be packed for removal. Delicate. Wondrous eyes up. The opulent eye sockets cupping snowflakes and the look of lost lenses. Quietness. Rolling over again. Centuries at a time. His face pressed to the breast of boulder. Kinking a wink from a sagged eyelid while the bone ropes relapse. Unbecoming like a knot being attempted again from a different start point. A fiddler without a bow. He lies there, a broken arrow. Splintered. Crushed golden into autumn leaves. Tobacco brown. Crumbly. An Icarus dropped by a jealous god. A doll of wooden pegs. Indeterminate zips of rain, cold metal, undoing the temporal bone still further to let light in. Blizzards biting at his ears to make him listen. He hears nothing while his eyes are shocked open to the absolute

foreverness of that day's death. He will take time to get over it.
Winter fingers have picked his teeth clean in readiness.

'We have to ask you again if you have any false teeth or
anything of that nature?' asked one of the theatre staff as the
rest of them began to crowd around the trolley bed I lay on.
They all knew my name. A pantheon of green gods taking me
away in a spaceship. Someone held my hand.

Skiers trod across his palms looking for compass bearings.
Unknowingly used his broken arm as a branch spring.

A chorus of friendly faces in surgical theatre caps surround
me. Criss-crossing arms with IV lines and drip feeds. Doing
things to force me, like a gang of pick pockets tousling a drunk
tourist.

Considerate of needs that I wasn't quite sure were actually
mine. Gentle, coercive, comedian. Famously fitting me up for
anaesthetic needles as though offering me pens for my auto-
graph. Smiling winning smiles towards me because I was
going somewhere 'strictly private'. A painting was situated
on the ceiling. Fine Art for the ill, the dying, the soon to be
better.

International teams of archaeologists arrived, trudging
through the snow to smooth over surfaces like frost flowers.
A helicopter orbited with a team of technicians. The police
had already taken some of his belongings back down. His skull
was birthed out of its glacial cervix of bin-bag slush. Drinking
from the puddled meltwater, his petted lip, one last time
before his corpse was lovingly bodybagged and dragged up to
date. The battering winds of helicopter blades stamping out a
dance of popped blossoms below. His map skin of burst roses
and ardent tatoos tucked into modern polythene. Unwrapped
by nervous technicians for intrusive computer tomography.
Surgical gowns were donned and tissue samples were taken
while ice was spread on a sterile operation sheet.

She was operated on for a little over an hour. The ileum

joined up to the sigmoid. She was wrapped in white hospital blankets to warm her from the frozen wasteland of anaesthesia. I decided to wait until I might see a flicker of consciousness thawing from under her eyelashes. The women came to move her to stop blood clots forming. The wound was ten inches wide. Stapled shut. The oxygen mask looked like a long thin icicle. Her breath smelled of fires. I would have given her one of my Norway maple leaves to chew on to take the bad taste away if she had been fully awake.

Private Enterprise

Jaohn Grace

K emp stumbled out of the tube station and into the freezing night. The cold hit him like a fist and he cursed his lack of forethought and his lack of overcoat. It had been warm in Edinburgh. You'd have thought it would be warmer still four hundred miles further south. He snuffled off down the street, shoulders hunched, his breath a white cloud, following the map in his mind. It was always a different pick-up point. Six years now. Twenty-three pick-ups, twenty-three drops. He had cut the pages out of an *A-to-Z* once: had stuck them together and put them up on his wall. God Almighty, what a size London was! You couldn't get your head round it. He had stuck pins in all the locations but they hadn't made any sort of pattern. Why should they? Daft idea. He crossed the road and turned right, left, right again, raced through an underpass – safer that way, he wouldn't want to get mugged with fifty grand on him. He found himself walking along a seemingly-endless chain link fence.

Three minutes later, he saw the sign. 'GENTLEMEN'.

'Bloody silly place to put a pisser,' he thought. 'In the middle of nowhere.' It was the only building still standing in a bulldozed urban wasteland. God only knew why. It was also a bit conspicuous, he thought, or it would have been, were it not for the near-pitch darkness and the fact that there was no

195

traffic at all on the street. He guessed the road must be closed. No pedestrians around either. He went in.

Less than a minute later he was out again and hurrying through the darkness alongside the fence, his heart pounding and his breath coming in short gasps. The return trip was always the worst – an icy tension between the shoulder blades and a feeling that his skin was made of eggshells. Was he being watched? Was he being followed? With two K's of unadulterated heroin on him, he would be looking at twenty years. He looked over his shoulder. Nothing. He hurried on.

This bloody fence was endless. He would be totally visible to any cruising cops. There was the underpass. He raced through it and out the other side. Oncoming headlights. Slow down, idiot! Nice and slow. He was back among people and traffic, inconspicuous now. At last! The underground sign came into sight. He was dazzled by sudden headlights and a flashing beacon. He froze at the shriek of the siren and his guts turned over. The police car screamed round a corner and was gone.

Minutes later, he was slumped, white-faced and sweating, in the seat of his underground carriage, rattling through the entrails of London. He closed his eyes. Never again. Not for a lousy two grand. This was the last time. Definitely the last time. So far his luck had held, but everybody's luck ran out sooner or later. And the people he dealt with frightened him. No. Stick to the theatre business; that was what he knew. That was what he was good at. He shuddered as he thought of the furtive transaction in the stinking, dimly-lit urinal: of the little man's brown teeth, his evil breath and his dead-fish eyes. He smelt of death and rottenness. Richard Kemp longed to be on the north-bound train and out of here.

The next morning he walked out of rehearsals. Not for the first time. Christ, this director was a pain in the arse. Nobody talked to him like that. Nobody! He was too long out of short

pants. Why did these guys always think they were God?
Wouldn't know real talent if it pissed on them. If only he
could get the real break – the big one. He was so sick of
working for equity minimum – of low-budget tours in crum-
my little theatres in cruddy little towns, performing crap plays
to idiots who couldn't keep their kids or their crisp packets
quiet and talked all through the show. How did you make any
headway in this business? It was one step forward and two
steps back. There was always somebody putting obstacles in
your way – always someone who had it in for you.

They were jealous. Simple as that. He didn't know the right
people, hadn't the clout. He tripped and cursed. Bastard
beggars! They were everywhere you went these days. Para-
sites! This bugger probably earned more than he did. Get the
punters' sympathy – sit in front of the most expensive shop in
town on a cold night with a threadbare blanket around you,
legs outstretched so you couldn't be missed and hold out a
shaking hand. Window full of bright consumer goods. Starving victim of capitalism on the pavement. Too easy. The
contrast was beautiful. Gah! He spat and walked on. He
hoped Anna was in. He needed to get laid.

'Why do students always live on the top floor?' he demanded as he breezed into the flat and threw himself down on
the sofa.

'Better than your basement grot-hole,' she replied. 'You've
got dogshit on your shoe.'

He kicked off his shoes and turned off the TV with his big
toe.

'I walked out.'

'What, for good?'

'Maybe. I don't know.'

'Silly bastard. They'll fire you one of these days.'

'Probably. God this place is a shit heap. Don't you ever do
any housework?'

'Between working my arse off at college and pulling pints for piss-heads like you, tell me when I get the time?'

'So how come you're watching TV?'

'It's a video. It's part of my course.'

'Yeah, well. Let's go to bed.'

'You're a silver-tongued fucking charmer, you know that?'

'It's my borstal background. Come over here and shut up.' He held out his arms.

There was nothing quite like sex in the afternoon, he decided afterwards, lying in the darkening room, Anna asleep in the crook of his arm. The trouble was it left you so empty afterwards and so . . . alone, somehow, with the long, flat, empty evening stretching ahead. He shivered and lit a cigarette with his free hand. Christ! He needed a fix! The thought panicked him. He hadn't thought this could happen to him – not so quickly. He'd only tried the stuff half a dozen times. Just for a buzz. It was fundamental. You don't sample your own wares. That's for the punters, the mugs, the junkies. Once more, he decided. Just one more time – half the usual dose to get him through the panic bit and then no more. He'd stick to the booze. He brightened at the idea, but he was already beginning to shake. He threw off the covers and leapt out of bed. He dressed quickly without waking her and let himself out. He hit the street running and looked wildly about for a cab.

Kemp got fired the next day, got out of his mind drunk the same night and the day after, was on a south-bound train with a hundred thousand pounds in his rucksack. He was scared shitless of needles, so he had swallowed his fix of Chinese white in the toilet and he was flying high: unassailable, invulnerable. He was alone at the table. Mothers ushered their infants quickly past the unshaven man with the glazed eyes and the wide grin. Three grand this was worth! The Vagabond Theatre Company could stick its play up its arse.

He giggled. He reckoned he was the kingpin of this operation: the bee's knees. Without him, they were nothing, nowhere. Without him, the deal wouldn't go down. They owed him. He was the one risking his neck so the big boys could make their fat profits. Three grand. Three lousy grand! Suddenly it didn't seem like so much. Suddenly it seemed like nothing at all. An insult. They were using him – treating him like shit. The same way his old man had treated him when he was a kid on a council estate in Edinburgh. He remembered the pain of the leather belt on his face, his buttocks, his back. He could still smell the stink of cat piss in the coal shed, where he was locked up for hours at a time for having the wrong expression on his face; could feel the hunger pangs, when he was sent to school without any food for one trivial reason or another; could smell the cheap booze on his father's breath and see the hate in his face. His mother had eventually seen the light and run off with a local scrap merchant. She hadn't really given a toss about him either.

He thought about his schooldays and all he could remember were the fists of the bullies and the fear of the teachers. Academically, he had always been in the middle – never top, never bottom – merely mediocre. Parents, teachers, the drug barons who paid his wages, authority in general – all began to merge into one, huge, hated figure that swam before his eyes like an evil genie. Well, he didn't have to knuckle under. Not any more. He was worth more than that. He was the kingpin, the pivot. He was worth more than the whole lot of them. He was the best. He had to be the best because all his life people had told him he was shit.

And he had a hundred thousand pounds in his rucksack.

He got off the train at Berwick on Tweed.

He hired a car in town and drove to his brother's country cottage, near Langholm, in the Scottish Borders. Michael

Kemp heard the engine minutes before he arrived and came out to meet him. He was a stocky, dour, inarticulate man, some ten years older than his brother and had got out from under years before Richard was able to. His background had made him suspicious and a little afraid of the world.

'You in trouble again?' was what he said first.

'On the contrary,' said Kemp emphatically, leaping the fence. 'I'm in the money!'

'You on something?'

'Couple of whiskies on the train, that's all. What's the matter with you?'

He put his arm round his brother and steered him into the house.

'Get me a drink and I will tell all!'

Kemp proceeded to spin him a yarn about winning a packet in a casino. Mike didn't query the story but neither did he believe it. He knew his younger brother was trouble. He was and always would be, a waster and a loser. That didn't bother him – he was practically a stranger anyway. He simply hoped he wouldn't stay very long. Mike was a smallholder. He kept a few sheep and grew his own vegetables and watched birds. He wanted a quiet life above all else. He wanted Richard to go away and leave him alone.

Kemp spent three days in indecision, walking the hills, swallowing heroin, drinking, sniffing coke and waking each night in a cold sweat of panic. He had to get away – out of the country. But how could he get that much money out with him? And his passport was still in his flat in Edinburgh. They'd surely be on to that by now? Maybe not, though. Maybe not yet. He'd always used Anna's flat as a contact address. In any case, his passport was well hidden – behind a loose brick in his unused chimney, along with his stash of smack and the cash for his last job. Anna was the only one, apart from himself, who knew about it. He'd have to leave the cash with Mike in the meantime – he didn't know what else to do. In the movies, they transferred it to Swiss bank accounts, but he didn't have the least idea of how to go about that without leaving a trail that could be followed. He left in the early morning of the third day, leaving the money in his brother's worried keeping. Two hours after his departure, Mike again heard the sound of an approaching engine. He sighed heavily and went out to meet his new visitors.

The dark powers that be of the drug world had resented the loss of so much venture capital. They had sent people to talk to people who knew Richard Kemp. One of these was Anna. They hadn't fucked about. They had slammed her against a wall, where two of them had held her, while a third poured acid from a small, green bottle on to her metal table top, where she could see it hiss and sizzle. He had held the bottle inches from her face and asked for information and addresses. She had held nothing back. They had tied her to a chair, but not very tightly. It took her fifteen minutes to work a hand loose and another five to jerk the chair across the floor to the phone. She wept into the receiver as, at the other end of the line, the number kept ringing and ringing and ringing.

Kemp had been careful. He had gone in through the back entrance in pitch darkness at four o' clock in the morning. Up the steps in his stocking feet, carrying his shoes and silently . . . in. He switched on a very dim pencil torch with an old battery in it: just enough light to guide him past the furniture. As far as he could tell, the flat was untouched – not that surprising, really, since nobody had an address, just a number. Still. Better to be safe. He retrieved the cash, the stash and the passport, threw some clothes in a suitcase, picked up the mail and got out fast. He threw up in the bushes and then disappeared into the night.

He took a cab to the airport and the shuttle flight to London. From there he would get the first plane out to anywhere. As the plane arrowed through the icy winter night, he shuffled through his mail. Among the bills and mailshots was a postcard from his agent, written in bold, red felt-tip. It said:

'Phone me, you bastard!'

Three men got out of the car and Mike Kemp walked out to meet them. He stopped dead when he saw they were all wearing balaclavas. They tied him to a tree. Then they took a hammer and chisel and shattered his front teeth. They doused him in petrol and rattled a box of matches in front of his face. One of them said: 'One question, Mr Kemp. And you're not allowed to get the answer wrong.'

They drove off with the money, leaving him still tied to the tree, weeping. The postman would probably find him on the following afternoon – if he had any mail that day, of course.

Kemp leaned back in his first class seat, high over the Atlantic, savouring the warm glow of his third whisky and the joy of his new-found freedom. He should have said goodbye to Anna, but that would have been so heavy – tears, recriminations – a whole heap of shit he could do without. He had phoned his agent from Heathrow, more out of curiosity than anything else. He had done a screen test, months before and had long given up on it, but it seemed somebody was interested after all. Harry had given him a name and a film company in Los Angeles. Could they meet up and talk about it? Kemp had simply put the phone down and caught the next plane to New York. He would deal with it himself. It was fate. It must be! Fame and fortune beckoned – and all the trappings of wealth: fast cars, good clothes. At last a chance to outshine all those smug bastards with their mobile phones and their BMWs and their Armani fucking suits! Christ, the women he would have, the coke he would snort, the faces he would grind into the dirt; the same way the world had always ground him into the fucking dirt! He grinned, and the grin grew wider and stupider as his fantasies burgeoned. He would be another Tom Cruise, another James Dean, another Superman – another King Kong, climbing fucking skyscrapers! He burped and giggled. And the snuggy bugle rug-rug-drug dealers would never find him. They had no-o-o-o way of knowing where he was. And anyway, he would pay them back. When he got rich and when he got so goddamn famous, they wouldn't dare touch him. But he would pay them back double – treble! Cause he was honest and . . . and honourable and he paid his debts and they would respect him for that. Loooads of respect for honest John. And now it was time for honest John to go to the honest John for a tippy top top-up! He fought the urge to laugh out loud. He rose to his feet and made his way, unsteadily to the back of the plane, taking his empty whisky glass with him. He entered the cubicle and locked the door behind him. He sat down heavily on the pan and reached over to half-fill the glass with water. Into the water he shook some white powder, spilling much of it on to his trousers. He paused, shrugged and emptied the rest of it into the glass.

'Can't take that through customs anyway' he said to himself and spluttered with mirth. He stirred the mixture with his pen and downed it in two gulps. He had time to frown in puzzlement at the unexpected taste of almonds on his tongue. Then he died.

If he had been in his flat earlier that morning, he would have heard the lock being picked; would have seen a dark figure let himself in and make straight for the chimney; would have seen him reach up and remove a certain brick; would have seen him add one white powder to another, mix them thoroughly, replace the polythene bag and the brick and leave, locking the door behind him with a specialist tool, for the man was a specialist. He would have seen all of this and understood its significance and, throughout the whole operation, he would have heard the telephone ringing and ringing and ringing.

Ninety-nine Kiss-o-grams

Suhayl Saadi

H e must've been mad tae have come here at this time ae
year. Either that, or desperate. Forty-five degrees in
the shade, and climbin'. And that wis just the official reading,
the wan they put in newspapers and atlases and tourist
brochures – not that ony tourists ever came here, mind you . . .

Sal looked up and closed his eyes. Tried to blank oot the
sun. But it wisnae like back hame. In the banjar zameene
around Lahore, the sun was like God; it wis cursed by everyone, fae jagirdaar tae bhikari, fae mohlvi tae kunjari. He
scuffed his foot aroon and stirred up the dirt, made it swirl
intae the air so that he began tae cough. Deep, wrenchin
coughs that were mair like big bokes. I'll choke on ma ane
land, he thought and then he almost laughed through the
tears but it wis too hot tae laugh. Behind him sat the stupit car
he'd used tae get here; it wis meant tae be *only twelve miles,
bhai, fifteen at the most*, but it had taken longer than the drive
from Glasgee tae Edinburgh on a rainy day, roadworks-an-aw.
But then there wernae ony roadworks here. The roads never
got repaired. Sometimes they nivir even got built. That wis the
thing about Pakistan. You never knew anything for certain.
Temperature, direction, distance, the future . . . it wis aw up
fur grabs. And money – well, money, that wis somehin else
again. That wis why he wis oot here, Sal reminded himsel. Tae

get money. And unlike maist ae whit went on here, it wisnae kala duhn he wis after. His dada had left aw his grandweans bits ae earth, thinkin that mibee wan day, they would come back tae Pakistan and build hooses, all in a row just like in the auld days. His dada had worked like a dog tae get enough money tae buy these plots just ootside ae Lahore. It wis the sixties, and everyhin had been lookin up and he'd been tell't that the city would expand along wi the population and that in twenty years, the same bits ae wasteland would be worth *ten times more, bhai, ten times more.* Sal looked at the straggly, brown grass so unlike the bright-green mud-grass of Glasgee, and wondered how anyone could have believed that this land would ever be anything other than dry shit. Far away, a row of scorched trees quivered against the horizon while to the east, in the direction of the Indian border, Sal thought he spotted a white-turbanned kisaan ploughing, behind a pair of bulls, through the yellow soil. He inhaled, slowly. This wis his country, the land ae his forefaithers and yet, the stink ae it sickened him tae his gut. That sweet smell ae rotting lemons, of uncollected rubbish, of unrepaired roads. Naa, he thought, and kicked the soil again, this isnae ma country. No ony mair. Mibee, it nivir wis. He'd been tae Pakistan three or four times before, but nivir tae a shit-hole like this, and nivir in the depths ae summer, for God's sake! The song he'd been playing, back in the car, seemed still to hover within the ripples of heat, the reel turning again and again as he walked slowly across the stretch of land. The groon wis hard, irregular like wild dog skulls yet it crumbled into powder as his sandals touched the surface. Suddenly, a big, black bird swooped down and landed on a branch above his heid. He felt its eye slide along his spine. A perfect, black globe. Sal stopped walking, and tried tae stare back but the light wis too strong, and his eyes began tae water. He wiped them wi the sleeve ae his kamise and removed a piece of paper from his shalvar pocket. Unfolded it. The sections came open uneasily and, when they did, they left behind dirty brown lines. Sal peered at the yellowed paper. The deeds. It had been written in Urdu script, and he couldnae read Urdu script. But right down at the dog-eared bottom, there were some letters in English which he'd tried tae make oot, all the way over, as he'd sat, bored and irritable, in the plane. They were probably meaningless, anyway. Most of the English here wis pretty meaningless. A kind ae jumbled-up mix ae auld Colonial-speak and Amerikan Gangsta talk. His dada must have worn this piece ae paper like a lover as he'd sweatit thru the pissin rain an soor terraces ae Scola on his way tae makin it. Only he'd nivir really made it. No like the big Cash 'n' Carry Families, or the Restaurant Wallahs. Naw, his dada had ended up like a chhipkali in a bottle, always slidin up the glass walls and nivir really gettin onywhur. He felt like cryin as he remembered his dada's tired face, the cheeks sagging and full of lines, one crease for every year in exile. He focused down on the writing. *Hauf-an-acre*, it looked like, but you couldnae be sure. Somewhur between the burnin grass an the red sandstone, somewhur over those strange, blue seas which they'd flash up alang wi the wee-whistle life jackets on the plane-flight, the exact measure of Sal's inheritance had got muddled, smudged, diluted. Sal jumped as the bird crowed through the heat. It had lost interest in him, and was gazing east, towards the land of Bhaarat. Now he'd come back to try and sell the land, to get what he could, and get oot again. But everything in Pakistan was cascading downwards like water from the Rawal Dam. The rupee had fallen from fifty-to-the-pound, to one hundred-and-thirteen (thirteen . . . for luck? Sal had wondered); the only things which held their value in this country were truth and the loudspeakers outside mosques. Truth was priceless, and it wis everywhere. Look under any bush (burnin or not) and there, you might find another truth. Sal thought that mibee this wis because it wis so close tae Hindustan, wi its million gods crawlin aroon all over the place, lookin fur worship. His dada had listened to wan version of the truth when he'd been telt tae buy these plots; the city was goin tae spread like the music ae the Beatles over everything and soon, the wee plots (the cotees all in a row, with the fair-skinned wives and the kala servants and the almost inaudible pulse of the air-conditioning) wuid be worth twenty times, *twenty times, bhai*, what they had been bought fur. And right enough, the city had expanded, aye, and laacs-upon-laacs ae cotees had sprung up like teeth all over the place, but the problem wis it had expanded in the wrang direction. It had gan north-east, not south-east and so his dada's plots had remained a wee wasteland. They might even have been shaam laat e shair, common land of the city, and then they would not have been his dada's, after aw. Nuthin wis certain here. Nuthin. Mibee you were alive, mibee you were deid. Mibee there wis a God, mibee there were ten thousand. Everyone had a different version of everything, and nuhin wis written doon. Or if it had been, then it would have got washed away in the waters of the Rawal Dam, the night had they had burst through stane and concrete and flooded the valley of Punjab, killing thousands. Or maybe that hasnae happened yet, Sal thought. It wis hard tae be sure. He'd not got very far, trying tae sell the plot; prices were dirt-low and almost no one wis buying land. Anyone who wis anyone wis tryin tae put money intae foreign banks, or tae get oot themselves. No one wanted land in a country that wis goin tae the dogs and the sand. He spat and his spittle landed on a hump of yellow earth where it lay but did not dissolve. Sal bent down and stared into the dome of the blob. He'd often wondered what he would do with the money. It wasnae gonna be a fortune. It might buy the wheel-trims ae a Merc; or else, a wide-screen TV so that his behene could sit an watch stupit Bombay filmi films. Three hours ae *rim-jim* and *roo-roo* and violins that screeched around yer skull. Or mibee he would invest it in the shop. Turn it fae a corner-shop intae a boutique like the wan his bitch cousin hud on Cathcart Road. Get merrit, huv a family. Naw. He had other dreams for his dada's land. In Sal's dream the money, converted like Sal from rupees intae pounds, would go tae buy a kiss-o-gram. Or, to be mair precise, ninety-nine kiss-o-grams. All blonde and bikini'd and stonin in a circle aroon him, and smilin at him wi thur thick, red lips . . . he saw himsel surroondit by them, their wee white breasts pushin intae his broon face, fillin his mooth, his body so that he couldnae breathe fur the whiteness. So that he could become invisible. But that wis jist a dream. In Scola, there wus nae room fur dreams; in Pakistan, dreams were all there wus. He scrunched up the deed and went to put it back in his pocket. Felt it slip from his hand. He bent down to pick it up but couldn't see where it had gone. There wis a clump ae grass, jis beneath his foot, but it wasnae in there. He swore aloud but his voice was immediately swallowed up in the molten air and, for the first time, Sal felt scared. He felt sweat spike along the line of his spine. His hair lay matted, dank over his scalp. He shouldnae huv driven oot here on his ane. The thought occurred to him that perhaps the deed might've slipped somehow (anything was possible) into the lining of his shalvar. He ran his hands over the smooth, white cotton, rapidly at first but then slowly, carefully as he held his breath and felt the heat enter him and swell in his chest. *Forty-six degrees, forty-seven . . .*

It wasn't there. It wasn't on the ground either, and the earth all just looked the same. It wisnae like Scola, wi aw its shades like the different malts; naw, from the plane, Pakistan wis jis wan, scorched broon. Suddenly he longed for the cool spaces ae Scola, the feel ae the rain on his back. He rummaged aroon wi the tip ae his shoe, but all he got wis mair dust. There wouldn't be another copy – God knew when and where his dada had got it from and onyway nothing would ever huv been written down, and, if it had been, then it would be a lie. Truth was held in the air like the waves of heat that burned his skin. He felt the glare of the bird on the back of his neck but fought the temptation to look back. He got down on his hands and knees and began to rummage his palms through the dry soil. The dust made him sneeze, and his eyes began to water but he took no notice, and let the tears drip silently on to the earth. The soil tasted bitter, like ajwain. Sal had heard that farmers sometimes tasted the soil of their fields, to test its quality. Eejeuts. His breath burned the lining of his throat and he needed a drink. There was boiled water in the car, but Sal didnae dare leave the plot. His grandfather had sweatit for this land and in the end, he hud died fur it and he wasnae goin tae jis let it slip away so that some fat zamindaar could come and swallow it up for nothin. A year back, his papa hud ran aff wi a goree and the whole family had been disgraced (as a result of this, his maa had developed five thoosand illnesses, all of which seemed tae afflict her concurrently, and his dada had gan tae his grave while watchin Madubala fling herself from the stone parapet in the video of the film, *Mahal*). Now Sal wis the man and, being the eldest, it wis up tae him tae save at least somehin ae the family's honour; he hud tae get a guid, or at the very least, a reasonably pukka price for this piece ae pure yellow shite and he couldnae go hame, empty-handed, he just couldnae . . .

There wis nae breeze but Sal thought he felt wan. He paused for a moment. His face wis covered in dust his clothes were no longer white but had acquired the dun chamois in which most Pakistanis over here seemed to dress. His hair fell across his eyes, and he brushed it back wi his hond but it jis fell forwards again. His mother had told him (countless times) tae get it cut *and why don't you try to look like a respectable bundha.* So he'd got fed up and, wan day, he'd gan oot and got it cut. A Number Wan. After that, she'd thrown her honds up intae the air and screamed, *Hai-hai!* and had taken to her bed for two days. You couldnae please them, no matter what you did. He hated his faither fur what he had done, but he hated him mair because he'd landed Sal right in it. Now Sal wis it. All eyes were on him, and he had tae succeed, or else he might as weil be deid. Mibee he wuid be better aaf deid; at least then, he wuid be a hero, or a martyr or, at the very least, someone not tae be spoken ill of. An image of the goree bein screwed by his father flashed intae his mind. He pushed it away. In the past, they'd sometimes talked aboot the men who'd been seen hauding honds wi mini-skirtit gorees an walking doon the street. And he'd despised those men and yet, at the same time, he'd wantit tae be wan ae them. Tae huv his ane long-legged, thin-waisted goree tae wave like a white flag at the world. And then his faither had gone an done that, and made it impossible fur Sal. Now, he wuid nivir be able tae surrender. Sal wus deid, right enough, deid an buried beneath the big, wet stanes ae Albert Drive. Beneath the big, white sky. He forced his mind back tae the deed, the plot, his honour. He had the insane thought of removing his shalvar and turning it inside-out to search for the piece ae paper. He looked around. There wis no one about. The peasant he had spotted earlier had vanished. He was far from anywhere. It would take only a few seconds. And onyway, time here wis different. Everything around him had grown silent. Or mibee it had always been like that, he wasnæ sure. He got down on his hands and knees and began to search for the deed. He felt the cotton ae his claes stick tae his back like a lizard skin. After a while, he stopped and rolled over.

Everything looked different. The sky was everywhere, and its blueness had faded into a shimmering silver. The bird was no longer in the tree, but was scarpering along the ground. Every so often, its head would flick down and then up, and, every time this happened, its beak would emerge empty, black. It seemed a lot smaller than before, its stupit wee deformed twig legs were like those of an auld wummin. It'll no find ony worms here, he thought. Sal began to feel uncomfortable. He felt as though he was sinking into the soil. His nails were all smashed and blood had begun to trickle from the end of his thumb. Slowly, he got up. The bird had disappeared. You couldnae even trust yer ane eyes. He removed his sandals and set them neatly aside. Spat again, to clear the dust from his mouth. He looked around, just tae check and in one, smooth movement, he slipped the elastic of his shalvar down and over his feet and stepped awkwardly out of it. He lifted it up, and shook the cloth so that a fine dust flew everywhere. Nothing. He turned it inside-out and shook it again but still, nothing. The dust smelt ae bhang. The whole country's gan tae pot, Sal thought, and then he laughed. He was about to put the shalvar back on, when the thought occurred to him that the paper might somehow have fallen, not into his shalvar but into his kamise. He threw the shalvar down on to the ground and slipped the long shirt up, over his head. The heat scalded his back, he could feel the cells begin to fry, one by one. His head felt like it was goin tae burst and his breath was coming in short rasps. *Forty-nine degrees, fifty* . . . He shook out the kamise but it, too, was empty. Exasperated, Sal tossed it aside and glared up at the sky which had become so bright, it held no colour at all. It was as though the sun had exploded and filled the entire sky with its burning substance. He tried to swear but his mouth was parched and no words came. He shook his fist at the sun, or God, or truth or whatever was up there. He fell to his knees and began frantically to search for the piece of paper which had hauled him across five thousand miles and three generations to the plot which he and his dada, both had dreamt of and, as he churned up the earth, the dust swirled into the air so that there, in the land that was his by right of inheritance, he had, at last, become invisible.

Suhayl Saadi

And because of the clouds of ochre dust which surrounded him, Sal did not see the bird up in the tree as it flapped its wings twice and took off into the burning sky.

Glossary

ajwain	a bitter-tasting spice, used in many curries and also used, mixed with salt, to aid excessive bloatedness
bhai	a brother (may also be used as a term of address from any one person to any other, regardless of sex)
banjar zameene	wastelands, scrublands
behene	sisters, or female relatives in the broader sense
bhang	marijuana
bhikari	a beggar
bundha	a man
chhipkali	a lizard
cotee	a house
dada	paternal grandfather
filmi	a style of film or of film music/songs pertaining to movies made by the Bombay film industry.
goree	a white woman (derogatory)
jagirdaar	a big Punjabi landowner
kala	black
kala duhn	'black money', i.e. money obtained or converted via the black market; most people change money in this manner, usually through shopkeepers since the rate is always better than the official one
kamise	a loose shirt worn by Punjabi men and women
kisaan	a peasant
kunjari	a whore
laacs	hundreds of thousands (one laac = one hundred thousand)
maa	a mother
Madubala	a famous Indian movie actress of the forties and fifties; she was usually a tragic heroine

213

Mahal	a film tragedy, made in the forties; 'Mahal' means 'palace'
mohlvi	a Muslim 'priest'
papa	a father
rim-jim	the sound which rain makes as it falls onto the ground; commonly used as a symbol of romance, particularly in films or in poetry
roo-roo	a meaningless word used commonly as a backing vocal sound in countless 'Bollywood' film-songs, and usually intoned by a female chorus
shaam laat e shair	land belonging usually to the city authorities, i.e. commonly-owned areas
shalvar	loose, baggy trousers worn by Punjabi men and women
wallah	a person, usually in the context of their job
zamindaar	a Punjabi landowner (a more general term than 'jagirdaar'; a zamindaar could be either a big, or a small landowner)

Clunker

James Robertson

Ye think it'll niver happen tae ye. Happen tae *you*. When it dis, it's like a knucklie cauldstane clunker skitin oot o Heiven an beltin ye ahint the lug. By the time ye get staunin again, ye're that uised wi the numbness ye canna mind whit like it wis afore thon meteoritic daud wheeched intae yer life. But by then it disna maitter.

Ye think ye hae a chyce but ye hinna. This journey's no aboot chyces – crossroads if ye like – it's aboot destination. If ye were religious ye'd say it wis aw in God's hauns. Ye'd accept it – the chib in the mugger's, the gullie in the surgeon's, they'd baith be in God's hauns. The yin cuts ye oot o badness, the tither seeks tae cut the badness oot, or sae it seems, but in fact it's no aboot bad, or guid. It's aboot luve an daith, an if there's ony luve tae be had afore the gash auld gudgie wi the scythe cums tae cut ye doun an stap ye in his lang poke. It's no the warld that maks yer sojourn in it hard tae thole; it's thinkin that ye're free tae gang doun that road or this, that ye hae that pouer, an then discoverin yer freedom's a mirage.

See in the auld days, the days ye find in thae buiks in the library, aw the auld sangs an ballads, there wis niver ony dout aboot daith in them. The word wis *deid* an nae joukin it: *Quhat is this lyfe bot ane straucht way to deid?* Whit *wis* life for some puir peasant wumman wi nae strength left tae wark, or some ootcast lipper wi hauf her face ett awa? As for luve, that wis only for some fowk; a luxury for maist. Unless ye were a laird or a priest, yer expectancy o life wud be that laich ye wudna hae time tae fash aboot luve. The ae thing ye'd ken for a certainty wud be daith, an that its sneddin wud be sune, sudden an sair as fuck.

Janice in the post-office queue. She wis young but her thochts were centuries auld. She shauchlt forrit throu the minutes o her lunch-oor ahint a line o grannies in for the pension. At the heid o the queue a TV monitor shawed the grannies hou they cud get a chairlift fittit in their hoose sae's they wudna hae tae flit tae a bungalow. A wifie glidin up an doun on it tellt them in douce English tones hou it michtna cost as muckle as they thocht, but she didna mention onythin aboot if ye cud get yer neibours or the cooncil tae chip in for ye steyed three flichts up a tenement stair. Whit she wis really sayin: this isna for the likes o you, it's for the likes o me. Janice had heard the spiel that aften she didna get mesmerised ony mair, that wey that had the fowk ahint ye giein ye a shuve tae snap ye oot o yer dwaum when the clerks were cryin oot 'Next!' Insteid she tuik in the Instants lottery signs stuck ower the waas an windaes, cuttin oot the licht wi their bleezing promises: CHRISTMAS BONUS, UK TREASURES, CASH EX-PLOSION, ACES HIGH. Somebody had turnt the post office intae a casino. She watched a granny gae up tae the nearest windae an get her siller, a wee skiff o tenners an three pund coins. Her knaggit auld fingers pushed the coins back: – Juist gie's three scratchcairds for them.

Janice tried no tae feel sorry for the auld dear. Awbody kent thae cairds were a rip-aff. The lottery itsel wis bad eneuch, but gettin yer pension peyed in Instants . . . ye had tae be witless. She tried no tae get angry aither. It wis a free kintra. Ye didna hae tae get involved. But it wis hard no tae, when ye were aye bein battert wi commercials shawin the pyntie finger o God destroyin yer ceilin an a muckle vyce shoutin IT COULD BE YOU. By the time Janice got tae be a pensioner probably a scratchcaird wud be aw ye'd get – Cash? Whit de ye mean cash? Three scarts an ye're oot, hen. The social-security system o the future.

It wis her turn. A windae freed up an she got her TV an phone stamps. It tuik the sting oot the bills but she hardly iver watched TV, an she got mair phone-caws than she iver made hersel frae fowk wantin tae replace her windaes or loan her siller for a new car or insure her against a disablin accident. She'd speak tae her mither a couple o times a week, that wis aboot it.

She queued again in the baker's for a piece, an then it wis time tae get back. Her mind wis on the grannies an their pensions: whit ye pit in an whit ye got oot at the hinner-en. At her wark past, Bob, the firm's salaries manager, had been talkin tae her aboot her pension. – Weill, Janice, he'd said, ye're no thirty yet, at your age I'd say it wis in yer interest tae opt oot o SERPS. Later it'll be in yer interest tae opt back in again.

– I'm no thinkin aboot retirin yet, she said.

– Course ye're no. But let's face it, by the time *you're* sixty-five the state pension isna gaun tae be worth a monkey's. Ye should think aboot a private scheme. If ye want ma opinion, disna maitter which gang o bandits is in government, the only interest that coonts ony mair is the state's. It's no in the state's interest if it iver has tae deal wi you or ony o yer generation iver again. I'm glad I'm the age I am.

– Weill, she said, I'll think aboot it.

– Dinna lea it ower lang, he said. He wis an auld dune kailyaird o a man: rampagin creashie hair, thistles growin oot his neb an lugs like castocks. She thocht hou awfy it must be tae be glad tae be the age he wis.

– Shair I canna persuade ye tae *jyne the syndicate*? he added. When he wisna coontin wages he collectit the lottery stakes.

The wey he pit it, it wis like bein recruitit intae organised crime.

– Ay, she said, I'm shair. She said it oot o principle. She didna ken whit the principle wis but she kent there had tae be yin. Mibbe it wis juist that it saved her a pund a week. Trouble wis, awbody else had surrendered their principles even afore the thing wis up an rinnin. Awbody forby Kevin in the mail-room, him that wis ower thrang faxin his pals' photocopies o his erse tae pey his pund. A richt tumshie she wis gaun tae luik if the nummers cam up an they aw walked oot the door wi hunners o thoosans each, leavin her an Kevin ahint. – Luik on the bricht side, said Kevin, there'd be promotion in it for us, an a haill crowd o new fowk tae boss aboot. Janice thocht aboot it, juist him an her an the photocopier. She near boaked at the idea. She wisna ambitious, Janice, but she wisna stupit aither. She'd left hame tae cum tae college in the city an she'd juist steyed. She liked bein hid in the city. Anonymous, mair or less. She'd hae a coffee or a gless o wine wi the ither lassies at wark an she earned eneuch tae pey the rent but forby these things her life didna connect wi theirs. That wis fine, she kept hersel tae hersel; read buiks, gaed tae the picturs, gaed back tae see her mither. She didna hae men chasin her, but that wis fine tae, ye cud dae athout the hassle. There wis Kevin, but he wis juist a nineteen-year-auld nyaff an his chase wis gey hauf-hertit, he didna coont. She didna care. In the simmer she flew tae a hot place for a week or twa an lay on the saun. Paradise. It set her up for the rest o that year's life.

She sensed in hersel she wisna whit ye'd cry a nice person. She didna set oot tae please. In the office she'd sit typin at her desk an fowk wudna cum near her. The men were feart o her: they cudna defrost her, sae hauf o them had her doun for a lesbian. As faur as she wis concerned they cud think whit they likit. She kent whit she wis. She didna hae tae be nice.

The simmer past she'd met a man on the beach in that year's

hot place. That wis whit she did maist years: fancied a man, got chattin, fucked him, forgot him. This time it hurt like Hell – aw burnie an chunderous. When she got back she gaed tae the doctor. They checked her records. – Have you never had a smear test? – Na, she said, must hae slipped throu the net. So they did yin. Then they did ither tests. Ay. She wis in the net nou.

That wis then, end o August. This wis nou, November, a month atween months, tae full the gap like. The lift wis aw streikit reid in the efternunes, the city a silhouette o spires an lums wi a brushstraik o reid abune it. Ivery November Janice mindit hou it wis aye like this, then she forgot till the next year. Autumn's mooth gantin at the stert o the month; by the end it wis winter, closin up, grey, cauld.

Janice in ither queues. Her life wis a queue – at the post office, the doctor's, the library, the chemist, even at the video shop on a Friday nicht, for God's sake. Fowk queued for awthin – seikness, health, sex, horror an ither fantasies. The only times she wisna queuein wis when she wis hame or at her desk. An hou lang wud that last onywey, afore Bob or some ither management type caad her in tae say, – Sorry, Janice, we're going to have to let you go. Whit they were really sayin: it's no in oor interest tae keep ye; ye're an inconvenience, an embarrassment. Luik at yersel, wi yer sneistie face an yer hingin-aff claes. But that wis whit she wudna dae, she wudna luik at hersel.

In Scotmid, gettin milk an biscuits on the wey hame at nicht, the haunles o the wire basket cut intae her airm as she watched an auld fella coontin oot coppers for a pokefu o tatties an fower tins o catfood. Ye caught yersel wunnerin aboot ither fowk's lives. Did the auld yin hae a cat or wis it for himsel? If ye bashed it up weill wi the tatties mibbe ye cud fule yersel. Wis he richt in the heid? Ye wudna ken yersel if ye werena. Then wan day ye wudna be there ony mair. Yer neibours wud complain aboot the smell an the polis'd brek yer door doun an fin ye turnin tae catfood on the flair, yer moggie lickin ye up at the edges. She hatit the thocht o that: abandonment; oblivion; purried Janice.

The line shuntit up. The fowk in it didna speak tae ither, didna luik. Some co-operative! Heids doun, prayin for rain. Only ye didna pray for rain in Scotland. That wisna whit ye wantit. Ye wantit a full hoose, a double rollover, 24 pynts on the coupon. Pou the puggie an pray for an on-ding o dollars.

Ootside somethin landit on her shouther, licht, an somethin else on the end o her neb. Snaw. She glanced up. The lift wis bowed wi it. Aw, an she liked snaw. Maist fowk hatit it, it gart them feart or frettin an aw they cud think on wis hou it wud be sliddery ablow their buits or their wheels. No Janice. For her it cam doun like a dream, millions o wee kaleidoscopes cascadin throu the air, contourin the kintraside like a weddin-dress. Aboot the only times she watched the news on telly wis nichts when they were reportin road chaos an closures caus o snaw. She luved the aerial shots o Scotland happit in white silk. She cud niver think on it as an emergency, a disaster. For her it wis like . . . whit? A new-made bed, mibbe?

Back hame the wee broun envelope lay like a sclatch o dug's dirt on her cairpet whaur it had fell throu the letter-box. She picked it up an pit it on the kitchen table. Gey slaw an deliberate like she tuik aff her coat an hung it up, gaed ben tae the front room tae lunt the gas, then back an pit the kettle on tae byle. Then she opened the envelope.

Ye dinna expect it. The clunker. But she kinna did. As sune as she read it her mind reset itsel so it wis as if she'd ayewis thocht it micht be her turn. An it wis.

She made hersel a cup o tea. Tea wis fine, if it wisna ower strang. She'd eat maistly wee scraps throu the day, an at nicht a biscuit or twa wis aw she'd fancy, sae the punds had been fleein aff her like – haw! – snaw aff a dyke, but she cud ayewis manage a cup o tea. Funny, ye felt seik an sair some days an ithers ye'd hauf-believe there wisna onythin wrang at aw. Ye'd cairry somethin aboot for years afore it surfaced: juist when ye thocht ye'd be alane foriver, oot it wud cum tae keep ye company.

She'd naebody tae phone but her mither. Tell her aboot the results. Aboot whit she had, whit they cudna dae aboot it. She'd no tak it easy, the mither. It must be bad when yer bairn phones *you*. Bairns, eh. Ye spend yer haill life anticipatin their illnesses, happin them roun, keepin them back frae schuil, thinkin they're cumin doun wi somethin. When *they* phone *you*, ye ken somethin's no richt. It's no fair.

Janice stobbed in the nummer. She let it ring tae gie her mither time tae hirple tae the phone. Ower the tap o the ringin tone she heard a distant vyce, a wumman's vyce oot there in the ether, ae side o somebody else's conversation. Ye cud hear her opinions in the rise an faw o her sentences, but ye cudna mak oot whit she wis sayin.

Her mither picked up the phone an the wumman disappeared. Janice began tae luik for wurds that she cud uise. She poud them oot o her heid tae tell it an, in between the phrases, she tuik deep braiths, rinnin her nail alang the wee scratch merks on the waa by the phone – merks that had been there as lang as she'd had the flat. She uised tae wunner aboot hou they got stertit, thae merks, whit bad news they'd chummed doun the line. It wis hard. Ye shidna hae tae talk aboot these things tae yer ain mammy.

Her mither soondit wee an thin an lonely. That wis because she wis. Janice tried no tae feel sorry for her. Or for hersel. It wisna as if she cud crawl back intae the wame an stert ower.

Efter, she keekit roun her curtains like a granny luikin for trouble in the street. It wis still snawin. The caurs were aw smoored an naebody wis aboot. She thocht aboot the snaw an hou she'd miss it, but she'd trade it richt nou for a beach an bleezin sun. Snaw ye cud keep, hospital-white an lourd as layers o blankets – she wantit blue sea an a bluid-orange sun papplin doun intae it. Style, that wis the thing tae gae oot in.

Later, sittin by the gas flames in a dwaum, she hauf-mindit the soun o that wumman's vyce frae the phone-line. The echo in her heid wis like a person greitin. She sat watchin the television even tho it wisna switched on, thinkin hou she kept cumin awa frae the video shop wi naethin because shite wis aw they had in there. She watched her ain pale shape in the dark deid screen an thocht aboot whit she wis gaun tae dae.

She kent whit. Aw yer life ye wait for the moment that maks it no yer life ony mair, for the threat o it bein taen aff ye. Efter that naethin can be the same. She'd mairch intae Bob's office the morn's morn, – Bob, I've made up ma mind. – Guid, he'd say. – I'm leavin, she'd say. Here's ma notice but I'm seik onywey, I'll no be in again. Stuff yer job, stuff yer pension, stuff yer bastartin lottery. Na, she wudna say she wis seik. She'd no gie him the chance tae get sympathetic. She'd juist wark her notice, she'd holidays tae cum aff it onywey. – Whaur are ye gaun? they'd want tae ken. She'd say she'd money saved, she wis gaun traivellin. An mibbe she wud an aw, borrow frae the bank or yin o thae patter-merchants on the phone afore they fun oot she wis chuckin her job. If she cudna affoord tae fly she'd hitch somewhaur. Onywhaur. Get some life in while she still had it. – Kevin, she'd say on her wey oot, I'm gaun tae lie on beaches an watch men stridin intae the sunset, men wi luvely wee roun bums that'll leave yours whaur it's aye been, in the mail-room. I'll send ye a postcaird.

She thocht aboot aw thae things. Insignificant things but they werena. An also she thocht aboot hou she'd mibbe ayewis been ower patient for her ain guid. Life ticked awa like a bomb an ye juist sat there waitin for it. She wisna feart nou, mair angry. The next girnin-faced bastart sufferin wi the cauld that gaed on aboot it, she wis gaun tae let flee at them, IT'LL FUCKIN GET BETTER. But mibbe it wudna. That wis the trouble wi onythin. Wha kent whit onythin micht turn intae?

The Greatest Whisky Ever

Brian Hennigan

G lenskinless, which in Gaelic means 'Glen of Vivisection', is in the heart of rustling country. Life is hard. For entertainment we go into the village shop and try on hats. Once or twice someone might take a bus to Elgin. They never come back.

And although many of the population enjoy a drop of whisky, none will ever pass my lips again – in either direction. Because I have tasted the Greatest Whisky Ever and no liquor will ever match it. It is also in tribute to my father and those other brave men who gave their lives on that tragic night that I do not drink.

Each clan has an ancient right to rustle a particular beast. For some it is cattle, for others, deer. My family had moles. My father and his father before him were the best mole-rustlers north of Dalwhinney. Grandfather himself had once rustled fifty right through the Achiltibuie Police Gala. I too had dreamed of the life, of damp midnight treks and strange towns at dawn. I would be the Kevin Costner of mole-rustling.

These dreams came to nothing. Having survived many troubles through the ages, including persecution by the eighteenth-century Mole Barons, we suffered at the hands of Europe. To the EU Hamster Hills and Gerbil Jungles were added the blight of Mole Mountains. The industry was destroyed. A man with a young family to support, I managed to get a position at the distillery. My dad and Uncle Bob were left to wander the heather, armpits aching for the warmth of a sleepy mole.

Glenskinless Distillery was a ruthless operation. The dedication of its founder, Milton McDuff, to the production of malt whisky was legendary.

There are only four basic ingredients in malt whisky but many thousands of variations in the formula. From what spring should the water be drawn? On what date should the barley be harvested? From which hill should the peat be dug? At what exact time should the yeast be added? Milton's life was spent in investigation of these matters, to the exclusion of all others.

My job was to deliver his daily nip. At precisely 11.30am I would cross the courtyard bearing a silver tray on which rested a single glass of whisky from that day's selected cask. Milton waited, blindfolded, on his chaise longue. I would enter, lay the tray beside him, and then slowly waft the whisky under his nose. After a period of contemplation he would open his mouth and I would place a single teaspoon of spirit on his extended tongue, which would then slither back into his mouth in a scene worthy of *Life On Earth*.

That was a terrible winter. The snow fell deep, the wind blew hard. At times the landscape was like a vast, frozen Sahara. Strange things happened. Old McPherson was found in the spring behind the bus shelter, looking at a timetable with a face of frozen disbelief. My dad and Uncle Bob were using a set of saucepans as snowshoes. They could often be seen tumbling down nearby hills, as the saucepans were nonstick. Through all this the distillery powered on, with Milton housing all workers on site. It was surely as a result of such dedication that the discovery was made.

In all other respects it was a typical morning. Silent John, our quiet Distillery Manager, had sent me over to Milton's office with a sample from cask 674. I had done my duty and was staring out of the window at the sad figure of my father building a giant snowmole. Without warning Milton leaped up, shouting, 'This is the greatest whisky ever!'

Minutes later cask 674 was sitting in the laboratory. Milton carefully removed the recipe attached to the side. He then addressed the distillery's twelve employees, hurriedly assembled in the boardroom.

'I have no doubt that this is the greatest whisky ever. We have much to be proud of. The name of Glenskinless will live forever. Let us now drink a toast to our future position in Scottish history.'

At that signal I brought in the silver tray, now with thirteen glasses. Trembling with pride, we drank. That one wee nip was enough to convince us all. For me, it seemed that angels were blowing softly across the tongue while my body was warmed by the fire of a travelling star.

Milton was on the telephone for most of what remained of that short day. Appointed temporary assistant, I overheard calls to lawyers, agents, distributors. And security firms. Milton ordered 'triple plus' protection from a company so secret that they refused to use real names. Our contact was a Mr Banana, who would arrive the next day with a crack squad of Tangerines.

Meanwhile – throbbing along wires, thumping off satellites, sucked down by antennae – word of the discovery surged around the globe as men in suits talked to other men in suits. We would not last until the next day.

The telephone calls were the first inkling that something was afoot. First one offer, then another, then another. The multinational drinks companies were quick to realise the threat. What would happen to demand for normal whisky?

Why would anyone buy such inferior products when they could have the Greatest Whisky Ever? No, these companies wanted Milton's whisky for themselves.

Orders were issued. Using the tractor, men, women and children were brought from the village and sworn into service by Milton himself, each placing their hand in turn on Cask 674. They were then assigned to one of twelve teams, each commanded by a distillery worker. Trenches were dug, fences erected, guards posted. My team stood outside the laboratory. We were the Elite Personal Guard whose duty it was to protect both cask and Milton.

Under the darkening sky everyone gathered round a central bonfire. Uncharacteristically Silent John got out his bagpipes and we warmed ourselves with traditional Scottish singing and dancing. And in small groups we talked of the wonderful life to come, the prestige, the honour. Perhaps we would even see the bright lights of Inverness.

A klaxon from the outer perimeter broke our enjoyment. We rushed to see. There, advancing across the snow-covered fields, were three black Range Rovers. A dumpy figure was running in front of them. 'It's me,' cried Fat Sandy: 'Let me in!' He fell to his knees, gasping heavily, 'It's the Minnesota Drink Corporation – their people want to talk to our people.'

'Is that right?' laughed Milton. 'We'll show them talk.' He waved his hand. From a nearby trailer were rolled three huge barrels of so-so whisky, originally called 'Grand Deluxe' and destined for England, but now put to use against the corporate devils. As they bounced towards the cars the casks leaked behind them a liquid fuse of Scotch. Milton took out his lighter and held the flame to the ground. Fire raced towards the casks and they exploded in mid-bounce, sending a burning spray over the Range Rovers. The passengers swiftly abandoned them, one or two being restrained by colleagues as they tried to rescue their mobile phones. So began the Siege of Glenskinless.

From the four corners they came; by jeep, truck and snowmobile. And each time they were repelled. The country-side was littered with the flaming shells of executive cross-country transportation. But even as victory appeared secure, tragedy beckoned.

It was only natural that, with so much whisky to hand, people would be helping themselves to wee drams, particularly on such a chill night. As the hours wore on the drams grew from 'wee' to 'muckle'. Behaviour gradually changed. Singing became louder, the troops more excitable. Suddenly the camp was echoing not to 'Ye Jacobites by Name' but the theme tune of *Home and Away*. People bumped into one another; curses flew. Long-forgotten feuds re-emerged. Full-scale fighting broke out.

My group alone remained disciplined. Taking Milton with us to the laboratory, we locked ourselves inside. The plan was to wait until dawn.

The Whisky-Boy Corporation of Tokyo had other ideas. Whisky-Boy is fanatical in its pursuit of anything new in the world of whisky. They timed their entry well. Having surveyed the fighting from above, they now parachuted into the com-pound. This was too much for the drunken villagers. They wailed in horror. 'Oh no! It's the ghosts of all the people who went to Elgin.' And with that the entire population fled screaming into the night. They were located the next morning inside the church.

As we hid in the laboratory Milton memorised the whisky formula then destroyed the recipe. Meanwhile Whisky-Boy executives tried to lure us out, dangling digital walkmans and mini-computers outside the windows. We had to hold down Jimmy the Postman.

Just before dawn there was a violent battering at the door. I peered over the window ledge. The Japanese had discovered our highland cows and were now riding them kamikaze-style into the door. Eventually, it had to give. We were seized and the barrel rolled out into the courtyard. The Japanese explained politely that they would not need the recipe; their scientists would simply break down the compound from a sample. The barrel was uncorked and a small test-tube lowered in. Milton wept.

Then there was a sound, a sound like a stampede, a stampede of hundreds of tiny feet. We turned as one – Japanese and Scot. Thundering towards us was a vast swarm of moles urged on by my dad and Uncle Bob. The Japanese froze in terror as the wave of squealing velvet burst over them. This was all the time that Milton needed. Jumping forward he drew his lighter, holding it up to the cask's open hole. I threw myself down. There was a huge explosion, then the sound of hundreds of tiny charred animals landing all around.

I came to several minutes later and got up. Through the smoke I made out my father's blackened body. I took his hand.

'Son,' he whispered through cracked lips,' I needed to do my bit, to protect the whisky. They can take our moles, but they'll never take our whisky.'

As I laid his body on the laboratory table there was a knock at the door. 'Good day,' said a man in combat trousers, 'I'm Mr Banana.'

No whisky has passed my lips since that dark dawn but not one day passes when I do not think of my father and the Greatest Whisky Ever.

Swans in the Spring?

Ian Brotherhood

I t's just that way. There's some things you don't do. Some
things you don't say. You don't have to be some kind of
genius to know that, know what I mean?

Likewise, if there's something wrong with you, maybe
that's different then, you know, if you're a bit dolly dimple
or whatever. But Parnie was never dolly dimple. No way. Not
him. Anyway, I don't want to talk about it. What's the point?
There's not much of this left. You asleep?

Do you mind that one in the paper a few years back about
the guy that got done cos his dog was barking at the milkman
or the postie or whoever? Mind that? It never even bit the
bastard, but your man gets had up anyway and they were
gonny do all sorts you know, put him away for contempt and
get the dog put down and all that, but maybe it was cos of the
papers getting a hold of it, I don't know, but it was madness
anyway, and you get these popstars making a song about the
dog. Barney, that was him. Barney the Death-Row Dog. It got
to number three or something. And what's his face, that guy
that used to be on *Nationwide*, remember him? Aye, him, I
think he was on *That's Life* as well, him, but anyway, he's
sticking his neb in and giving it Barney! and all that, sad
bastard just wanted people to take pictures of him again.
Member that? Well, Claude was the same kind of dog, you

know, only Claude was a cross collie Labby, and that other guy's was a cross collie Alsatian. Doesn't matter anyway. But Claude was a beauty of a dog. My wee man he was.

So that was him next door, that Parnie. For all the use there is talking about it now. You got any skins there? You going to sleep? Eh? The skins. Cheers.

Maybe we're in the house, what, three month? Not much more than that anyway, and no hassles at all, right, everything's just hunky-dory. There's a few of the young team round that way are a bit wild right enough but where are they no? And she was well happy with it cos of the garden, and she was always on about getting a dog as soon as we ever got a garden you know. She had a dog when she was with her old dear. That was just one of those wee terriers right enough, and they're alright for in the high-risers, they can run up and down the hall you know. But she was broken hearted when her mum wouldn't let her take the dog, said she needed it in the house for company with them all away and her old man dead and all that, so I promised when she moved in with me, I was like, no problem, doll, as soon as the wee one's arrived and we get a house I'll get a dog sorted. So that's another three years before we get out of that flat what with her losing the first two you know, dodgy insides she's got and the weans just come away from her you know, very sensitive on the insides she is, so when Tricia came that was it, really fast they give us the option on this two-up-and-down at the back of the spring on the new wee scheme, you know that one you can see from the bypass, that's it, right. It was only just open, you know, the first few houses are took and the punters are moving in and it's all this shite in the papers about the dealers are right in there and it's gonny be a ghetto before it's even got off the ground, all that pish, so I wasn't giving a fuck anyway and neither was she. I mean, that was us managed to stick out the Hill for near enough four year so there's no way it was gonny be any worse,

so thanks very much, that'll do us, and the next thing we're in
and there's a view down the canal and the noise from the
bypass isn't that bad and the air's fresh. Honest, we used to go
walking down the canal and watch swans swimming and all
that. Swans, man. In the spring? I'm telling you, well sorted.
So that was us.

– LIGHTS OUT! NIGHT-NIGHT, LADIES! NIGHT-NIGHT!

Bastard. Here, pass us that lighter. You still awake? Right.
Aye, so that was us. Takes a while getting in and that, and I'm
just started that job in the Arcade so I'm doing nights, she's up
all hours with the wee one, but it's fine you know, it's that way
you're busy but you don't mind cos you're getting stuff done
and that, you know. But it's coming up for her birthday and I
get off sharp this Friday morning, head up the cat and dog
home and have a swatch about. Nothing doing you know, it's
nearly all cats and pure sad-looking mongrels and that, but the
lassie on the desk says to have a decko at the board cos they get
a lot up there, and there's this one saying they just want a
tenner for a collie Labrador but you've got to take one right
away and it's dated like a week old, so I'm thinking they'll be
well away cos they're only wanting a tenner. But I call it
anyway and she's like aye, come round, there's two left, and
she gives us the address and it's on the way home anyway. So
no problem, get there, and it turns out this one. Angela her
name is, she was at school with me, like two years under me
you know, and I couldn't mind her at all when she says right,
so she takes me in the living room and this is like ten minutes
I'm playing with this wee thing you know, maybe it's like it
knows I'm taking one of them so this one's making a bid to
impress, all big eyes and being cute you know, and the other
one's not bothering its shirt you know, it's just sort of crashed
out by the sofa and it's not asleep but it's just not bothered.

So she comes back in with the tea and sits right beside me
on this two-seater, so right away your old da's like, oh-ho,

here we go, and she's all smiley and knees touching and asking me about my Gerry and what happened to him, cos he was in her year, so I tell her about the Viking and she's like totally shocked, like the last she heard he was working the rigs but she never knew he was on it when it blew, so she starts greeting and sniffing and, oh, I must've been devastated and all that so your old da's right in there and it's a wee cuddle and next thing she's getting the shirt off me, so that was it, straight into the bedroom and she's not even made the bed yet you know, so that's a bit weird thinking her man's probably not long out the thing; but we're about an hour in there, magic by the way, really needed it you know.

So I'm like, oh-ho, better get this dog sorted out and get back, you know. I mean. I was already well late and she's a right worrier you know. I mean, she wouldny think twice about phoning the work even with me telling her, you know, I says don't phone the work unless it's like a real emergency, they don't like it, they make a note of personal calls coming in and all that, so I'm like, look doll, I'll have to be getting up the road and she's like, you'll have another cuppa and all that so I'm like yeah, on ye go and I get back in to see these wee ones and make my mind up. So she comes in then again with more tea, but when she opens the door this fucking huge black Labby comes striding in after her and it's like that, boosh, right over to me. So I'm like that, ho, up with the knees and trying to cover my baws and my face at the same time cos this is a big fucker right enough, and for a second I was like, maybe she's took the spur cos I'm for the off and she's getting this big bastard to keep me in you know, like trap me so she can use me as a sex slave or something like that you know, but the thing comes up and it's all licks and tail going ten to the dozen so it's a friendly big bastard and turns out it's the mum of these wee ones, so I'm like nice girl, nice girl, giving it big pets and letting her lick my hand and all that, and she's like, she likes you, she definitely likes you.

Turns out the mum's quite fussy about who she likes and this Angela knocked back a couple of folk just on the strength of the mum not liking them you know, giving it growl and not going near them and all that, so that's a good sign, and she's like which one? So I'm dithering and looking and this one's still sort of jumping up and looking well keen but the other wee one's still rubber-earing me down at the sofa.

You want some of this? You asleep? Want some then? Suit yourself.

So anyway, this wee one by the sofa, it's not asleep mind, it knows what's happening, so I'm like, that one, so I go over and I get it up and it's like moaning and having wee nips at my hand and all that even with it shaking cos it's scared and whatever, but this Angela's giving it can ye not stay a bit and all that and she's probably into it again you know, but I'm like, got to split, hen, really, so she gives me this wee sort of towel thing and I wrap up the wee one and offsky.

So that's it. She's over the moon you know. It's not her birthday till the next Wednesday, but she's not bothered and it's pretty mental with Trish still staying up half the night and that, but the wee one's no bother, you know, really good for that age, doesn't chew much and makes for the papers whenever he wants a pish. Cos I've got to hand it to that Angela, that was the big black Labby had the six of them you know, and that's a right handful, but she managed to get them so they wereny bad with the old toilet training you know, it was maybe a fortnight or that on the papers and maybe the odd wee shite lying here and there but he soon knew to go out the back. Don't get me wrong, it's not like he got belted. That's a lot of folk do that and it's not right you know, it just makes them scared. They're babies, you know, they don't know what they're doing wrong and they just want to keep you happy. Jesus, they'll die for you, you know, a decent dog, it'll do anything for you. So all I would do, and I made sure she was the same, I was like, you find a shite, don't lose the rag, just ignore it, and make sure Claude's out every hour. It was her called him Claude cos she likes him, you know, the kick-boxer guy. So half the time the wee man's pottering about in the garden sniffing about and that, and if it's dry he's happy to sit about out there and listen to the birds or have a wee scrape at the grass, whatever. And Jesus, you want to see him piling on the weight. You know, it was like we had wee Trish there and she's like totally tiny and greeting non-stop and there's the wee fella getting bigger by the day. Mind you, I still don't reckon he was eating anywhere near enough for that age, cos this is him just like seven, eight weeks you know, but he shoots up all the same, fills out grand.

So that must've been just after he gets his second jag, maybe ten, eleven weeks. And it's the same week the health visitor's like, no no no, something wrong here, you know, with Trish and, Jesus, she's pure freaking out, you know, really giving it panic, and I'm like come on, we don't know, so we gets her stuff packed and I take them down to the unit and we're there half the day before we get to see this woman doctor and she's like, we don't know, the tests are not conclusive and all that, we'll have to do more, so she's wanting to stay but the nurse is like, no way, so there's a bit of a stramash you know and she's saying she'll no leave her, but eventually I'm like, come on, this is no use, leave her, they know what they're doing, so it's down to her old dear's and I'm like, best you stay here, cos it's easier getting to the unit if they hear anything, and that's me offsky, back to the wee man, and you can tell he's no been a happy camper you know, there's shite all over the kitchen and it's like even when I open the door he's like crying and pishing you know, like he's scared. Right enough, that was the first time he was ever on his tod, and that was near enough seven, eight hours, so he must've got a fright right enough, but that night I let him kip in the bed beside me.

Want the bones of this? You asleep yet? What?

So, Trish is dead. Just like that. Heart failure. She was two hundred and fifty-five days old. And we wereny there cos it happened so fast. We knew it was bad right enough but what're ye supposed to do? She stays at her mum's cos she says she can't face coming back. That's me and Claude boy on our tod.

That's when the job went. No one to look after him at night. He's still just a baby as well, what's he done to deserve that? So I jack the job, tell that tosser Allan to stick it right up him, walk out the door. She goes mental, what about the rent, blah blah blah. What's the fucking use anyway when she won't come back? So I'm like, get your head sorted and get back in. We can try again. No way, she's saying, no chance, not until you get another job sorted, maybe then, just maybe, so I do the rounds a few weeks but the old heart's just no in it you know, and I'm just walking daytime, doing the canal out to Kirky and back with the wee man, getting a few cans in night-time. She stops calling. The boys from the council come round a couple of times about the arrears and that, but I just give them her address at her old dear's and leave it at that. Walking out the job? No chance. No fucking chance.

It was a Wednesday. I signed that morning, so I couldnae take the wee man cos he goes mental if you tie him up outside, so I went up on the bus, had to hoof it back but, no dosh, and soaked I was too. But I'm just in the door, just through it, and there's this voice behind me, like ho, you. So I turns like that, and there's your man Parnie looking over the fence, and he's standing at his own door under the wee canopy bit out the rain, so I'm back out, and he starts giving it your dog hasnae shut it for the past hour and if you don't shut it I'll shut it for good, so I'm like, is that right? and he steps down. It was all dead fast. He starts on about do I not know who he is? and if I'm wanting sorted as well as the dog he'll see to it and all that, so I leans back inside the front door and takes up the old snooker butt, cos I always keep it there you know, and steps back out and takes it right off the fucker's head. Down he goes like a sack of King Eddies, and that was it. Next thing, his missus is out shouting the odds. I goes in, sees to the wee man. Shite all over the place, like the old tex ritters you know. He wasnae well. That's how he was barking, cos he knew he was needing but he couldnae keep it in, god love him.

I never knew Parnie was supposed to be any kind of ticket. He was only in the house a month and never once cracked a smile or says hello or whatever, so how was I supposed to know? See the bastard of it too, the wee man's likely with someone like him now. Someone who wants a guard dog, a big barker. Some scumbag dealer wanting a dog to do the scary stuff for him. But Claude's not like that. He really isn't. Ach, what's the point talking about it anyroad.

You still awake? Eh?

A Musing Tale

Lesley Affrossman

S o what ye have tae understand, like, is that I never expected tae meet a muse. And all because the wife got infected by Culchur. Tae be honest, it's nothing mair than a big Hoo Ha tae me. I mean they gave us all that culchur back in 1990 and still didn't bring the price of a pint down. Now if they'd asked me (which I might add, they didnae), but if they had, I'd have said, bring the price of a pint down. Mair Scottish genius has been found at the bottom of a glass than ever came frae having an opera hoose. If ye don't believe me, just ask old Rabbie, himself. 'Tae A Moose' wasnae written after an evening with Pavarotti, now was it?

But anywise the wife doesnae see it like this, and she goes and joins the Cessnock Ladies' Social Club and Art Appreciation Society. Well, if she wants a wee interest, apart from the budgie, that's all right by me. But the next thing I know is, we've got free tickets to see an exhibition of modern art. 'That's nice, dear,' I say, when she tells me. 'Let me know what it was like.' But no, I have tae go, with her. And it's that or listen to the speech about, 'how her mother never liked me anyway'. So I go.

When we get there the speech about her mother doesnae seem so bad. There's all these people, milling about, wearing torn jeans and T-shirts (she's made me put on my funeral suit). They're saying things like, 'It's a superb example of post-Impressionism in the milieu of modern subjectivity.'

It's a what?

I hear one of them saying, 'He's really captured the sensual quality of womanhood this time.'

And his pal says, 'It's a gift, just an absolute gift. You could almost reach out and touch the breasts.'

Well mibbe art's no as bad as I thought. I walk up, all kind of casual like, just to have a wee gander. But what I see is a big ball of string, some of they polystyrene chips and a widden orange box. 'Is that it?' I ask. Thinking that mibbe the artwork was inside the box, and we were admiring the wrapping.

'Ah, sublime,' the first one says. 'Eve's daughter is truly divinely inspired, do you not think?'

He seemed to be asking, so I said, 'Well, the wife looks worse in her curlers.' I laugh, but they just look at me, like my head's on backwards, so I wander off tae see if the wife's ready tae go.

I find her in the 'Tube Room', which is really the only room that's well named in the whole exhibition, and it's no the artwork I'm referring to. Over in a corner, I can see the wife, and her teacher, fair gone on the auld art chat.

'Och, I know, Orlando,' she's saying. 'I really do think that it is a unique example of Neoplatonic forms transmogrified into the spatial dimensions of contemporary social structures, so it is and that!'

That's it. I've had enough art tae dae me until the next year of Culchur. And she'll never notice if I slip out for a wee breath of fresh air and mibbe a pint. Just the one.

It must be about ten o'clock that a find myself in Kelvingrove Park. I know I meant tae go home, and I know that this is the wrong direction, but somehow I can't think how tae get back in the right direction. Something's preventing my brain from proceeding in an orderly fashion. 'I know what the trouble is,' I say, 'I'm as drunk as a monkey.'

'Too right ye ur, pal,' a voice says.

I stop in my tracks. Now, I've been known tae talk tae trees when I've goat a drink in me, but this was the first time one o them talked back.

But there it was, one of they big, beech things, with all the branches and wee, green leaves, and it was saying, 'You are stoatin, Jimmy. I've goat mair chance of walking out of this park in a straight line than you have.'

'Hold on a minute,' I says. 'Just you come on out frae behind that tree.' But all that happens is that the big widden punter starts tae laugh.

'I'm no behind the tree, Jimmy. I *am* the tree.'

Now, I've had a lot tae drink, but I've no had that much. There's some kind of head case hiding behind that tree, and I'm alone with him. I know what my chances of running away are, so I try tae humour him for a wee while.

For a couple of minutes there's silence, cause I canny think what tae say tae a tree, but eventually I try, 'So, have ye been here long?'

He starts laughing, and says, 'Actually I havnae. Ye see I'm no really a tree.'

'No? Well that's a relief.' I just hope he's no going tae say that he's really one of they psychopaths.

'I had ye fooled though, didn't I?'

'Aye, well, I canny deny it.' Mibbe, if I run fast enough, I can make it tae the gate.

'Naw, I'm no really a tree. I'm a muse.'

'A what?'

'A muse. You know, Art, Music, Dance . . .'

'Aw, the jigging, I know about that.'

'Aye,' he says, 'that's the game. There used tae be only nine o us, but since the advent o the microchip there's thoosands o us.'

'Which one are you, then?'

'Och, I'm Art. I'm in charge of drawing and painting and that. No graphics and design though. That's been subcontracted.'

'Well izat no amazing. I've just been tae a big do at the McLellan. Ye know, the gallery.'

'Aw really,' Art says, interested. 'What did ye think?'

I thought about being honest, but decide I'd better be polite. 'I thought it was rubbish actually.'

'That's cause ye didnae understand it,' Art says. 'Look, I'll show ye.'

There's a big bang and a flash of light, and the next thing I know Art's no a tree anymair. He's turned into a rusty, auld fridge, with a pair of rotting trainers on the top of it.

'That's disgusting,' I say.

'Naw, it's naw. It's art.'

'Look, I'm mibbe only an ordinary, wee punter, but that is no art. Art's about pictures of wimmen and flowers, and big statues made of marble. You're just an auld fridge an some mouldy gutties.'

Art sighed. 'Ye don't get it, dae ye? I'm no just somebody's auld kitchen appliance. I'm an allegory about the state of the world. I'm using art to represent decay.'

'Why did you no use Govan then?' says I, but Art doesnae see the funny side. Instead, he turns into a big pile of builder's bricks, and a self-assessment form from the tax office.

'What ye don't understand,' he says, 'is that it's no what it is that makes it art, it's what you put into it, yourself, that counts. Ye might look at me and think that form's on the wrong side o they bricks, or you might think politics is the destructive force that's bringing about the ultimate downfall of society. It's no what the artist did that's important, it's what you see that makes it art. Dae ye follow me?'

'Aye,' I say, nodding. 'I see what yer saying. But if it's only up tae the punter tae see the art in something, what dae ye need the artist fur?'

There's another flash and a bang, and Art's standing there, like a seven-foot-tall Greek statue, pointing a big, marble finger at me. 'Who are you?' he booms.

'Me? I'm nobody. Well, I'm no nobody. But I'm nobody special, no like a muse or anything.'

Art puts his finger down. 'Aw, that's all right. I thought ye were an art critic for a minute. It wouldnae dae if they asked questions like that. It could ruin the whole deal.'

'What deal?'

Art goes all mysterious then, and starts looking over his shoulder tae see if any of the trees are listening. They arnae, so he leans forward, and says, 'I'm going tae tell you, cos I like you, Jimmy, but keep it tae yersel, awright?'

I nod, feeling a bit glaikit, and he starts tae tell me his wee story.

'Well, it's like this, see. A wee while ago, roon aboot the beginning of the century, I'm getting bevied out o my skull, down at the Curlers with a punter I met there.'

'Who was that?'

'Haud oan, I'm getting tae that. I didnae know who he was at first, but it turns out later that he's a muse as well.'

'Another one?'

'Och, aye, we're all over the place. This one's the muse of Retail Insurance Investments. It's a right cushy number that one, I can tell you.

'Well, then he asks me how come the money's no so good in art, with all them van Goghs and da Vincis floating about. "The money's all right," I tell him, "but ye have tae wait till after the artist's dead before ye make anything on them. And even if they're popular while they're still alive, they take forever tae get one painting out the door." Retail Insurance says there must be a way round it, and then he suggests that I go in for insurance myself.

' "Not oan your life, pal," I tell him. But he says, "Calm doon. It's no like ye think. Instead o spending all yer time inspiring the long-haired layabouts with the paint brushes, why dae ye no go and work the auld magic on their agents?"

'At first I don't see how that'll help, but auld Retail Insurance explains, "If the agents think that their wee laddie's producing genius, they'll want tae insure it. The artists can produce all sorts of rubbish in half the time it used tae take, and, as long as I inspire the agents, the critics will put their money into it." '

'So that's what we did. At the end of the day Retail Insurance and me clean up on the profits.'

'Can an art muse dae that?' I ask cautiously.

Art shrugs. 'Nobody's said anything so far, and I get two holidays a year in Marbella, and a ski-in trip at Christmas, so I'm no complaining.'

'Zat right, then? *Two* holidays in Marbella? Don't suppose ye need any help?'

'Naw,' says Art. 'We've got it all wrapped up. But I'll keep ye in mind just in case. Anyway, dae ye fancy coming for a wee bevy?'

'Naw. Thanks, but I'd better be getting back tae the exhibition. Been nice talking tae ye though.'

'Och, any time,' says Art. 'If I'm no here I'll be at the Curlers. Ye canny miss me. I'm the big mental-looking one with the flares on.'

He waved as I headed back to the McLellan.

My luck was in. No one noticed I'd been gone. The wife had her back tae me, looking at a wee picture that was hidden away in an alcove. From behind her I could see the painting. It was called, *The Way O Things*, an, in it, a wee, drunk-looking man was standing in a park, no unlike Kelvingrove, talking tae a tree. Under the tree was a big pile o bricks and a self-assessment form from the tax office.

'That's me!' I exclaimed.

'Don't be stupit, ya wee eejit,' the wife says. 'Who'd want tae put you in a painting?'

And, right enough, it's no exactly the sort of thing ye can explain. If I tell her I've spent the night talking with a muse, she'll be doon seeing her lawyer before the milk's in tomorrow.

'Naw,' I say. 'I didnae mean it was me. Not me the person. I meant it was a symbol about the common man. It's an allegory.'

The wife shakes her head in disgust. 'Honest tae God, you know nothing about ert, dae ye? That's no an Allegory. He didnae paint in oils!'

ABOUT THE AUTHORS

Lesley Affrossman is thirty something. She is a technical author based in Glasgow, and has published a number of short stories and technical articles. She lives with her husband and two little extra-terrestrials trying to pass themselves off as her sons.

Alan Bissett grew up in Falkirk and was an English teacher before deciding to study for a PhD at Stirling University. His thesis is on the devil in literature. He is co-organiser of *Growl*, monthly reading events in Stirling. His work has been performed at the Traverse Theatre, Edinburgh and at the Stirling Youth Theatre.

Gavin Bowd is a poet, essayist, fiction writer and translator. His previous works include *Decades* (1996) and *Technique* (1999).

Ian Brotherhood is a 36-year-old Glaswegian Art School graduate. He works as an editorial assistant for *Variant* magazine and runs the Three Towns Writing Course. He has published many stories in *Variant* and his work has appeared in *The Edinburgh Review, West Coast Magazine* and on BBC Radio Scotland.

Sheena Charleston was born on the 4th of June 1964 at 7.05 AM (Astrologers) in Edinburgh. She is a freelance psychic who studied Divinity at Edinburgh University and lives with her child, her parakeets and her quails. She is deeply grateful to Mr R. G. Wilson at the Western General Hospital and to Ptakchmylol.

Linda Cracknell was the winner of the *Macallan Scotland on Sunday* short story competition in 1998 with *Life Drawing*, her first published work. Since then her story, *The Fall*, has been published in The Keekin-Gless anthology, and another short story, *Death Wish*, will appear *Something Wicked*, to be published by Polygon this year. She lives in Highland Perthshire where she works for an environmental charity.

Chris Dolan lives in Glasgow. His short story collection, *Poor Angels*, was published by Polygon in 1995, the year in which he also won the Macallan/Scotland on Sunday award. He adapted his story 'Sabina' for the stage, winning a Fringe First in 1996, and the play has since been performed in Spain and Italy. 'Conviction' will appear in Polygon's *Something Wicked*, to be published this year. His first novel, *Ascension Day*, will be published in August 1999.

Morgan Downie

> 'As I walk away she asks
> "Why did you write it?"
> I say "I did it for you"
> She looks suddenly puzzled, as if her memory

About the Authors

Had tricked her into forgetting.
And faintly, she smiles.'

Lizbeth Gowans was born, raised and educated in Scotland. She wandered the world for some years and is now married and settled in Yorkshire, growing fiction from real seeds and slowly learning Gaelic. Her short stories have appeared in several anthologies and she has also published three books for children.

Jaohn Grace is a writer, singer, songwriter, actor and painter. He fled the city in 1986 to live in the back of beyond and grow organic vegetables and plant trees.

Iain Grant lives in Edinburgh and works as an editor. His first novel, *Small Town Antichrist*, was published in 1999. 'I Shall Fear No Evil' will appear in *Something Wicked*, to be published by Polygon.

Brian Hennigan is Scottish born and bred. He recently quit a lucrative business career to become a successful writer. He can now be found on street corners, holding a 'Golf Sale' sign or begging.

David Kilby has published short stories in a variety of anthologies. His stories have been aired on radio and a full-length play was performed in the Edinburgh Fringe in 1991. He was born in Glasgow, but now lives in Cambuslang and is married with a son. His mother says he gets his talent from his Uncle Jack.

Carolyn Mack lives and works in Glasgow. She was a runner-up in the 1997 Ian St. James Award, and her work has appeared in various women's magazines and in the New Writer. She currently works on *The Northender*, a community newspaper based in Possilpark.

Michael Mail is originally from Glasgow and is now living in London, where he is a Director in an educational charity. He has been writing for several years, mainly short stories and screenplays.

Lynda McDonald grew up in Grimsby, Lincolnshire when it was a thriving, bustling fishing port, but she has lived in Edinburgh for over twenty years. She has previously published a children's story and short stories in magazines.

David Millar was born in Edinburgh in 1955 and his short stories have appeared in various publications. A play, *A Meeting with the Monster*, was performed at the Edinburgh Fringe (1995) and at the Traverse Theatre (1996).

Mitchell Miller was born in Edinburgh and graduated from Edinburgh University with a degree in Politics and History. He is currently completing research.

About the Authors

Yseult Ogilvie grew up in New York, London and Inverness. She left Inverness to study in Oxford and London, and qualified as an architect in 1999. Previous publications include 'Blow Out', published in London Magazine. Her first novel is well underway.

Sian Preece was born in South Wales in 1965 and came to Aberdeen via Canada and France. Her work has appeared in *Scotland on Sunday, Chapman, West Coast Magazine* and on BBC Radio. Her first collection of stories, *From the Life*, will be published by Polygon. 'Second Hand' will appear in the forthcoming *Something Wicked* from Polygon.

Wayne Price was born in South Wales and now lives and teaches in Edinburgh. A number of his short stories have been published in anthologies and journals including *New Writing Scotland, Panurge* and *Stand Magazine*. He has recently completed his first novel.

Tom Rae was born in 1960 and lives in Glasgow. He writes poetry, short stories and drama. His work has appeared in print, on radio and on stage at the Edinburgh Festival.

James Robertson was born in 1958 and grew up in Bridge of Allan, Stirlingshire. He studied History at Edinburgh University. Previous published work includes *Scottish Ghost Stories*. His first novel, *The Fanatic*, will be published in 2000.

Suhayl Saadi was born in 1961 and is based in Glasgow. His first novel, *The Snake*, was published in 1997 under the pseudonym 'Melanie Dermoulins', and he won a major prize in the Bridport Competition in 1997. He is currently working on another novel.

Sarah Salway lives in Edinburgh where she works as a journalist. She is currently completing a Masters in Writing at the University of Glamorgan and writing her first novel.

Rachel Seiffert was born in 1971. She has previously written and directed two short films, and has worked as an editor on many others. She is currently writing a novel.

Kate Thomson loves writing because it lets her go anywhere and become anyone. A Glasgow creative writing MLitt student, Katy's current project is a novel about lap-dancing, *Psychedelic Pussycat*.

Eric White graduated with an Honours degree in biochemistry at Strathclyde University. After working in a fund-raising office, he went into banking. Hobbies include music and guinea pigs.